A sensual gar

"You're alone?"

"Not anymore," Ma
"Though you might want to choose a better line."

St. John hadn't been fully prepared for the deepness of her voice, or that it might rival her sultry exterior. As the surprise washed over him, he grinned.

"Also, there's a rule about having to dance while on a dance floor," she said, swiveling side to side so that her hips lightly brushed against his thighs.

His reaction to the unexpected touch came in the form of a jolt of pleasure that streaked through his body. Her life, her energy and all that fire in such a fragile body, were heady draws that, for a fleeting moment, made him remember what it was like to be a man, aroused.

A sensual game of Russian roulette.

IMMORTAL OBSESSION

LINDA THOMAS-SUNDSTROM

All rights reserved including the right of reproduction in whole or in part in any form. This edition is published by arrangement with Harlequin Books S.A.

This is a work of fiction. Names, characters, places, locations and incidents are purely fictional and bear no relationship to any real life individuals, living or dead, or to any actual places, business establishments, locations, events or incidents. Any resemblance is entirely coincidental.

This book is sold subject to the condition that it shall not, by way of trade or otherwise, be lent, resold, hired out or otherwise circulated without the prior consent of the publisher in any form of binding or cover other than that in which it is published and without a similar condition including this condition being imposed on the subsequent purchaser.

® and ™ are trademarks owned and used by the trademark owner and/or its licensee. Trademarks marked with ® are registered with the United Kingdom Patent Office and/or the Office for Harmonisation in the Internal Market and in other countries.

Published in Great Britain 2014
by Mills & Boon, an imprint of Harlequin (UK) Limited,
Eton House, 18-24 Paradise Road, Richmond, Surrey, TW9 1SR

© 2014 Linda Thomas-Sundstrom

ISBN: 978-0-263-91405-4

89-0914

Harlequin (UK) Limited's policy is to use papers that are natural, renewable and recyclable products and made from wood grown in sustainable forests. The logging and manufacturing processes conform to the legal environmental regulations of the country of origin.

Printed and bound in Spain
by Blackprint CPI, Barcelona

Linda Thomas-Sundstrom, author of contemporary and historical paranormal romance novels, writes for Mills & Boon® Nocturne™. She lives in the West, juggling teaching, writing, family and caring for a big stretch of land. She swears she has a resident muse who sings so loudly she virtually funds the Post-it company. Eventually Linda hopes to get to all those ideas.

Visit Linda at her website, www.lindathomas-sundstrom. com, and the Nocturne Authors' website, www. nocturneauthors.com.

To my family, those here and those gone,
who always believed I had a story to tell.

Chapter 1

Death was coming in the form of a cold, hard blackness.

Christopher St. John looked for it with his eyes wide open.

He gave the woman down the block a cursory glance, drawn to the shivering gleams of silver coming off whatever she wore as she passed beneath a streetlight, sensing something else about her that he had no time to explore. Though intrigued by all that shine on a gloomy night, no unnatural darkness floated in the woman's wake, so he couldn't afford a second look.

Where was death hiding?

The air he breathed carried an odor of old boots and had the slimy feel of an oxygenated oil slick, as if something nasty had left an indelible imprint. Alerted by that, St. John turned his head and caught sight of an ooze of movement so subtle, human eyes would have missed it.

He watched the shadow pass into the alley on his left. Tuning in, he fired up his senses to determine that shadow's status and to name and categorize the anomaly, which was just another thing that shouldn't exist, but did, hanging on to darkness as if it needed, ate, breathed, required the worst part of a day. Midnight.

"Shade," St. John said, disgusted.

Shades were evil suckers. Unable to possess actual physical form, they couldn't be touched or destroyed by regular physical means. It took cunning, guts, and a whole lot of properly functioning know-how to take down something so substantially unsubstantial. And like flies on a fetid carcass, the presence of this Shade meant some poor fool had died in that alley, probably minutes ago.

St. John's fangs dropped, pressing threateningly against his tongue. He worked his jaw to relax himself. It was imperative that Shades and creatures like them were kept away from London's human population, and that they remained underground. He'd have to follow this one and do his bit to mop up the danger before anyone found out.

Taking a step toward the alley, he paused, his attention disturbed by a sudden prickle at the base of his neck. Cutting his eyes to the left, he saw another shadow hugging the building beside the alley. Then he saw a third.

His fangs began to sharpen automatically, chiseling into lethal points as if they recognized danger all on their own and were getting ready to face it. In this case, the fangs were harbingers of doom. Three Shades in the area meant three dead bodies, since Shades were entities uninterested in sharing their spoils. Three dead bodies in a row suggested the presence of vampires. Probably more than one. These Shades had likely been attracted to leftovers.

Death tonight had manifested in the form of a blood-suckers' blood fest, a vile breach of etiquette in London's trendy West End. Most vampires here, unless newly made, knew better than to trespass on ground owned by their older immortal cousins. The careless vamps heralding the Shades were either really stupid, had been freshly bitten, or they had a death-after-death wish. Same difference in terms of the results.

"Too damn close to mortals to be excused."

St. John again glanced down the street, to where he had seen the shapely woman in silver walking alone. He looked at the row of lights announcing the first of the West End's string of nightclubs, thinking as he always had that these clubs and the people they attracted had become too tempting for the city's extended list of subterranean inhabitants.

The lights were, in essence, like big neon arrows pointing the way to an all-night buffet. But this particular grouping of night creatures currently flouting the rules were truly on the wrong path if they assumed they'd get away with leaving corpses in alleyways so near an immortal's domain. Especially his. Nobody liked gore on their front steps.

Closing his eyes briefly, St. John again felt death's dark touch, a blackness he knew intimately. In a distant part of his subconscious, he pinpointed the nearness of the other uninvited creatures in the area. Vampires, yes. Rogues, giving off signals of rage and insatiable hunger, things he had long ago mastered, though his fangs were empathetically aching.

Something else nagged at his attention besides the five young vampires emerging from the far end of the alley sporting haughty expressions and exhibiting no evidence of their recent kills. Some other warning had caught hold of him, mixed up in the brief gleam of a woman's silvery light.

Shaking that warning off, St. John watched the tight group of young vampires, reminiscent of a group of wild animals on the prowl, boldly cross the street, heading for the biggest club on the block. The same one the woman in silver stardust had entered.

Striding past the queue of waiting guests, the rogues looked the club's controller up and down until that man stepped aside, but not before he'd sent St. John a silent signal of alarm that rippled across St. John's skin in the form of a really good chill.

St. John nodded his head to the man in reply, wondering if perhaps these ignorant fanged parasites had also seen that dazzling young woman and had been attracted. Scavengers, like crows, loved anything that glowed.

Or maybe they were just trolling for dessert.

A wave of apprehension rolled across his scalp. Keeping tabs on the ever-increasing hordes of fledgling vampires would have been a full-time job for a small army. Keeping them out of his own territory was a personal necessity.

Drawing his hands out of his pockets, St. John pressed his lips over his pulsing, aggression-seeking incisors.

"Wrong road, wrong night, boys," he said aloud,

adding in honor of whatever Shades were lurking nearby, "I'll be back for you."

Thinking of what a bunch of unrepentant, openly visible monsters might do to an unsuspecting woman like the one in the intriguing silver getup they were no doubt salivating for, and knowing that *mercy* wasn't a viable word in bloodsucker vocabulary, St. John set his shoulders, squinted at the club's lights and started off in that direction.

He wasn't called the *Protector* for nothing. And that woman, still very much on his mind after only a glimpse, didn't have any idea of the extent of the trouble about to strike.

Chapter 2

It wasn't the first time Madison Chase had downed one too many drinks lately, and by the look of things, it wasn't going to be her last.

She had accepted a martini from the guy dressed in head-to-toe leather at the bar and a shot of something foul from the stiff in the business suit who smelled faintly of clove cigarettes. Some people thought drinking was sexy. She wasn't one of them.

She had tossed those drinks back like they were water and should have been pain-free by now, but the never-ending ache inside her still hurt like hell, not in the slightest bit blurred by alcohol.

Tonight was no different from all the rest of the past three days: roaming around, tempting fate by taking too many chances. Clearly, she was headed for a breakdown if she kept this up. All the signs were present.

She just couldn't seem to back off from the wave of momentum sweeping her up.

She might be placing herself in jeopardy by wandering alone in an unfamiliar city, in another country, at night, but an uncanny, persistent idea suggested that a solo recon might turn up information about what had happened to those missing college girls from the States—the reason for ten American television crews, including her own, taking up residence.

An even more important objective, and the reason for this club-hopping, was the search for her brother, who'd been MIA for a full three weeks.

Hopefully, if her stars were in alignment, she'd find Stewart, her fraternal twin. She just needed to do some of her sleuthing after-hours and alone, since the camera crews usually following her around tended to scare people off.

Plus, there was no plausible way to explain to the network guys that she was almost supernaturally aware of her brother's presence in this part of London because the uniqueness of the bond between twins defied explanation.

Stewart Chase, her womb-mate, and younger than herself by only one minute, felt close enough to reach out and touch. His life force seemed to float in the air, whispering things just out of hearing range.

Madison searched the faces closest to her, finding nothing familiar. Yet she knew she'd be the one to find her brother, if anyone could. Respected Florida attorneys like her twin didn't just disappear when sent by their firms to pursue the legal details of a headlining missing girls' case. Neither did most attorneys believe in the paranormal, she'd be willing to bet.

"But you do," she said to Stewart, wherever he was.

The discovery that he had hidden certain aspects of his life from her had been a shock. More surprising still was the magnitude of the secretive research her brother had gathered on the existence of monsters. Stewart thought that monsters had taken over jolly old England's capital, as well as other cities like it, in the manner of a spreading plague.

Monsters. The kind with fangs.

Vampires, for God's sake.

After cracking the password on his laptop and sifting through Stewart's files, she had learned that her brother had been obsessed with the undead for a while. So, was she to conclude that someone that smart and savvy had become mentally unstable in the past year or two, hiding a loose mental screw from her and everyone else? Although gray, aged London was a place where any gothic idea might seem possible, vampires would be the underworld's dirtiest little secret society.

Stewart had listed this nightclub in his notes.

"Absurd. Disgusting. To hell with you, baby brother, for bringing this up and for vanishing without a trace," Madison muttered, worried her instincts were wrong this time about sensing him near her. Worried also that in sharing genes with Stewart, and thinking about vampires, her own mental screws might someday loosen.

She was here on company time. Her ticket to ferreting out why so many people had gone missing in London in the past month had been presented to her in the form of a golden opportunity not to be missed. Accepting the network's assignment to follow the story of four missing Yale grads, now officially being dubbed in the media as the *Yale Four,* had been a timely move.

And though the streets outside of this club were creepy at night, London's hotspot of the moment, called *Space,* was teeming with people.

Conscious of eyes turned her way, Madison again searched the area around her. The guy in the business suit raised his glass. Shaking her head, she said beneath her breath, "Not going to happen. Not with you, buddy."

She turned her attention to the dance floor. If her brother's research had any merit, this was one of the most dangerous clubs in London for humans, and run by a vampire community whose roots ran deep.

That was nuts, of course. Most of the people here seemed normal enough, and were having a good time. Still, the only way she could maintain any hope of getting her brother back was to explore all scenarios that might explain his disappearance, and those included the most fantastical ones.

So, if she were to *try* to believe her brother...

"What the hell is a vampire supposed to look like, anyway? Other than exposed fangs, how would anyone tell them apart from anyone else?" she muttered.

Stewart's notes said that some vampires blended fairly well with the human population. Then again, rumors about vampires in nightclubs could just as easily be a well-planned advertising campaign for thrill seekers to get off on, and completely make-believe.

This was her third club, in as many nights, looking for Stewart and his monsters. The number three was supposed to be charmed—some kind of supernaturally charged digit. With that in mind, Madison continued to scrutinize the faces around her, picking out likely candidates for fangdom in the crowd. Males seemingly too sober, too intense and darkly expressionless as they lurked in the shadows.

There were a few.

However, slightly suspicious males were also the usual fare for dance clubs, so how in hell could Stewart have been sure of what was what? How could she?

Monsters should be required to wear bells.

And okay, now that she had stooped to considering monsters, Madison wondered how someone with a loose mental screw could tighten it.

Her gaze dropped to the table beside her. Another drink would make the tally what? Three? Four? One awful-tasting alcoholic beverage for every monster she thought she perceived around her. Just to take the edge off the game. For more fighting spirit, in case there was any way Stewart had been right, and there actually were vampires everywhere.

"Another drink is definitely the way to go," she said to herself.

Grabbing a glass off the table, Madison sipped the contents, realizing she was walking close enough to the edge of an abyss to see the steep drop. Why? Because it was impossible to delete from her mind the part of Stewart's research proposing that death didn't have to be the end of existence.

And if anything bad had happened to her brother because of his ridiculous beliefs, some part of her actually hoped he was right. Without Stewart, she felt like only half of a whole. At the moment, a tired, ornery half.

The decibel of the music raining down from overhead speakers drowned out her thoughts. With the burn of alcohol in her throat, Madison closed her eyes and picked up the rhythm of the beat. Moving her head and her hips, she began to wind her way through the people on the dance floor, heading for the center of the room where something other than fear, sadness and regret would hopefully, for a time, give her some peace.

Regretfully, that peace remained as elusive as ever. Someone still watched her. She picked up on this, she assumed, with the special sense of connection to others that some twins possessed. Whoever this particular watcher was had a gaze like a laser beam that made her feel as if she were naked.

She glanced up at the balcony and found the culprit. Her breath caught. Behind the ornate railing stood one of the most beautiful men she had ever seen. Every working woman's version of a wet dream.

Tall and broad-shouldered, the wickedly handsome observer leaned against a pillar with a self-assured, languid pose. Immaculately dressed in black, a visually stunning contrast of fair hair surrounded his sculpted, angular, aristocratic face.

Having noted his interest, Madison figured that any other woman would have run right up to that balcony and handed him her hotel key, desiring his touch and to hear his haughty British accent. Happy to have been singled out by such a creature, they'd have wished for a kiss, a condom and the luck of being chosen as his one-night stand.

Any *other* woman.

She didn't have time for that sort of nonsense, or for anything other than this one dance. It was after midnight, and she'd be on camera in the morning. Plus, finding this guy observing her so intently, her inner warnings about him automatically upgraded to full alert.

He was staring at her rudely. Something in his expression made her imagine he possessed the ability to read her mind, and that what he found there was amusing.

Blinking slowly to break contact and announce to him that she had no intention of accepting his unspoken invitation, Madison ignored the rise in her pulse that he was causing. No one on the planet was that good-looking. She should know; she had interviewed a lot of movie stars up close.

What would Stewart have said about him?

Maybe this guy's beauty was unearthly because he actually was unearthly?

Though that seemed ridiculous, she took Stewart's reasoning one step further.

Maybe one of her brother's secretive research subjects had just crystallized, and the awe-inspiring male exterior encapsulated something not so fine at its core. Hidden inside that full, slightly insolent mouth of his, could be a pair of long, pointed teeth.

Thanks, brother.

Madison now regretted the drinks, and vowed to never touch another one. Defiantly, she whispered to the man on the balcony, "If there are such things as vampires, though, there'd be no doubt about you."

Disturbed that her brother's extraordinary inner world had folded into her own, she gave herself over to the dance, keeping an attentive eye on the other men that were ogling her as if she were an appetizing after-dinner snack.

St. John settled his shoulder against a pillar and stared down from the balcony, his gaze riveted to one particular woman on the dance floor. He had found the woman in silver. When a sensation long dormant in his chest stirred, he hardly recognized it as a bead of honest interest.

Her hair was bloodred. A brilliant, fiery riot of untamed curls that glowed like bonfire flames in the dimness. Hair like that was the colorful embodiment of passion, intelligence and sex. Moist with sweat, several silky strands clung to her pale neck like crimson streams leaking from a puncture wound as she danced, dead center in the room and in the middle of the fifty other gyrating bodies, on the gritty stainless-steel floor.

St. John had never seen anything like her, or the way she moved. She waved bare, slender arms over her head sinuously, with her eyes closed, as if caught up in a trance. Her hips swayed in time to the heavy bass beat of music in a fluid, seductive display.

As she wove intricate patterns with her body in the tight area she'd carved out for herself, heat rose from her in visible waves. All that heat and flame in one sleek outline made it easy for him to assume he wasn't the only male in this club whose gaze was fastened on the sultry redhead. Certainly not the only one with fangs.

No being with functioning genitals, either dead or alive, could have failed to be drawn in by Madison Chase's enticing performance. This close, he would have recognized the American newscaster anywhere.

His fangs remained lengthened and ready for action, which meant that the rogue vampires were here, and nearby. A subtle scent of well-turned soil pervaded the area below, underscoring the rising drifts of sweat and expensive perfume.

The five bloodsuckers he'd seen on the street had been lured from the anonymity of the crowd and onto the outskirts of that dance floor. He sensed them as cold spots in the overheated room. They were bits of darkness broken off from the night outside, misplaced black holes with no perceivable pulse of their own. Deviations among the world of the living, and nothing at all like him, though their eyes and instincts were also trained on the redhead they had followed here.

Bloodsucker presence in this club was unacceptable. Problem was, he was finding it difficult to concentrate on that situation. His body had already started pulsing in time with Madison Chase's.

Rather than searching out the specifics of the creatures he had tracked here, he continued to stare down at her. The sexy femme's solo performance was an added bit of trouble. The fact that rogues had also zeroed in on the lithe dancer leaned toward a notable multiplication of the problem.

That nagging something he'd sensed in the back of his mind while outside, on the street, had reappeared in the form of a woman. He wasn't sure why her presence affected him, beyond the obvious fact that Madison Chase was nothing short of magnetic.

His reaction to her was visceral and soul-stirring. But he had seen Chase on broadcasts and heard her on the radio, and knew why she had come to London, along with all the other television crews from around the globe.

Madison Chase, famous for her determined attitude of withholding nothing newsworthy from the public, could turn out to be a royal pain in the backside if she persisted in nosing around where she didn't belong. It would be even worse if she were here to track vampires and their body counts, taking up where her brother had left off.

Damn, though, if she wasn't a tantalizing half-naked problem, and keen to his well-honed senses.

The parts of her that weren't bare were skimpily covered in a mesh concoction of silver sequins and spandex that was anything but modest. Calves, knees and most of her shapely thighs were exposed. She wore impossibly high-heeled shoes that sparkled and made her long legs seem endless.

He supposed nice girls might be allowed in public underdressed like that in the States, in the current decadent decade, though for this particular woman to call so much attention to herself here was an act approaching suicide. The world wasn't as safe as it once had been.

Tonight, because of her sumptuous looks and moves, Madison's appearance was a health hazard. Her way-too-personal, provocative dance was raising not only the room's temperature, but some of the room's occupants' hormone levels, taking those things precariously close to the critical zone.

She was playing Russian roulette with her life.

"The gun's chamber might be empty this round, but it's only a matter of time," St. John said to her from his observation perch. "Surely you can hear the fangs gnashing?"

She looked up right at that moment, as if she'd heard him. Her eyes widened. When her lips moved, St. John knew he had been right about the trouble. He'd heard what she said.

"If there are such things as vampires, there'd be no doubt about you."

"Such a pity," he said, because it wasn't his business to warn Madison Chase about anything. Nor was it his job to rescue her from herself or anyone else. She wasn't supposed to be on his radar at the moment. There was only room for one Chase twin at a time.

All he had to do was turn his back, lure the rogues outside and take care of them. If he didn't do this soon, it looked as if the mindless monsters might make a move on Madison right here. They were stalking her in public, in one of London's busiest, most successful clubs owned by a consortium of ancient immortals—beings who wouldn't condone misbehavior of any kind. Though the Ancients were themselves old vampires, they hated the fanged fledglings as much as mortals would, if mortals truly believed vampires existed.

"Do you believe it, I wonder?" he said to the feisty dancer stirring things up, and who had the potential to become a thorn in every vampire's hide if she were a believer like the brother who looked almost exactly like her, minus the good parts.

"I guess you haven't been paying enough attention to the roadwork your brother laid about the danger," he said to her conversationally, as if they were side by side.

Actually, she probably had no idea how far and how deep the creatures she'd called vampires had long ago dipped their fangs into London society. Likely she hadn't a clue that immortals owned more land in England and had stockpiled more cash in this country than the Queen.

It also had been made abundantly clear, by her reputation as an aggressive television personality and by her visit here tonight, alone, that Madison Chase might be as tenacious as a vine in digging out newsworthy scoops.

No doubt she was here to find her brother.

"Ah, but you are so interesting. So tempting," he said. "It would be a shame to let the monsters have you. Not to mention how quickly your disappearance would become an international incident. I suppose, in that case, I'll have to intervene."

Descending to the dance floor by way of the stairs, instead of taking a graceful, telling leap down, St. John added, "All that glorious, disturbing heat…" as like a wave of barely disturbed air, he edged himself through the crowd.

Chapter 3

St. John came up behind Madison Chase on the dance floor, eyeing two of the vampires who quickly turned away from the sternness of his gaze. He spoke to her in a husky tone that he willed her to hear above the music.

"You're alone?"

"Not anymore," she replied over her shoulder. "Though you might want to choose a better opening line."

St. John hadn't been fully prepared for the deepness of her voice, or that it might rival her sultry exterior. As the surprise washed over him, he grinned.

"Also, there's a rule about having to dance while on a dance floor," she said, swiveling side to side so that her hips lightly brushed against his thighs.

His reaction to the unexpected touch came in the form of a jolt of pleasure that streaked through his body. Her life, her energy, and all that fire in such a fragile body, were heady draws that for a fleeting moment made him remember what it was like to be a man, aroused.

He quickly compartmentalized the sensation.

"It's crowded here. Would you like something to drink?" he asked, hoping he'd get her to stop this indiscriminate sexual display and back her temporarily into a safer corner, while at the same time hoping she'd go on dancing. She was so very good at what she was doing.

"No, thanks," she replied. "I never drink while I'm working."

Working? Yes, she was working it hard. He'd attest to that. And she had lied about not drinking. The sugary fragrance of an alcoholic beverage emanated from between her lush, parted lips.

This woman, he decided with mixed feelings, was sex on legs. Without thinking, he reached out to touch her wrist with a quick stroke of his fingers, desiring to touch something so fine, but backed off before doing so, satisfied that she really was as hot as she looked. Heat to someone like him was the ultimate turn-on, and so very dangerous for the mortal radiating this much of it.

Out of the corner of his eye, he watched the two disgruntled, freshly christened vampires circle the floor, checking him out. He sent them a second silent warning.

"You're still not dancing," Madison said, looking at him with slightly dilated, incredibly lovely blue eyes.

Aware of the fact that he was beginning to stand out

by standing still, St. John matched his rhythm to hers. As he started to move, he searched her, head to toe.

Madison was indeed genetically gifted. She had a fine-featured, delicate face, with flawless skin. Small nose. High cheekbones. Arched brows. The damp red curls clinging to her cheeks were darker than the rest of her hair and a stark contrast to her skin's paleness. Her mouth was glossy with a scarlet lipstick so dark, it had a blue cast under the lights. Much like dried blood.

Only the force of his willpower kept him from grabbing her. The urge to lay his lips on hers, to taste that red shine and run his fangs over her pretty, pale cheek, was close to overwhelming, and an affront to his monk-like existence.

He couldn't recall the last time he had been so taken with a woman's appearance that he'd allow one to lead the direction of a meeting. And if he was so affected, the young monsters nearby had to be in a state approaching frenzy.

He had to get her out of there for her own good, but in spite of the danger edging closer, he wished for more time with her.

"Perhaps you don't like meeting new people," he suggested when she tossed her head, raised her taut, toned arms and continued to sway in time to the beat.

"I like men," she said, "if that's what you're asking."

When viewed in silhouette, her body was slender to the point of sleekness. Her shoulders sloped toward fragile arms and small, firm breasts. No hint of a bra covered those breasts beneath the mesh dress, which led him to focus longer than he should have on a bit of pale pink nipple. Hell, he actually was aroused. His aching fangs weren't the only parts stimulated by the woman.

The reactions to this sensational dancer had hit surprisingly hard, as if he had dived back in time to when those kinds of physical reactions mattered. He nearly smiled again, though keeping his fangs hidden was imperative. Some people might consider him a monster, but he liked to think of himself as a gentleman, when all was said and done.

"You like men, just not this one?" he persisted. "You might prefer a darker complexion or a smaller frame. Maybe you only like Americans."

She shook her head, sending her red curls flying. "You're too good-looking. Hurtful to the eyes. I don't need more pain in my life."

St. John accepted the unusual compliment with another burst of unfamiliar pleasure. Nevertheless, the fact remained that Madison was more naive than her brother had been if she didn't understand how easily he could make her do whatever he wanted with one whisper in her ear. No self-respecting centuries-old immortal hadn't mastered such a basic trick, and he'd had more opportunity than most to use them.

"Is that a compliment and a rebuff, all in one?" he asked. "Also, it's a strange comment, since I believe you haven't really looked at me yet."

"The truth is," she said, stopping so suddenly, she bumped into the person next to her, "I saw you on the balcony. You're hard to miss. Besides, you're not really affected by my comment anyway, are you, since you're not actually a man at all?"

St. John's eyebrows went up out of sheer curiosity. She had pegged him as a vampire, though she wasn't

acting as if she truly believed it—which meant he had
to consider the possibility that she wasn't serious, and
merely engaging in an unusual bit of titillating fantasy foreplay.

He had heard about vampire fans and groupies of
popular horror fiction pretending to be bloodsuckers, playing with the concept without confronting the
downside. However, this was Stewart Chase's sister,
so he had to take care.

"Not a man. Damn. That's probably not good," he
said, eyeing her carefully, trying to decipher what she
might be up to.

"Not good for the unsuspecting people here," she
agreed, exhibiting an outward calm, though he sensed
her heartbeat had begun to rev inside her chest, and
the pink buds of her nipples had hardened. Her beautifully bare, formerly fluid shoulders became tense
and riddled with chills. Long lashes veiled her eyes.

"If not a man, what do you suppose I am?" he asked,
his concentration dropping to the dazzling net of sparkling silver mesh encircling her frame like a garment
composed of pure, unobstructed moonlight.

"Don't you know?" she countered with a lilt of cynicism far too worldly for one so young. "Don't you know
what you are?"

"For all I know, this could be some kind of test."

"Vampire. You're a vampire," she said. The nonchalant way she stated this set his fangs on edge. The
comment also increased his interest. Possibly the Chase
twins had done their research together, after all.

"You believe in vampires?" he asked.

She shrugged.

"If you believe I'm one, why aren't you running?"

"You're bigger than the other monsters here and have twice the presence. You outclass them by miles, so I'm guessing you're a lot older, have more experience, and that if I stay here, on the floor, doing what I came here to do, you won't hurt me. At least not in public."

Unable to help himself, St. John let out a soft bark of laughter. Madison's idea of foreplay was exotic and chancy. For him, sexy, brazen and intelligent were characteristics adding up to a deadly irresistible mix.

Yet she had also proved herself to be somewhat enlightened about his breed, and this was cause for concern. And she was scared. The metallic tang of fear seeped from her pores, adding texture to her woodsy perfume and telegraphing to him that there was a fair chance she might actually believe what she was saying.

"You said *work*. Do tell me what it is that you came here for, exactly, given that dancing isn't the only objective," he said.

"One of my goals was to find you," she replied with a further outward calm containment of nerves that St. John supposed could have earned her an award.

"Find me, personally?" he said. "You know who I am?"

She nodded. "And what you can do."

St. John sobered slightly. "Should I be flattered?"

"Are vampires vain enough to accept truth as flattery?"

Now she had even more of his attention, if that was possible. "Of course," he replied. "Some of us, anyway. It's so rare that we deal directly with mortals who aren't sprinting in the opposite direction, you see. So, if you came here to find me, and saw me watching you, then your dancing might have been to lure me to the floor? To you?"

"It worked."

He grinned, conceding the point. Her intention had, in fact, been accomplished to perfection. He had felt in his bones that she'd been dancing for him, and had been drawn to her light and heat like the proverbial moth to a flickering flame. This was an interesting deviation of his character, and one to be considered carefully.

"Now that I'm here, do you want to tell me why you were looking for me?" he asked.

"I've merely been seeking truth in the rumors."

"There are rumors about me?"

"Now who is being naive?" Her gaze rose a few inches, though she didn't make eye contact. She had not resumed her dancing.

"Actually, I was thinking the word *naive* applied to you." St. John alluded to her outfit with a pointed finger. "I came down here to tell you so, and to warn you to watch out for yourself, though not quite so directly. I'd hoped to use some tact."

"Yes, well where I come from, directness is not a flaw. I know what I'm doing."

"I seriously doubt that, Miss Chase, or you wouldn't still be here talking to me."

When she used lean fingers to press a strand of hair back from her face, St. John knew he had surprised her with his own frankness and the use of her name. Her heart rate exploded, one loud boom after another visibly pounding against the bare skin of her long, lovely neck.

His gaze hesitated on that stretch of creamy skin longer than was prudent before realizing that two of the vampires in the periphery had also sensed the rise in Madison's pulse. Out of the corner of his eye, he saw them take several steps onto the crowded floor.

"You know who I am, then?" she asked.

"We Brits aren't as backward as you might think. Some of us even have television sets."

"What else do you know about me?" Her tone was husky now.

"I believe rumors on this end have you as the bane of anyone's existence who tries to get in your way. Is that a fair assessment?"

He expected her to dash for the exit now that personal truths were being revealed. Instead, she replied with equal candor, "It's a good enough description, I guess."

"Since you're here alone, and looking for vampires, you know pathetically less about us than you give yourself credit for," he said.

"*Us,* as in Brits, pick-up artists or vampires?" she countered.

Right after, and as though something had disturbed her, Madison's attention shifted to one of the ravenous rogues. "This has been fun," she said. "But the question in need of an answer is if you'll help me, now that we've been introduced?"

"Help you how?"

"I think there are others here who are looking at me strangely." Her expression remained unreadable, with her blue eyes again cloaked by lowered lashes. "Will anyone try to harm me right here?"

Had she somehow sensed the other vampires? Nailed that closest rogue as one of them? She had looked directly at the fledgling.

"Not here," he said, checking that fledgling out. "No ruffians will harm you here."

"Why won't they?" she asked with obvious distaste.

"For several reasons, not the least of which is that bloodstains may be difficult to remove from the floor.

She didn't respond to his remark. Didn't smile. Her expression remained unreadable, even for a master like himself, which made him wonder what she might be thinking.

Her heart gave her away, in the end. It beat dramatically, each strike lifting the skin beneath her right ear.

She truly was scared.

Was all that thumping in honor of the presence of the others she thought might wish her harm, though, or due to his nearness to her? St. John couldn't quite get a handle on that, or which Madison Chase was the real one… The dancer, with her loose, inviting body, or the intruding, borderline-aggressive, slightly frightened and very nosey media insider, who might or might not have a nose for vampires?

He decided that the unique mixture of all those ingredients was what had fascinated him, and also what made him unexpectedly excited by their continued closeness to each other.

"These ruffians you mentioned are also vampires?" she asked, and followed that question rapidly with another. "If that's true, or even if it isn't, will you see that I get out of here, or at least as far as the door?"

The way she tilted her head exposed another dewy length of ivory skin. Her tension made the enticing lacy network of lilac veins in her neck stand out like a road map to the source of every vampire's inherent need. And though he wasn't a vampire, *per se,* he had been created by drinking of the blood of his Makers, and was reminded of this now by a treasonous thud in his chest.

"Then again," she added, "if I'm to be the bane of anyone's existence, including yours, why would you help me at all?"

Since she preferred directness, and was still thinking in terms of vampires, St. John answered in kind. "Isn't it possible, since vampires were once like you, they're not all heathens? If you can't believe this, I wonder about your sources, Miss Chase."

The spine that had so mesmerizingly taunted him just moments ago snapped straight. The rigidity made the woman beside him seem even younger, and more vulnerable.

Had she taken him seriously? She who had brought up this vampire game?

Her sudden show of frailty sent a reactionary shock of emotion, with the force of a fist, slamming against St. John's rib cage, kicking his nerves into overdrive. He didn't want to hurt her; didn't want anyone else to hurt her. Madison Chase was like a rare, glittering jewel, no matter how her mind worked.

"You wanted to find monsters, and that's it?" He spoke to cover his tremendous need to touch her.

"Yes," she replied. "Maybe."

"Now you'll go? Simple as that?"

"If I can."

"If you were hunting vampires, expecting to find some here, I take it you planned for an escape route?" he said.

"Aren't you that escape route? My free pass out of here?"

"Why would you assume so?"

She glanced up. "Don't they call special beings like you Protectors?"

That stunning announcement actually stopped his breathing for a while before St. John reminded himself to take in a lungful of stale, sweaty air. He withheld a blasphemous oath.

It was possible for Madison to know superficial things about his community, since her brother had been interested, but it was damn inconvenient for her to know about his position within it.

Protector.

No one knew of this. This precocious woman's brother certainly hadn't known it when he'd come nosing around. Yet reason told him that if Madison hadn't been kidding, and that if she knew what kind of beings ran this club, as well as about Protectors, she had to have an informant. One too close to the fold.

The question, though, was still whether she had really pegged him as a vampire? Beyond that, did she actually know that by asking a Protector for help, he was bound to oblige?

The game had changed. Gaining knowledge about what Madison Chase knew about his society was crucial, as was the importance of finding who her informant was. She almost certainly hadn't seen her brother, or she would have been running for the airport to get as far away as possible. If she'd truly been looking for vampires, would she have come to the club alone?

He wasn't sure, couldn't read her. For the sake of the immortal community, as well as his own well-disguised presence in it, though, he was driven to find the answers.

The room seemed to darken somewhat. He had always loathed the dark when there were so many genuine surprises hidden in it.

"You are far from your home and out of your league on this one," he warned, noting that Madison, with good reason, seemed more and more uncomfortable, and was trying hard not to show it. Her arms were taut with long lines of anxious, wiry sinew. Her pretty jaw had set.

He went on. "There will be trouble if you roam the city alone, and probe into issues that don't really concern you. It's best that you forget about this club and the word *vampire* before some real blood hits the fan. There are all sorts of monsters, you know."

Although her lips parted and he expected a comeback, she didn't offer one. The word *blood* had an effect on her. They had wasted far too much time. He had to get her to move. The only way to make her believe the seriousness of her predicament, as well as seek those answers he needed, would be to get her to safety with a minimal amount of damage to anyone here. Two of the rogues, partway onto the dance floor, were losing patience, being taken over by a bloodlust too ferocious for anyone's good. Their gaunt faces were feral in the fallout of the club's neon lights.

"If the word you use for bodyguard is *Protector*," he said over her silence, "I can help. But if you persist in taunting ruffians of any species, they might hunt you down for sport."

In fact, they already were. And Madison would be like Easter candy to creatures so much better than television journalists at going after their prey.

"To the door, then," she said, bringing him back to

those wide blue eyes that nearly met his. "Please escort me there."

"Well, since you asked so nicely…"

Of course, he knew it would be easy to get her to the door, being who and what he was, and also that it was too late for her to take ten steps beyond the exit by herself. Madison, in all her silver-sequined glory, had attracted the attention of too many creatures tonight. The place virtually hummed with ill intent.

Three of the five miscreants had already cleared out, though the dark, gaping hole by the exit suggested they were out there, eagerly awaiting her departure. Their anticipation, excitement and tangible bloodlust rolled across St. John's skin as if it were his own.

When his fangs raked his lower lip, he imagined what using fangs on the woman beside him would be like for those others. They might take their time biting into her, using quick flicks of their teeth to tear apart her flawless flesh. Would they offer a tender kiss to her throat before the final bite, though, or whisper a caress?

Probably not, since those things were issues of control that had to be learned over long spans of time, and most vampires didn't make it past their first year. Although fledglings had Makers, they lacked tutors, as well as self-restraint.

He told himself to stop imagining kisses and caresses and fangs and throats. All of those things were too erotic with his libido this fired up. Care had to be taken not to maintain his closeness to Madison for too long. An immortal's idea of foreplay was different from the norm.

Damn those rogue vampires. Besides needing information from Madison that necessitated his continued contact with her, he wasn't ready to have her removed from the world—and not for any altruistic reasons. He wanted to bask in her heat awhile longer. Part of him longed to feel the remembered humanness and anticipation of indulging in an all-encompassing man-woman attraction. Since mortals and immortals didn't mix or play well together, he'd had no desire before this to explore those things.

Madison Chase was different.

And he was a sucker for redheads.

"Would you trust me with my help beyond that doorway?" he asked, observing the daring sideways movement of the two remaining rogues. He knew he'd be unable to take care of them here, with so many mortals around.

"You have got to be kidding." She sucked in her cheeks. Her chest rose and fell with each staggered breath, so that her breasts were close enough to touch. Only inches away.

"I've never been more serious," St. John said as his heart fell in sync with hers, virtually stealing her rhythm and adapting it as his own—a trick that happened with all vampires and their superior immortal counterparts when confronting a victim or an enemy. They tuned in, sensing every move, beat and thought.

The bloodsuckers closing in on Madison would know how frightened she had become and would be anticipating her departure with their fangs gnashing.

Following his gaze, she glanced to the exit. "Do you know something I don't?"

"The answer to that would take time that you don't have, I'm afraid."

She threw a second glance to the doorway, visibly

shaking now. Her little silver sequins made tinkling sounds that only he could hear.

All that femme-fatale bravado on the dance floor had indeed been a show, St. John realized. Her expression had changed. The scent of her fear was stronger.

Maybe the dancing act had been for him, or merely to satisfy her own private needs, but getting Madison away from Space would not only save her life, but possibly also the lives of countless others in and out of the club. Newly turned blood drinkers were mean, fast and exceptionally hungry. When thwarted, *bloodbath* described the results perfectly. These rogues were barely hanging on.

When he held out his hand to her, Madison winced. Nevertheless, it was necessary for him to touch her. His scent would disguise hers, up to a point, until they were out of sight.

"There's a back way out," he confided.

"So, you really are going to be my Protector?" Her voice wavered.

He turned his palm up insistently. "In this case, you just might be right."

She wasn't going to touch him, no matter what, even after soliciting his help. Her anxiousness tangibly thrummed in the air, part real and part false, the falseness signaling to him that she wasn't completely dissatisfied with his offer.

Time was pressing. St. John took her hand, thinking to speed things up. Immediately, with the first feel of her fingers in his, he became immersed in an inferno-like flood of heat, shockingly molten and similar to getting too close to the sun. The onslaught of sensation hit so powerfully, so unexpectedly, he briefly closed his eyes.

It had been years since he'd touched a mortal for any reason, and centuries since he'd been one of them, yet in that instant, as their hands met and she looked into his eyes with what he knew was the fearful fire of both intrigue and disgust, St. John sensed that there was much more of this story to come. In order for him to find out about that story, he'd see to it that Madison Chase stayed out of the hands of London's monsters and stayed alive.

His job description of Protector, meant originally not for guarding people, but the special blood in his veins, had been changing lately, and had just morphed again to include Madison.

She might hate interruptions in her agenda and fear forward strangers, but the sparks crackling between them said it all. Underneath her fear, she reached out to him. She wanted to know more about him, and was drawn to him. Whether she actually believed him to be a vampire, or not, would remain to be seen.

As for himself…for whatever reason, he had made an instantaneous connection to her from afar, outside, on that street, in a way that defied description.

He was equally aware of fact that the Ancients, called the *Hundred* because they had all lived past that milestone in time, would get wind of this small indiscretion—his willingness to help a human, and in particular this one, tonight—while allowing rogues to get away with murder on the streets. They would know about this breach of protocol before he left the building.

Every action had risks.

This one might be worth it.

Tugging Madison to him before she had time to register his move, St. John gathered her body to his. He ran his hands over every glorious angle she possessed, exploring her with his eyes and senses wide open, looking for the secret to this unusual attraction.

The Ancients present who were observing this might assume he merely desired the kind of steamy sexual encounter a mortal like this one could provide. Taking a woman or man to bed wasn't completely forbidden by this fanged community. Biting them for anything other than pleasure was.

He laid the flat of his palm against the smooth bareness of her back in an intimate touch that moved him way down deep in memory and made Madison shut her eyes.

Daring to slide his fingers downward, beneath the loose silver fabric and over each bone of her naked vertebrae, one at a time, toward the curve of her buttocks, he heard her sharp intake of breath.

"You bastard. What the hell are you doing?"

She had meant to say *monster*. He heard this as if she had actually shouted the word.

He didn't stop touching her, feeling her, caressing her. It was imperative his flesh touched hers, skin to skin, and equally as important for him to scare her out of her crazy solo reverie.

With a gentle lightness, his hands retraced their way over every inch of her anatomy, floating briefly over off-limits sensitive spots in what would seem to her a ghastly transgression. He did this, not because he wanted to distress her further or pleasure himself at her expense, but because it really was necessary on so many levels.

"I have to make them believe you're mine," he told her, leaving her most vulnerable spot for last. Nothing could be left out of this scent transfer. Not one part of her.

With his knee between her legs, as if they were merely engaging in a slow dance of lovers, and with his mouth next to her ear, he lightly stroked the V between her thighs that was covered by damp, lacy lingerie. Touching her there seemed to alarm her. Hell, it shook him up more than he had anticipated.

In a flash as ephemeral as a dream, he imagined easing that lace aside and slipping another part of himself in. Amid the crowded frenzy of the dance floor, if he held Madison tightly enough, close enough, possibly no one would notice the rise of her dress, and how easy it would be for him to claim that hottest and holiest of spots between her slender, silky thighs.

What then, Red?

She gasped with a sound that suggested she might want the same thing, and that this torrid fantasy had been one of her creation, all along. She had admitted she'd been dancing to lure him to the floor. To her.

So, was he helping her for her sake, the public's sake, or merely indulging himself?

Stopping his exploration of her body, St. John rode out a series of aftershocks rolling through Madison that echoed his own. In tandem, their pulses soared. Their heated breath mingled in the steamy air.

She wasn't completely against his actions. When his exploration had been completed, neither of them moved. The seconds ticking by were unexpectedly rich, and roughly textured by doubt. Two strangers were pinned together for whatever reason had drawn them together, and sharing an incomprehensible desire for more.

Sadly, seconds were all the time they had. They were the wrong kind of strangers, opposites in every way, from the true rhythm of her heartbeat to the name she had called him and what it meant. *Protector.*

Riding the crest of the temporary time stall, and reveling in the enormity of the pleasure this awkward intimacy gave him, St. John waited to see what she'd do next. Which of them might finally break the spell.

With her chest against his, the beat of life within her seemed strong and slightly intimidating, coming from an organ that monitored itself and needed no reminder to function. He had forgotten how loud a mortal heart could sound. The noise filled his ears.

The heat she radiated was the best thing of all. Soaking it up as though he had never been privy to such warmth before, and as though he'd never get enough, St. John whispered, "What I'm not telling you may come back to bite us both. You will be marked now, from this day forward, as mine. Because of your request for help, and because this is the only way to accomplish that, you will forever crave this touch as much as I will."

His sigh stirred her fine, baby-soft hair. One lustrous strand tickled his face.

"There is payment due for every action, you see," he went on. "This closeness is mine."

With his mouth in her hair, he heard the blood rushing through her veins, beneath her ivory skin, sing a song that called to him as seductively as her body had. That blood meant life. Living, breathing, life. Fragile. Heated. Special. Mortal.

*Take me...*Madison's blood sang.

Drink me.

But those were the rogue vampires' thoughts, not his own. He was tapping into their desires, too, which only somewhat paralleled his. Distance had to be encouraged from the delicate arteries just centimeters from his lips. He wasn't one of *them,* and never had been. Christopher St. John had never bitten anyone... for sport.

With that protest live in him, St. John reluctantly and with the greatest effort allowed Madison to tear herself away from his embrace. Once free, she raised her hand and slapped him hard across his face, as he'd known she would. For all the world, he wouldn't have stopped her.

"Ready?" he asked.

Smiling grimly, and without waiting for a reply, he took a handful of silver spandex and backed up, pulling her overheated, angry, extremely luscious body through the oblivious crowd.

Chapter 4

The suddenness of finding herself fleeing from the dance floor came as a surprise, and meant that the arrogant bastard beside her might actually be keeping his word about getting her to safety.

After all the touchy-feely personal exploration that she'd had no ability to stop, and may even have helped along in a moment of complete mental lapse, Madison didn't know what to make of any of this. She refused to look closely at the guy holding on to her, afraid of actually believing her brother, and that gorgeous British males could potentially be vampires.

Surely this guy had put a goddamn spell on her?

She had always believed Stewart, one hundred percent, in the past. So, what if vampires were real? Conversely, what if Stewart's research amounted to a pile of nonsense, which was much more likely the case?

As this guy whisked her through the crowd, Madison kept unuttered cuss words to herself. Shouting obscenities in a night club would be a very bad idea. Any incident centered on her might make the headlines.

Every nerve in her body twanged from the illicit touch of the man who had hold of her. In the case of a quick exit, though, he appeared to be helpful.

At least they were moving.

The fact that her pulse raced was an annoyance. This gorgeous guy leading her might have wanted to help her for dubious reasons, but in his brief embrace she had nearly forgotten about everything else—all the bad things, all the work she had to do.

This was a grim reflection on her present state of mind. She wasn't often fooled by offers and false ardor from people who wanted something from her, either because of her job or merely to score points by bedding a minor celebrity.

Probably, this guy wanted one of those things.

The arrogant male hadn't introduced himself. He hadn't rejected the vampire foreplay, or shunned the title of Protector, a term her brother's notes had listed as being the vampires' liaison to the rest of the world's population.

Of course, this guy could simply have been playing the game she'd started, toying with her by making spooky small talk. She had brought the whole monster thing up. Without that freaky conversation, their meeting might have gone in a different direction, despite her former resolve.

Protector and *predator* were probably interchangeable terms in swanky nightclubs.

"This is far enough," she said after passing through some of the club's back rooms.

"Not nearly far enough," he countered in that deep masculine voice of his, speaking over one impressively broad shoulder.

They moved on.

He'd said there was a back door somewhere.

The club was aptly named, and much larger than it appeared from the outside. Striding through dim corridors, dodging people doing all sorts of activities that shouldn't have been open for public viewing, Madison began to breathe in the dank, stale smells of the original portion of the old building. Eventually, the hallways narrowed and the people disappeared.

They were moving quickly through a dark area. She had voluntarily trod the fine line between remaining safe and tiptoeing toward trouble by going out alone tonight, and by asking this stranger to help her. Whatever happened next, she was responsible.

Damn though, he seemed to have the eyes of an owl. A twinge of concern surfaced over that, because she couldn't see a thing.

Maybe he had vampire eyes?

Wanting to kick herself for the cynicism, she quickly replaced that thought with another.

Her strange bodyguard was rescuing her from a bunch of idiots bent on trouble, but he could just as easily be taking her from the club for nefarious purposes of his own. He, or someone like him, could have taken all four Yale girls away in a similar manner, pretending to take charge of their safety. Those girls had just dropped off the face of the earth.

Finally, her strange guide led her through an unlocked back door. They emerged into an alley. Hit by a blast of cold night air that seemed extreme after the closeness of the club, Madison sighed with relief. This guy had done what he said he would, but her nerves remained jumpy. Her skin felt red-hot where his hand fastened to her wrist.

He didn't stop in the alley, or show signs of slowing. Rounding the corner of the club's exterior, Madison dug in her heels, sliding on a filthy stretch of pavement.

"It's quite possible this won't be far enough," he said with a tug that effectively got her moving again.

"Wait a minute. Stop." Madison swallowed gulps of the chilled night air. "You're saying those idiots watching me might follow us all the way out here?"

"Yes," he replied.

"Pursuing you, or me?"

This earned her a lingering look.

"Okay. So, why me?" she asked, deciphering his look. "They recognized me?"

"You're beautiful, exotic," he said. "In that outfit, you look like a piece of some distant constellation, and yet you feel like the sun. Who wouldn't want to be close to that?"

"Even taken as a compliment, is that supposed to make sense?"

"It does if you know what your pursuers are, and what drives them," he said.

Before she could address that, he pulled her off balance, tipping her sideways onto the hood of a conveniently parked car. She landed in a compromising position with her skirt hiked up and her bare legs dangling over an icy metal fender. No blaring car alarm went off to warn anybody within hearing range. There was no one around to respond to a shout.

Primed to fight, Madison struggled to get up. "You can't tell me this position helps in a getaway."

"Yet it demonstrates how easily you might be overpowered by someone stronger than yourself."

She was held down by her companion's hands as he arched over her. His outrageously angular face came close enough to see each shadow that outlined his face in the faint illumination of a nearby streetlight.

"Okay. I get that," she said.

Light eyes searched hers intently. She avoided the scrutiny by glancing away. Adrenaline spiked through her in a sharp, nasty flood. Usually she thrived on this kind of scrambled energy.

"I need you to listen, and to pay attention," he said. "You requested my help, and I am helping. At least I'm trying to, because danger is close behind. Can't you sense it, smell it? Aren't journalists supposed to have a nose for danger?"

"My reactions to everything so far have danger written all over them," she said pointedly, referring to her current position on her back. "What I'm smelling is bad, and way too close to me right now."

The comment hadn't been lost on the man hovering above her. He had the audacity to crack a smile, and said ominously, "Do you want to continue to argue, discuss the mysteries of the world, or get away from what could turn out to be your worst nightmare? *They* are coming."

"Then it might be a good idea to let me up and dial whatever the hell the emergency number is in England."

"What will you do then? Run? How far do you think you'd get on your own, not knowing the city?"

"Farther than this."

Her next intake of air drove this guy's scent deep into her lungs. The masculine odors, topped by the faintest trace of musk, had nothing artificial or perfumed in them. No hint of aftershave, because it was highly possible, she again thought cynically, that vampires, being the walking undead, couldn't grow a five-o'clock shadow.

"Just who is the danger here, anyway?" she demanded.

When he turned his head to listen to a sound she didn't hear, another round of apprehension struck her. He sniffed the air, in the manner of an animal detecting its prey.

"What the hell?" She resumed her struggle to rise. He held her easily—this mystery man who possessed a graceful, threatening, controlled elegance that made him more than a little frightening and at the same time disarmingly seductive. Sort of like a big, sleek panther decked out in a really expensive, perfectly tailored suit.

His eyes might have been blue. She upheld her refusal to check them out. Every horror movie she'd ever seen proposed that it would be suicidal to meet a vampire's gaze, though the same should be said for all predators.

She figured that looking into the eyes of any incredibly chic bastard would be the equivalent of handing him her hotel key. On her back like this, underdressed and on a side street, she wasn't going to take that chance.

Screw the heat beating at the air between them. Get-

ting away was urgent. This man was too darn sexy for
anyone's good, and pushed all her buttons, some of
which shouldn't have been up for debate.

Kicking out with her legs, she managed to sit up.

She froze.

"Oh, shit," she said, the sound of her pounding heart
nearly drowning out everything in the surroundings.
"You weren't kidding, were you? I think I hear them."

Her companion nodded. "They're young and persistent. They've found the scent."

"What scent?"

"Yours," he said.

That reply, made so casually, brought on a quick
stab of real fear. "Let me go," she demanded.

He obliged.

St. John let Madison slip off the car, regretting the
necessity. Emotions, long ago buried along with his
mortality, had no place here.

He was helping her, not completely for personal reasons, but in favor of keeping bloodsuckers away from
the unsuspecting crowds. At the same time, he was
preventing another international incident.

The oncoming gang of young vampires demanded
action. Their imminent approach needled his skin like
tiny pricks from the point of an annoyingly icy blade.
He needed them to follow, and had allowed them to
play catch-up.

But something else nagged at his conscience: Madison Chase's heartbeat. When he had pinned her to the
hood of the car, their hearts—the beats, rhythm and
pulse—had shared an intimate moment on a subcon-

scious level of awareness, as if they'd met like this before.

He didn't fully understand this new sensation, and found it disturbing.

"Go now," he said, and she rocked back on her heels as though unsure of how to respond to her sudden freedom.

"What will you do?" she asked tentatively, brushing fiery strands of silky hair back from her face.

"Wait for them."

St. John wanted to touch those flaming strands, and press them close to his face. He wanted his hands back on her.

"By yourself?" she asked. "You'll wait for them by yourself?"

"Go," he repeated. "I recommend that you start right this minute."

She turned, and started walking. Then she stopped as though halted by a hidden roadblock, and just stood there.

St. John found himself wondering why she'd blow her chance to get away from him, as well as the others, if she was scared. He wasn't holding her there physically. He hadn't imposed his will.

For a fleeting, perhaps untrustworthy moment, it seemed possible that she had hesitated, not because of the bond he'd set in place between them on the dance floor, but because she was contemplating the same strange attraction to him that he was experiencing with her.

There was no ignoring the heat of having her so close. He fisted his hands to keep from reaching for her.

"What part of *right this minute* don't you get?" he said.

"The part you're leaving out."

"The devil is in the details, Madison, and he's not very attractive."

"I'm familiar with the devil."

"Somehow," St. John said, "I don't believe that's true."

His shoulders ached as the metaphorical knife pricks got deeper, warning that the time for discourse with Madison was over. He felt a pang of remorse over that. She was beautiful, radiant and alive, but it was nearly too late to keep the identity of the approaching vampires from her. One look at those rogues, up close, and Madison would know for sure that their vampire foreplay on the dance floor hadn't been a game at all.

His interest in her had to wait. All five of the misbehaving misfits were rounding the corner. The sight of the group caused Madison to stumble backward.

"Do this for me, if not for yourself," he said to her. "Run."

"Not without you." Her voice quivered.

"You're afraid of me," he pointed out, using up precious time they didn't have.

"But more afraid of them," she admitted.

Bloody hell! The woman was interfering with the unnatural order of things by sticking her pert little nose where it didn't belong. She couldn't be privy to his dealings with these creeps, and not facing them, not dealing with them in the manner they deserved— the manner necessary for maintaining his community's anonymity—was already weighing heavily on him.

He wasn't used to distractions or abandoning one

cause for another. This went against his grain, an impressively nonhuman grain. The purest form of immortality animated his body, forging within him a direct link to the source of all immortal blood on earth. Only six other beings in the world could claim this, if in fact they still existed.

They had been the special Seven. Seven men chosen for the gift of life everlasting, and all that came with this gift. A fraternity of souls designed for an endless quest.

He had lived through numerous crusades, continent expansions and too damn many world wars. Given all that, what would be the cost of the possible loss of one woman, met at random, in comparison? Why risk anything for her?

When her eyes met his, perhaps accidentally and perhaps because he had unknowingly wished for it, the impact of the connection struck him like a fresh wound to his chest. He knew that losing Madison, if she were to be harmed, or if she ran off into the night, would be not only a shame, it would be unbearable.

He craved the fire. Her fire. He craved her heat, and the beautiful body radiating so much of it. He tried to get a handle on this as he held her gaze.

Her blue eyes, large, round and wary, hinted at depths that contrasted her scandalous state of undress. In those seconds, with their eyes meeting, St. John confirmed that Madison Chase was indeed much more than she seemed on the surface. More than heat and sparkle and a partially naked display.

She was a fighter, strong-willed, confident, and maybe even slightly mad. These were characteristics she shared with her brother, and the very traits that also made her a threat.

Did she want to be like her brother, pursuing vampires? Had she come to London for the same reasons that Stewart Chase had come here for, using the missing girls as a ruse to further their own agenda?

The uncertainty obviously fueling her visible tremors hadn't budged her. Five vampires heading her way didn't have her running. For all her wariness and his warnings, when faced with the unknown, Madison Chase was concerned for him.

The Protector was being aided by the damsel in distress.

You really are going to be a pain, Red.

Smelling death's fetid breath, feeling its presence surf across his senses, St. John whirled. Fighting for control of his automatic reactions that would have made him walk toward that oncoming darkness and confront what was hidden within it, he instead took Madison's hand.

She had kicked off her shoes. They lay at her feet, looking on the black asphalt like spiky bits of fallen silver stars. He found himself smiling joyfully, in spite of everything. After enduring years of an empty, benign lack of emotion, he had experienced several in the last half hour. With her.

Holding out against a surge of possessiveness so strong it threatened to take him over, St. John said to her, "Just this once," and started to run.

Chapter 5

Shudders rolled over every inch of Madison's body, stemming from the electrical charge that came with this man's skin meeting hers.

Again, she found herself sprinting through parts of London with a stranger. She may have made a stupid mistake by trusting in him in the first place. It wasn't like her to take this many chances.

They were sprinting through a maze of narrow side streets. Her bare feet were taking the brunt of both the pace and the debris littering the ground. She vowed to complain if things got weirder.

No sound came from behind. Only the rush of blood echoing inside her head filled the silence. Her companion's legs were twice as long as her own. His shoes, striking the streets, seemed to be working in mute mode. He wasn't laboring, wasn't breathing hard. He was definitely the one in better shape.

With all the twists and turns they'd made, she lost all sense of direction. Since they hadn't slowed, it became obvious that her companion knew the area well. The hour was late, well after midnight. The side streets were quiet. They hadn't passed anyone since leaving the trendy West End. If she shouted for him to stop now, or asked where they were going, would the idiots behind them hear?

If they were still following.

Around the next bend, a set of steep concrete steps loomed, looking in the dark like a stairway from hell to whatever lay above. Madison tackled those stairs in her guide's wake. His hold on her hand never loosened. Tiny bursts of electrical charges continued to pass from his fingers to hers, his skin to hers, each surge bringing up more questions and fresh rounds of anxiety.

She was harboring lusty, ridiculous thoughts about one-night stands with strangers. With no idea who her companion might be, or where they were, the drama and the obvious electricity between them turned her on, despite the situation.

They reached the top of the steps with her heart working near to full capacity. She sucked air through her mouth without the ability to catch up or stabilize her breathing. Her bare feet were sliced up pretty badly, and probably bleeding, leaving a blood trail for vampires to follow, if, as in Stewart's world, blood was their drink of choice.

If she got out of here, she might not be able to wear shoes for a week.

When her guide suddenly slowed, she wanted to cheer, until she sensed movement from their left. A subtle shifting of shadows in the distance produced a new layer of gray on black that her companion noted with a sigh.

She heard voices, laughter. Her heart careened wildly.

With a smooth tug of his arm, her compelling stranger shoved her against an old stone wall. What air Madison had left in her lungs whooshed out as he pressed himself close, as though he would shield her from whatever was out there by grinding his body tight up against hers.

His body was hard, taut, and her reaction to him was swift. Her legs and arms began to shake with expectation. Her breasts strained against his chest.

"Damn you," she whispered.

The fabric of his pants felt soft against her bare thighs. His breath warmed the side of her face. This sensual stranger felt solid, human and exactly like a man in every way that counted. In spite of that, her breath suspended, because there was something about him she couldn't mentally digest. Her instincts warned that something wasn't quite right.

What was it?

Before she could think about it further, he brushed his lips over hers so softly that Madison wondered if she'd made those warning signals up.

A flush of heat rose from her chest to her neck, and into her face. Her thighs began to simmer, despite the chill of the London night.

"So," she said breathlessly. "You think I owe you just because you saved my ass?"

His hands were on the wall behind her. Madison felt him looking at her, sensed those big eyes continuing their careful observation in the same darkness that wouldn't allow her to reciprocate.

"I have never forced myself on anyone," he said.

The pressure of his body against hers was erotic. Way down deep, she shook with a series of internal quakes. An insistent drumming beat out a warning that had the words *no good* attached to it.

This closeness was wrong, somehow. At the very least, it was distracting, when she had to keep focus. For the sake of her sanity and self-respect, she had to get away from this man who might brag about an intimate liaison with a TV celebrity, or post illicit photos on the internet.

She had to escape this predicament in spite of the fact that the hips tight up with hers fit in all the right places, setting those places on fire.

This was too freaking unbelievable.

Her reactions were unsound. They were in some godforsaken alley, and part of her didn't care. Part of her wanted this, and him. She just couldn't resist his magnetism and graceful animal allure. Against the onslaught of physical reactions, she stood little chance of thinking straight. Her last one-nighter had been a very long time ago.

"This isn't like me. I'm not this person." The words stuck in her throat. As a rule, she didn't lose her wits. Couldn't afford to. Yet the urge overtaking her at the moment wasn't to run away, but to lock her mouth to his mouth, so hot and close and beckoning. The impulse was to tear at his clothes with both hands in order to maximize a crazy, all-consuming and insatiable hunger for him.

When her exotic companion spoke in the gravelly,

velvet-clad tone of a man unfulfilled, she knew he was experiencing the same thing.

"Madison," was all that he said, but the word caused her body's deep throb to intensify. She was certain this man knew it. He had to be feeling each beat.

His lips danced across hers lightly, without lasting pressure. His face moved to the crook of her neck in a slow slide of his smooth, cool cheek over hers. She felt his lips touch a spot beneath her right ear before he moved on to place a soft, almost tender kiss on her shoulder.

She was getting hotter, hornier.

"All right." Her lips formed those words against his lips. "Damn it, all right."

He didn't react or respond until her hands crawled up his back. Then he made a faint sound of startled acceptance. After that, the night became a hungry, mindless blur.

His hands were back on her. In a replay of the naughty touch on the dance floor, they slid between her legs with a dangerous spontaneity.

The hem of her silver mini rose. His fingers moved under it, drifting over her lace-covered mound.

When her thong began a feathery, downward descent, Madison wanted to shout at the time this was taking. Spontaneity didn't mix well with taking the time to consider the possibility of mistakes. She wanted him now, inside her, hard and fast. She wanted to get this over with, because it was insane and unavoidable, and too late to do anything about.

He lifted her up. Her back hit the stone in a scrape of sequins. The lace panties fell silently to her ankles, and then to the ground. She was naked from the waist down, and his fingers flowed over her sensitive places like some kind of molten liquid. Confidently. Possessively.

He urged her to wrap one leg around his hips with a slight motion of those hips, and her bare, moist, sensitive parts met with his swollen groin as cool palms danced over her thighs.

Madison loosened her grip on his tensely muscled back just enough to make room for a second brush of friction; his fingers on her folds without the thin, almost indecent barrier of lace.

The subtle external caress, accompanied by the silky seduction of his golden hair sweeping across her face, kicked up a rolling internal rumble that rushed toward this personal touch. Each breath she fought for was shallow. She could not have opened her eyes, no matter what.

The guy dealing out this exquisite level of pleasure hadn't yet even fully participated, and she was already on the verge of a climax.

But the deep-seated evidence of his seduction also seemed to carry something else in its wake. A dark shadow rode this seduction like an unwanted hitchhiker.

Something was wrong.

Madison whispered a throaty, "Stop!"

The hand pleasuring her stilled upon her command.

The inner chaos of her approaching orgasm hovered some time more before eventually starting to recede. Her insides ached for its loss. Her mind whirled.

He hadn't reached that place she'd so badly wanted him to reach. His hand remained on her quivering slit, and she couldn't allow him to move.

She had no idea where the protest had come from, or what that darkness was that she'd felt so extremely. Yet as the orgasm she hadn't quite reached disappeared, the dark haze lifted from her sight, leaving her and this stranger motionless, and glued together in a compromising position.

It was a truly awkward moment.

He moved first. Her would-be lover set her on her feet, and backed up a step, forcing her to overcome the weakness in her knees.

"We will meet again," he said in an unsteady tone, and gently pushed her toward the concrete stairway, where she was again out in the open without her shoes, without her panties, unsatisfied, alone and exposed.

The transition from being in his arms one minute, to being on her own the next, was too quick.

Was it possible that this hunk of a man might give her to the creeps who had chased them, turning her over to them after having his fun? He and that gang couldn't be some kind of kinky, faux-vampiric tag-team, out to separate tourists from the crowds?

She supposed that anything was possible. She had been uncharacteristically gullible, but at least they hadn't had sex; no penetration and going all the way. She was lucky that her companion had let her get away with this protest, and had stopped when she'd asked him to.

Would he have done so if this was part of some scam?

Hearing laughter echo off the buildings, Madison spun to face it. This was men's laughter, loud and unrestrained.

Were they laughing at her expense?

She gazed into the dark, to the wall she had been pressed to, no longer able see the man she'd been with. Panic shot through her as she pressed her dress down, and glanced at the steps.

Someone shouted at her, too close for comfort.

Rigidity overtook her. It was too late for retreat.

The laughter became a roar in her ears.

Balling her hands into fists, Madison turned as another shout came. Two more shouts followed, sounding like…greetings. Sounding, in the vast stretch of foggy, foreign darkness surrounding her, vaguely familiar.

Nerves revved, skin tingling with fear, Madison felt a scream claw its way up from her chest. On wobbling legs, she processed the familiar lilt of a voice, unable to confront the rush of relief she began to feel.

"Hey, Madison! Is that you?" Theodore "Teddy" Jones, her network cameraman, called. "What are you doing out here?"

Collapsing with relief was not an option.

St. John watched the four mortal males surround Madison. In a swirl of his own shadow, he silently leaped onto the wall at the edge of the alley. Walking quickly along the top, he backtracked along the same route he and Madison had taken.

The rogues were heading this way.

His sexual escapade with Madison would have been short, if allowed to continue. But he had been up close and personal with the American media anchor twice, enough to ensure that some of her scent had rubbed off on him, as well as the other way around. Smelling like her, he would lure the rogues away from where he'd left Madison, and lead them to a more secluded area.

Fledgling vampires tended to squeal like teenaged girls at a party when taken down. If it weren't for Madison's scent, saturating his pants and jacket and hands, the murderous villains wouldn't even see him coming.

On the downside, her lingering fragrance was as enticing as it was delicious, and a heady distraction from his usual routine of avoiding mortals whenever possible. His coat smelled like an orchard of trees basking in Florida sunlight. His fingers, having dipped inside her glorious heat, smelled like…heaven.

He stopped midstride as if pulled to attention.

Something wasn't quite right about either scent. In the heat of the moment, he had missed that.

He wanted to turn around, find her again, and to hell with the Americans he'd left her with at the steps, as well as the bloodsuckers on Madison's trail. He wanted to know what had just happened, what this new scent was and why she had been the one to step on the brakes.

Madison had been willing. He hadn't imagined this. The spike of electrified current he'd experienced with her, with every touch, in every breath, had also caught her up. She had been soft and supple. And yet she had only gone so far.

Had she heard the others approaching, with inferior mortal ears, or had she merely had second thoughts about a sexual liaison in a dark alley?

She hadn't pulled away or raised a hand to slap him a second time. Her sensational body had ached to give in to the bond he'd set in place in the club, just as his ached.

But he had begun to detect the anomalies in her as soon as his mouth had met with hers. Although it had taken him awhile to process the information, he'd tasted the thin layer of darkness that Madison kept tucked away, hidden.

That's what the unusual scent also had to be. Darkness. She may have hair the color of flames, and lips like heaven...but all of that was tinged with a subtle layering of shadow.

He had sensed a similar darkness hovering about her brother on the one occasion they'd met.

This gave him pause.

Nevertheless, he couldn't afford to reason things out at the moment, with his responsibilities here only half over. He'd gotten Madison to safety, and although her safety was important, his initial task remained.

Taking off again, St. John jumped from the wall and landed soundlessly. The nearness of the young vampires ruffled his nerves beneath Madison's darkened, woodsy fragrance.

"Job to do," he said aloud, with determination.

With Madison's scent in their noses, the fledglings searching for her like cats after a rat would never give up. After one whiff, these vampires would follow her until they found her, however long it took.

They had to be stopped before they did, stopped before they encountered other people on the streets tonight who got in their way. Fledglings didn't know how to curb their appetites. These upstarts had outlived their welcome in the West End. Madison was far too intriguing to wind up as pulp on a damp sidewalk.

Miss Chase had to be around for a while longer, so that he could see her again.

He intended to learn how much she knew about her brother's research, and what part she played in it.

But the truth was there were more personal reasons for keeping her safe that had little to do with whistle-blowers, hidden inner darkness and her capricious, lacy lingerie. He just wasn't sure he wanted to accept those reasons.

As St. John kicked up his speed to a pace that made him little more than a blur to any onlooker, he admitted to himself that it was entirely possible that, darkness aside, Madison smelled nothing like a Florida orchard. Since he'd never been to Florida, he might be wrong about that.

One more alley...

He paused in an open-legged stance, listened, waited. When the five savage youngsters, probably no more than a week or two old as vampires, full of themselves and finding comfort in their numbers, stopped on the opposite side of the lane, sneering at him with their fangs exposed, St. John shook his head.

"Now that," he said, "just makes it easier all the way around."

Then he waited for the stupid bastards who knew no better, and knew nothing about him, to attack.

Chapter 6

Sleeping had been tough before. Trying to keep her eyes shut now amounted to torture.

In her unair-conditioned hotel room, located a short hop away from Buckingham Palace, Madison tossed and fretted on the mattress, struggling to relax, finding it impossible.

Fresh air might have helped, but there was no way she could open the window when the man who had rescued her from those thugs had freaked her out about who might be out there. Hell, he had sent her imagination into overdrive. Possibly, that damn loose screw was at that very moment turning inside her head.

She didn't even know that man's name.

She had stood in the shower until the hot water turned lukewarm, and scrubbed her skin raw with a washcloth, and she still smelled *him* on her skin. Wool and musk and that other more elusive undercurrent that permeated the air around him as he'd taken her for a midnight run were still there.

Her hotel room smelled like him. So did her sheets. Her oversize white T-shirt had picked up the smell. It had been impossible to rid her freshly washed hair of this lingering fragrance of seduction and mystery.

She didn't know why he had initially played along with Stewart's vampire games. Admittedly, though, the guy she'd been groin to groin with was too special to be a mere mortal, any way she looked at it. And way too sexually exciting. From the start, it had been obvious that something had clicked into place between them. Lust at first sight was a powerful incentive for tossing inhibitions aside.

That stuff about *them* following might have been a ploy for him to get her alone. *Them,* as in what, London's version of a low-life street gang? Certainly he didn't mean the monsters her brother would have her believe frequented London's crowded places. That had just been a game. Strange foreplay.

"Vampires. Jesus." She made a face.

The man she'd been tight up against hadn't been some ephemeral bit of mythological mist. He had been solid, and interesting in all the right places.

"No mistake about that."

If she hadn't come to her senses, she'd be even sorrier now about the whole ordeal.

Madison smacked the mattress with her open hand. She had placed herself in a bad situation, and luckily had come out of it reasonably well. But she had also been distracted, big-time, from the after-hours search for her brother. Distractions she couldn't afford.

"So why does this hotel room lack a minibar, as well as an all-night pharmacy in the lobby that could cough up an aspirin or sleeping pill?"

Her nerves were shot, she couldn't breathe properly, and there was no way she'd open that window, a crack, even if she didn't really believe there were vampires or some other *things* out there.

Flipping over on the bed, she knocked over the half-full box of Band-Aids that Teddy Jones, now holed up down the hall with another member of the television crew, had graciously provided after seeing her safely back to the hotel. She waggled her toes, lacerated with superficial cuts and fairly sore, though she'd been fortunate enough to have avoided broken glass.

Losing her expensive shoes was a drag. She had discarded the designer Choos somewhere near the club and would have to replace them with a cheaper pair. The silver stilettos had been a rare twenty-fifth birthday splurge last year.

"Shall I send you a bill for the shoes?" she asked.

If she met the handsome maniac at the club again, she'd register a complaint in person. Going beyond that, she might also press charges for scaring the wits out of her. Again, she glanced to the window to make sure it was closed.

"Sucker," she said.

In the morning, in the daylight, and prior to her crew's meeting for updates on the Yale Four case, she would hit a department store for some forgiving footwear. She'd already done ten interviews with the families of those girls, as well as some potential witnesses. The morning broadcast cameras wouldn't need to include any shot below her knees.

She'd also need to use extra makeup to cover the dark circles that would no doubt appear from a lack of sleep, and perfume to mask the scent haunting her.

Tugging on the edge of the rumpled sheet, Madison looked to the window for the twentieth time.

"Feeling claustrophobic," she muttered.

In Miami, in her modern high-rise condo, the windows were always open at night. No one in their right mind would attempt to climb up the outside of a twenty-four-story building to bother her, unless they were related to Spider-Man. No one would probably bother her here, either, in this busy hotel, in her cubby-hole on the sixth floor, unless the invader happened to be one of Stewart's vampires. A Protector, maybe.

She blinked slowly, in disgust, and said, "Don't even start."

On the desk were stacks of files pertaining to her assignment. She had a few more interviews to do. If she had stayed in tonight to work on those files, none of this would have happened. No chiseled, fake vampire. Nothing embarrassing.

Then again, hindsight wasn't worth much these days. The four young women who had vanished while vacationing in a civilized country didn't have the option for a do-over.

She hoped to God those girls were alive. After tonight, she could see how one false move might have been the key to their downfall. If her crew hadn't shown up when they did, there might have been a chance she wouldn't have made it back in one piece.

Next to those case files on the desk sat her laptop, loaded with her brother's files on monsters. She'd had to work hard to crack his password.

"Absurd," she said, her gaze straying to the window. No one could actually be out there. Her memory pulled up something. A warning, or a threat, issued by a blond stranger that she hadn't registered at the time.

"You will be marked now, from this day forward, as mine."

"Frigging nonsense," she snapped.

Nevertheless, she found herself at the window, searching the street below.

She saw nothing out of the ordinary. A few people meandered toward the palace and Green Park. Other than a handful of cabs and cars, London had gone quiet.

Leaning against the wall, Madison smoothed her hair back from her face. The movement caused the masculine scent she'd tried so hard to get rid of to waft over her. Coughing once, she lunged for the bed.

On her back, with the blanket pulled up to her chin, she traced small visible cracks in the ornate, slightly luminous white ceiling plaster, hoping counting cracks would be better than counting sheep. Hoping to avoid erotic fantasies about strange men...with fangs...

Even though her hand had already slid under the elastic band of her underwear, to the same spot *he* had touched.

St. John felt Madison sink beneath the surface of consciousness. Cautiously, he climbed over the window's iron railing and entered her room.

He was trespassing, but the need to see her was great. Dark had a tendency to draw dark, which was a viable reason for him being here, and maybe why the fledglings had been drawn to Madison as well.

There was something about her.

She lay curled up on the bed, with her knees to her chest. A thin, well-worn white T-shirt replaced what had earlier passed for a dress, and was equally as sexy.

Her lithe body took on softer aspects in sleep, when she didn't expect surprises, though her position told him she wasn't comfortable. Faint sounds came from her each time she moved—noises so very inviting to a hungry soul.

"I'm far too interested in you," he said, watching Madison's eyelids flutter as if she might sense him beside her.

"For the first time in a long while, I hunger for a mortal. I am a man, you know. Not in the way other mortals might define the term, but my desire remains the same."

A twitch in Madison's right cheek made him want to touch her, but he didn't dare.

He was aware, even now, of the darkness she harbored. It sat beneath her taut, ivory skin. She and her brother had come here under the auspices of following the case of the missing American girls, yet her brother had already shown his true hand. Stewart Chase had ulterior motives for arriving in London, and look, St. John wanted to tell Madison, where that had gotten her brother.

"Are you like him? Do you share your twin's need to find creatures that aren't mortal? Do you also hunger for the supernatural?"

There were so many kinds of vampires, he thought. Those who drank blood, and those who soaked up the very essence of others in a different way, by taking away their freedom.

Mortal souls thrived on freedom. Madison's soul

needed more freedom than others, he supposed, which is why she took chances. Madison Chase, the gutsy newscaster, went to any lengths to unearth a story. This is what made her dangerous to his cause. Exposing the immortals in this city would be a stupid move.

"I wanted to look at you when you aren't looking back or looking away," he said to her. "Few women turn the heads of beings like me. Few cause us to look beyond ourselves and our long pasts."

She wasn't awake, or listening. Her fingers moved restlessly on the pillow.

"A moment more. Only that, Madison."

St. John leaned over the bed.

Breath. Touch. Skin. Scent...

He ached for the woman on those sheets. His fangs were extended, and throbbing. She had made him hard. She had made him laugh, severing the bottomless world of melancholy from which he never completely escaped. Madison Chase had lightened his world for a few brief moments, and then she had left him wanting.

Her fine crimson hair spread out over the white pillow in coronas of radiant sunfire. Transparent skin stretched beautifully over the planes of her delicate face. Staring at her made St. John wonder if he might find some kind of salvation in his nearness to her, if only for a while.

There was no real future here. They weren't alike. Though his body and hers would fit together perfectly, her life's spark was what separated them.

"Can you blame me for wanting what you have to offer? I can feel your heart and your heat from here."

If allotted the time to get to know her better, Madison still would have been hard to handle and out of bounds. If there were to be a replay of their intimate moments in the alley, he might actually learn to care for someone like her, when his agenda couldn't strain that far.

Madison was a television darling, but she hadn't dealt with the likes of the Hundred who ruled this city and what went on there. For them, and the ring of immortals surrounding the Hundred, there could be no long-lasting peace if they were discovered. The world wasn't ready for what they represented.

A low murmur escaped from Madison, as if she had heard that thought. St. John didn't step back. He was experiencing longings formulated from centuries of ignored, pent-up emotion.

He had to know everything about Madison, and he had to stay away from her. He wanted to settle himself between her long legs, and could not do so. It was essential for him to find out how much she knew about Protectors and vampires, when even this small closeness brought pain.

"You must not find your brother," he whispered to her, observing how his breath stirred one glossy strand of her hair. "You won't like what you'd see."

His hungry gaze traveled down the length of one pale arm to find the imprint of a breast, outlined behind the thin fabric of her shirt. His body pulsed with the effort of his restraint. He snapped his fangs angrily.

He had to get away, quickly. The turn of her head had exposed more flawless skin, and his attraction to that bit of naked flesh was disconcerting.

"I'll leave you now."

Turning from the bed, he tucked in his fangs. A weaker being would have acted on the cravings, but

he had never been weak. He had, in fact, been chosen
for his strength and honor. The gift of immortality
had been bestowed upon him because his Makers had
known he would uphold that honor at all cost.

At the window, St. John spoke again. "You have
never come across the likes of the Hundred, and must
keep off their radar, Madison."

Filled with regret so tangible that he could taste it,
St. John left his sleeping beauty, refusing to look back,
turn back or change his mind…already hating the necessary separation.

Chapter 7

The knocking sound seemed to come from a long way off. Annoyed, Madison rolled over.

The sound came again.

This time, she came fully awake and glared at the door in the haze of the early-morning light coming through the window.

"Chase, you in there?" Teddy called from the hallway. "Open up."

A surge of adrenaline propelled her into alertness. Grabbing the blanket off the bed to cover up with, she padded to the door and yanked it open.

"Ted? What's up?"

"Why didn't you answer your cell?" Teddy's voice was tinged with wary excitement.

"It didn't ring." Madison looked to the bureau, where she usually put her phone. "Great. I must have left it somewhere."

"Well, that's bloody inconvenient," Teddy said. "Get dressed and be out here in five."

"Why?"

"I'll tell you then. It's something you'll want to hear."

Knowing better than to prolong the five minutes Teddy had asked for by demanding more details, Madison closed the door. There was no time to worry about the dreams, or that damn window. The dimensions of the room were small enough to prove that she was alone in it.

She knew the routine. Her makeup case sat in her bag by the desk, ready in case of emergencies. Clothes were on hangers and easy to grab. Shoes... Hell, her feet hurt just standing on the carpet.

She wiggled into jeans, pulled a loose black sweater over her head and slipped her aching feet into a pair of worn athletic shoes. With everything she'd need to be camera-ready in hand, she stepped into the hall in just three minutes flat.

Every member of her crew was there, crowded into the narrow hall and looking rumpled. Madison tossed her things to the assistant in charge of details, and tore an elastic band off her wrist to tie back her unruly hair.

"Dish," she said.

"There's news," Teddy explained as they headed for the stairs. "The police have found something they think might be important."

"Pertaining to the girls' case?"

"In lieu of you not answering your cell, I got the wake-up call to get our butts in gear and get over there to find out."

"There's a hotel phone in my room," Madison pointed out.

"Have you heard how loud that thing is? It would have woken the entire hotel and scared the pants off everyone, including you."

"Yeah, and a rap at the door wouldn't do that."

"It was a gentle rap," Teddy said.

Madison threw him a sideways glance. Teddy appeared to be more rumpled than the rest of the guys. That call for action he'd mentioned must have just happened. Then again, Teddy always appeared to have just gotten out of bed. His short dark hair stuck up at odd angles. He hadn't shaved. His blue shirt was partially unbuttoned, and untucked. It appeared that Teddy had also had a sleepless night.

"Where are we going?" she asked, racing with him and the other crew members down five flights of steps, hearing the bump of the equipment bags they carried striking the walls.

"The London Eye," Jerry, the new assistant, said.

"That's the big Ferris wheel thing," Teddy clarified. "By the Thames."

"What do we know?" Madison brushed through the lobby toward the revolving glass doors that showed a white van with its door wide open waiting curb-side. The crew had gotten the rented vehicle here quickly.

The others began storing the equipment inside. After they'd jumped in, the metal door slammed behind her, and they took off.

"Okay. What?" she said, looking to Teddy.

"Clothes," he said. "They found some clothes."

"Belonging to the girls?"

"No."

The fine little hairs on the back of her neck lifted.

"Whose clothes?" she asked.

"There's a whisper about a possibility they might belong to your brother."

Although Madison tried to take this news in, she had a hard time digesting it.

"Stewart?" she managed to say.

Teddy nodded. "The network told me that the authorities are hoping you might be able to identify the items. I said we'd be there shortly, before the morning newscast, and that we didn't want the police coming to get you."

"Thanks."

It was a miracle she'd gotten that one word out. No further conversation seemed possible. Someone had found what they believed might be her brother's clothes? Clothes he wasn't wearing?

Her empty stomach turned over.

The ride was short at that early hour. As the sun rose in the east, the London Eye appeared above a sparkling glint off the Thames—a humongous, permanent carnival ride perched on the bank in front of a block of centuries-old buildings. She had always wanted to go up on the Eye, in one of the glassed-in baskets that provided a bird's-eye view of the rooftops of London. Now, the contraption was still, and slightly ominous in its silence.

"Are you going to be okay?" Teddy asked.

She nodded. "When were these articles discovered?"

"Either sometime last night, or early this morning. That's all I know."

The van stopped in front of a line of yellow crime tape. The sight of that tape rendered Madison speechless.

A male uniformed officer met the van, but Madison hardly took in the guy's features. She was out of the van in seconds, with Teddy showing his press badge behind her.

She rushed toward the three men in suits standing near the ticket booth for the Eye. Suits were always the guys to see in situations like this.

Situations. Hell, what have they found?

"You're expecting me," she said to them without taking her attention from the Eye itself.

Where were the clothes she was to identify? How had they been found? Who had found them and why did these cops assume that whatever had turned up might belong to Stewart?

Most of all, she wanted to know how they knew Stewart was her brother, and where to find her.

She thought about asking all of those things before any of the men had offered a greeting. She was on the other end of the crime spectrum here, not only reporting on missing cases, but involved on a personal level. She had to keep it together, somehow. As a representative of her network, she had to stay grounded.

"I'm Madison Chase," she added for clarification.

One of the men turned to her. Six feet in height, with close-shorn brown hair, dark eyes and an age she gauged to be approaching forty, he said solemnly, "Sorry to get you up so early. I'm D.I. Crane. Thanks for coming, Miss Chase."

She nodded at the detective inspector. "You have something for me to see?" There was no time for any "cut to the Chase" jokes that had become so prevalent in her job. This detective wore a serious expression.

"We do. Can you step this way, please?" he said.

He moved away, and then stopped to wait for her. Swallowing her fear, and knowing she would have to look at whatever they had found, no matter how sick she felt, Madison followed him, passing several other uniforms until she and the detective had reached the entrance to the Eye itself.

She looked up at the mechanical beast with trepidation.

"We won't be going up," D.I. Crane said.

"You think you might have found something of my brother's here, on this thing?"

Crane gestured for her to step toward the open door of one of the Eye's baskets. "The supervisor stumbled upon this when he got to work this morning."

Madison was starting to feel really panicky.

D.I. Crane seemed to understand. "Right here," he said. "Can you take a look? Are you up to it?"

"There's no body or anything?"

"Nothing like that. Just this." He carefully lifted up something dark that had been stuck behind a pole.

Madison recognized what it was immediately. Though her whole body tightened, she kept the reactions in check with a stern warning that this was just a coat. A black leather jacket, to be exact, with worn patches on the sleeves.

The coat was very similar to the one Stewart often wore in his off time, though reasoning suggested that there wasn't only one leather jacket in the world, and that this one could belong to anybody. There was just one way to find out if this one belonged to her brother.

"Can I touch it?" she asked D.I. Crane.

He shook his head. "We'll take it to the lab for processing."

"Can I smell it?"

That question earned her a raised eyebrow from the Detective inspector.

Madison leaned close to the jacket, and inhaled. *Stewart, is that you?*

What came to her was a shocking nightmare of images. Stewart, running. Being chased. Hurt. Limping to this spot. Removing his coat to see whatever damage he'd been dealt. Leaving in a hurry.

Oh, no. Stewart...

She kept her eyes shut for what seemed like forever as her heart pounded with a fury suggesting it would never slow down again. She feared that if she opened her eyes, she'd scream, and that if the scream came out, she'd lose consciousness.

"Miss Chase," D.I. Crane said.

Just a minute more, she wanted to say. *Please.*

Stewart had been hurt. She had seen that, or so she thought. Their connection ran deep, but she had never felt as though she was inside his skin. She felt like that now.

But Stewart had been alive here, and alive when he left that morning. She didn't want to believe that any lingering aura of death stuck to his jacket, discovered only that day. There was no trace of blood on it that she could see. If there had been blood, the investigators wouldn't have allowed her to get so near to it.

So there was hope. God, yes, a chink of light had

opened up after a long dark spell. She felt her brother's presence here.

"Miss Chase?" D.I. Crane repeated, resting a hand on her arm.

"It's his," she said. "The jacket belongs to my brother, Stewart Chase."

To the detective's credit, he didn't ask how she knew this by smelling the coat. Maybe he was saving the hard questions for later.

"It's his scent," she said to gain some credence with the trained detective. "The only scent he wears. Have you looked in the pockets? What made you believe it might belong to my brother?"

D.I. Crane said, "We found your brother's business card in the pocket. Since he has been reported as missing by both you and his law firm, your ability to identify the jacket could help our investigation."

He held up a plastic evidence bag. "What about this? Do you know what this is?"

Madison gaped at the item in that bag with a disbelief that bordered on horror. The bag contained a pointed wooden stake.

"That's an odd item to be carrying around," D.I. Crane remarked. "Don't you think so, Miss Chase?"

She couldn't possibly answer. Having just gotten the word *vampire* out of her mind, she found that the word again began to blink with the vibrancy of a Vegas neon sign.

St. John felt the chill that riddled Madison's body and knew she was thinking of him. How easily he read her. This was the way the connection he'd set into place between them worked, and the result of helping her out of last night's mess.

Glad of the tip about this meeting at the Eye, he stared down at Madison from his penthouse above the Thames. He saw her sway in reaction to the sight of a weapon made for piercing the chest of a vampire.

He didn't like this.

Hell, he didn't like anything about this.

With his enhanced senses and superior vision, he watched Madison's features go from shock to relief, eventually settling into an expression of defiance. Already, she was putting two and two together, rerunning their interesting vampire foreplay of the night before.

Stewart Chase had been a fool to leave such a thing behind. Finding that stake in her brother's jacket had just upped the ante of not only his strained relationship to Madison, but also endangered her safety.

Each minute she remained in London, now that she and the detectives had viewed an example of her brother's strange obsession, the degree of risk to Madison's security would escalate. Cameras were everywhere. Eyes other than those belonging to law enforcement were watching. If she set her agenda to causing more trouble over this, she'd become a liability.

Two Chases in a row.

That ungainly adjective, *tenacious,* blinked in St. John's mind. Madison was in a state of wary suspension right now, but when the initial surprise wore off, she'd be bolstered by what the detectives had found and driven forward by it.

She'd assume she had discovered a clue to her brother being alive, and tonight she would double her efforts to find him, whether her twin was dead, alive or occupying the space in between.

She would start by going back to the club where Christopher St. John hadn't laughed at her vampire game, and had, in fact, played along. She might demand answers about her brother's research. She might wield a similar weapon to gauge his response.

"Don't you be foolish, too," he whispered to her, his throat tightening due to the knowledge of how dangerous her next appearance at Space could prove to be.

"Take your time and think this through. If you don't believe in vampires, there must be another explanation for that wooden stake."

The way she was staring at that stake made him frown. The way her hand opened and closed, as if she wanted to wrap her fingers around it, left him uneasy.

An icy chill crept up his spine.

He narrowed his gaze.

Madison looked different.

He thought...

But couldn't be sure...

Had some kind of alternate reasoning been awakened in her just by seeing a damn sliver of wood? Was this a reason for the darkness trailing her?

It was possible, and terrible. St. John leaned against the window frame as if those few inches could get him closer to her.

"Are you like your brother, then?"

Anxiously, he tossed the cell phone she had dropped in the alley from one of his hands to the other. Madison would be missing her phone, but for the time being, it was the only piece of her accessible to him. It was another link, if he chose to use it.

Restless, St. John shifted on his feet, forced to think ahead. It didn't take a master to predict how the Hundred's thoughts would go. Getting rid of Madison would be necessary if she showed her face again at Space waving sharpened sticks and muttering the word *monster*.

If she, as a media insider, came sniffing around, an edict would be issued that she had to be dealt with, from the same beings trying so hard to blend in with society.

Hell, it was not only dangerous for him to see her again, but crazy to do so. This was an untimely distraction that threatened his agenda, when he had spent several years shoring up his own well-cultivated place in the vampire community in order to flesh out the identity of the one traitor that had infiltrated the Hundred.

If Madison were to come nosing around, he'd be faced with a choice. Find that traitor, and let fate have Madison, or forget all the time and effort spent on finding that traitor and his degenerate vampire cult, in order to protect innocent mortals, and ultimately the secrets of his kind.

The situation was grim. Even so, he had to choose one of those options. He knew Madison well enough to guess she wouldn't back down on the issue of her brother.

St. John stiffened suddenly. His skin grew colder as his gaze moved to the detective who had placed a hand on Madison's arm. The man had stepped closer to her, offering comfort of sorts in a way that he, himself, could not do.

His fangs flashed. He gritted them in distaste.

And he knew why.

Christopher St. John, one of the seven Blood Knights fashioned for the task of protecting the sacred blood of the immortals, was experiencing a pang of jealousy that nearly choked him.

The little cell phone case snapped in his grip. An old curse left his lips.

A woman like Madison could no doubt have any man she wanted. But she was so much more than a *mere* woman. So much more than a beautiful face. Madison Chase was intrigue in a delicate package. She was light tinged with dark, a challenge and an enigma. She was the keeper of her own secrets, and the temptation of the damned.

And that hellish weapon taken from her brother's coat had made her awareness prickle, as it had his. It had opened her up to taking a second look at her brother's obsession.

Oh, yes. It was necessary for him to meet her again, if only to discover why his bond with her, his snare, so carefully set into place on that dance floor, had worked the other way around...ensnaring him.

His purpose for being in London had hit a fork in the road, a five-foot-six, redheaded fork in the road.

"Tonight," he said, his attention riveted to Madison. "Tonight, if you are going to be foolish about this, I will be waiting for you. Be glad it's me, Madison."

Chapter 8

"I will be waiting for you."

Had she heard that? *Couldn't have.*

"Do you know what this is?" D.I. Crane asked, but she tuned out his voice in favor of the distraction that had come in the form of a disturbing mental touch; a whispered voice that struck like quick, exploring fingers, leaving her feeling violated, and vulnerable.

Trying to locate the origin of the voice that no one else seemed to have heard, Madison looked around, then up at the Eye. When the detective beside her removed his hand from her sleeve, she reluctantly returned her attention to him.

D.I. Crane gestured for Teddy to join them.

"We won't need you for anything else at the moment," he told her as Teddy approached. "Why don't you get some breakfast." To Teddy he said, "Where are you staying?"

"The Doncaster," Teddy replied.

"Can you see that Miss Chase gets back there, and remain in the area in case we need something further?" the detective asked.

"No can do," Teddy said. "We're off to work right now."

"Ah, yes." The detective glanced to the van and the crew standing beside it. "I forgot about the press call."

When Madison glanced down, there was no awful pointed stake or leather jacket in the detective's hands. Another detective had taken them away, saving her from the unwanted scrutiny of her crew, if not the rest of the cops present.

"I'll be around," Madison said. "There's more than one case to be solved here."

"There usually is," the detective concurred. "But we'll have questions, such as what your brother might have been doing here at the Eye, and when he left the jacket. I suppose you'd have no idea about that?"

Madison shook her head.

"Well, I'll be in touch, Miss Chase," D.I. Crane said before walking off in the direction of the other officers.

"That was your brother's jacket in the detective's hand?" Teddy asked.

"Yes."

"If they found it this morning, then your brother must have left it here."

"Him, or someone else."

"Are you okay with that, Madison?"

Stewart running. Being chased. Hurt. Limping here. Removing his coat to see whatever damage he'd been dealt. Leaving in a hurry...

Those flashes replayed in her mind, over and over

in a continual loop. There was no way to be okay with that if the images were real. But were they real?

"I'm fine," she said. "If it means my brother is alive, I can't begin to tell you how happy I am."

But as she headed toward the van, Madison had to shake off a spooky chill of acknowledgment that the voice in her mind had just issued a warning for her to be careful.

"Are you like your brother, then? Don't be foolish...."

She could have sworn she heard those words, and tried to shake off the notion that there was one too many sets of eyes on her back.

"There are press teams here from all over the world," Madison said on camera, holding a microphone in both hands and trying to keep herself together after the shock she'd had.

"It's a good start on the Yale Four case. With all this coverage, surely someone will come forward with a tip, a break."

She held up a piece of paper and moved it closer to the lens.

"We've just learned that the reward for the missing girls has been bumped up to a million dollars, and that the prime minister will formally announce this in a live interview this morning. That interview will take place in less than one hour. We will be covering his speech, keeping you informed and updated on all the efforts to find those girls. *Our* girls. For now, this is Madison Chase for CRTS Television."

Teddy gave her a nod as the camera lowered. "Good sentimental call at the end there with the *our girls*.

It's possible the prime minister might mention your brother eventually."

Now that the camera had been turned off, Madison's insides were churning. Stewart might have been alive that very morning. He might be hurt. She needed to find him, do something, and was stuck here for a few more hours.

"We have time for breakfast if we can find a restaurant close by," Teddy said. "I've been more or less ordered by that detective to make sure you eat. I think he liked you."

Madison shook her head. "You go. Take the guys. I feel like walking."

Both of them turned as noise broke out above the din of several other crews talking things over. In the span of seconds, the area around them fell silent, and a whole bunch of interested faces focused on the ruckus going on in front of the Parliament building.

Teddy grabbed and hoisted the camera, already focusing as he strode that way.

Madison took a step, stalled, whirled back, drawn by the strangest sensation of being called.

She saw him. Her mysterious stranger from the club stood in the shadow of an open doorway, looking as tall and chic and intimidating as he had the night before. Maybe more so, because of her nocturnal fantasies about him.

The arch over the doorway kept his features hidden. If he saw her, he made no move to indicate recognition. But she knew him without the necessity of a close-up. Her nerves had begun to vibrate with a low-pitched hum. Her heartbeat ramped up to a tempo she didn't like and sure as hell didn't appreciate when the guy's scent still clung to strands of her hair.

"Teddy."

Her cameraman pivoted back with a nimble camera-balancing act.

"Can you get the front of that pub on tape?" she asked.

Teddy did so, then took off with the others.

"Got you for posterity," she said, swinging around to find that the man of her secret nighttime desires had already gone.

Running after him as fast as her wounded feet would carry her, Madison stumbled into the crowded pub, where at eight in the morning news crews from all over the world were killing time until the prime minister's speech.

New and familiar faces were swapping anecdotes, information and jokes. In spite of the seriousness of the press call, these seasoned veterans of the information highway knew how to relax when time allowed—a necessity to their health and well-being in a job that detailed loss and sadness on a daily basis.

Lots of faces glanced her way, none of them the one she sought. The mystery man had given her the slip. Yet if he wanted to avoid her after the alley escapade, why had he been here?

Leaning against a portion of the long, gleaming, mahogany bar, Madison looked around for a back exit. He liked those.

Conversations ceased abruptly as someone else entered the pub. Her attention strayed to the front door, where a man had stopped. His gaze found hers. He headed toward her.

"Miss Chase," D.I. Crane said in a lowered tone.

"Detective," Madison acknowledged with another unwelcome jump of nerves.

"Would you please come with me?" he said.

Everyone on the room listened with the uncanny instinct all newscasters and journalists possessed for a potential story in the making.

Madison frowned. "Have you found something else?"

"Please," he said. "Step outside for a minute."

She preceded him to the door, then to the sidewalk, where two other officers waited.

"What is it?" she asked, really antsy now.

D.I. Crane pulled an item from another ziplocked plastic evidence bag he was handed.

Good Lord, had they found something else?

When the item in the detective's hand appeared, Madison was so taken aback with relief, she almost laughed. He was holding up one of the silver shoes she had lost.

"Yours?" he asked, addressing, she assumed, the surprise written all over her face.

"Yes. Where did you find it?"

"Where did you lose it?"

"Somewhere between a club called Space and the street beside it."

He nodded. "You're sure this is your shoe."

Madison looked to his other empty hand. "Hell, do you only have one of them?"

"Only one." He held it higher for her inspection.

"It's mine. Would you like me to try it on, like Cinderella, to prove it?"

"Would you do that?"

She was glad he grinned. Until that moment, she hadn't been sure folks in the law-enforcement profession were capable of humor.

"I kicked the shoes off so that I could run faster," she explained.

The detective's right eyebrow went up quizzically.

"The hour was late. I had to get back to my hotel and couldn't find a cab."

This, she realized, was known as withholding information from the police. Private, personal information about her hunt for her brother, and the man she'd found instead in the club her brother believed housed creatures that went bump in the night. All these things were best left out of any conversation with the authorities.

"You just left your shoes behind?" D.I. Crane asked.

"After three drinks, let's just say I lost them, and leave it at that," Madison said.

Crane's grin thinned out. "We thought the shoe might belong to one of the missing girls until one of your roaming cameramen identified it. I wonder how he would know what you wear?"

"A lot of people have seen me in those shoes, on more than one occasion."

"That's what the guy from your crew confirmed when he saw the shoe arrive at the Eye."

"I'm sorry it doesn't help on the Yale case. We would all like to come up with a clue as to their whereabouts. After finding my brother's coat, I understand why you jumped on this."

The detective shrugged. "Is the shoe expensive?"

"You have no idea."

"In that case, we'll keep a lookout for the other one." He handed her the silver stiletto.

"I'll offer a reward if you do," Madison said.

D.I. Crane made to turn without quite getting all the way around. "May I offer some advice, Miss Chase?"

"I'm all ears, Detective."

"That club, Space, isn't the best place for tourists."

"Has there been trouble?"

"Lately, it seems there has been trouble everywhere."

The detective dug into his pocket for something, and handed her a business card. "You can reach me at this number, day or night, if you want to talk about your brother. We are looking for him, Miss Chase."

"I'm glad to hear it," Madison said.

He had more to say and wasn't shy about getting to it. "I'd prefer you heed my advice about that nightclub and the others around it. And if you lose more shoes, please let me know before we get our hopes up."

"I'll do that."

Wearing a good rendition of the perfect cop face, the detective said, "It's getting to be a habit…finding bits of your family's clothing lying about."

"At least I'm not missing."

"Not yet, at any rate."

The detective left her with that cryptic remark. Yet it wasn't his warning that tugged at her senses; it was the feeling that the mysterious stranger was somewhere nearby, and that she hadn't been entirely out of his sight since they'd met.

Her sigh was one of exasperation. A handsome, brazen stranger and a cryptic cop? What the hell was going on in London?

She should have been more concerned about the cops actually helping to find her brother than wondering about that stranger, and the fact that the words she heard in her head had become like the melody of a subliminal song.

"Don't be foolish..."

"Yes, well, I'll try not to disappoint you," she said aloud, earning a wary smile from an innocent passerby. "And I'll raise you one pointed stake."

Chapter 9

St. John stood on the rooftop of Space, looking down at the dark street, waiting. Would Madison's rebellious streak get the better of her? Would she show up when she had been warned to stay away?

He was dressed in black, his usual choice, not only as a metaphor for the loss of his soul, but because black was perfect camouflage for slipping in and out of darker places.

He and his brethren, called the *Seven,* had chosen ebony for the background of their crest, highlighted by a golden cup centered between two parallel stripes of crimson. One red stripe to represent the blood of the mortality they had left behind, and one for the first drink of the new blood that changed them so radically and forever.

They had painted this design on their shields with

fluid from their veins, and etched the same design into the skin of their upper backs with the tip of a heated knife.

The tattoos were there now, between his shoulder blades; an ever-present reminder of what he had become and the goal he served—all of those things so much bigger than anyone knew.

He remembered, as he stared down at the crowd gathered by the club's entrance, how people had once flocked to him and his brethren for aid. And how, over time, those same people had run from the sight of the fated knights who never aged.

Times had changed, but his goals hadn't. Presently, he was more or less in disguise as just another immortal amid the world of London's immortals, playing a part, acting less than he was after a long, self-imposed exile.

He would break the very heart of the Hundred if necessary to find the being responsible for the creation of so many fanged monsters rummaging around in this city. His vow, taken so long ago, dictated that he find and eliminate the beast whose habit of biting and turning innocent people into bloodthirsty vampires created havoc on the streets.

His job was to guard the innocent, and protect them from the spread of vampirism, though the Seven had long ago all but given up on stemming the bloodred tide taking over the shadows. As the population of mortals exploded, so did that of the beasts. The Seven now had to settle for doing their best.

The wind whipped through his hair and St. John briefly shut his eyes. No one alive or dead, except for his six lost brothers in blood who were scattered around the globe, was privy to the reality of what his function in the world was. No one else knew that his quest continued to this day. Now, with rogues and Shades turning up all over the place, one woman threatened to challenge his goals by getting in the way.

And here she was.

"I didn't want to believe this," he whispered as Madison's fragrant scent filled him.

She stepped from a cab with her body cloaked in a black sheath and her hair glowing like urban wildfire. Stunning, contained, leggy and luscious, she had arrived tonight with a personal army in tow. Four of the men he'd seen around her that morning flanked her.

"You assume this might help, Madison?" he said.

She was tight, tense. Her presence ruffled across his nerve endings, urging him to move. She had ignored his warnings, but carried no questionable weapons.

"At least you had the sense for that," he said, sadly.

St. John braced himself, accepting the implosion of willpower that removed evidence of his superior strength by sucking some of his power inward and away from his outer shell of muscle, skin and bone. He left only enough of that power visible on the surface to firmly set his most recent, well-moderated, practiced persona.

Although the tattooed sigils stretching between his shoulder blades protested the loss of power with a warning sting, he shrugged it off.

"Just another run-of-the-mill immortal at the moment, attempting to ward off disaster," he muttered, taking the quickest way down.

* * *

This time, Madison had come prepared.

Arriving at Space armed with her crew, she hoped the four guys in her entourage would amount to testosterone camouflage.

The day had been disappointing. The prime minister's speech hadn't lived up to its expectations of offering anything new on the Yale Four, except for raising the reward. Since there were no new clues about the girls themselves, there had been plenty of media chatter and a lot of standing around after the necessary interviews.

Tired beyond belief, and emotionally drained from thinking about her brother's jacket and what the cops had found inside it, Madison kept a sharp eye out for any sign of hoodlums on a bender. She had mixed feelings about a rematch with the one man she figured might be here, because after finding that wooden stake, the vampire game they'd played seemed particularly dirty.

She had gone through her brother's research again after the incident at the Eye. Space remained the club of choice for finding vampires, Stewart had written. That chiseled stake only served to press home the fact of how serious her brother's quest was to find the fanged gang.

She had to take this equally as seriously if she were to find Stewart.

"Open your mind," she said. But embarrassment made her hope she'd make it through this night without meeting the fair-haired hunk who had nearly had his way with her in a cold, dark alley.

No such luck.

Two steps inside the club, she sensed him, possibly in the same way some animals sensed an oncoming storm system. The acknowledgment made her waver on her new black pumps.

"What'll it be, Madison?" Teddy shouted over the blaring music. "First one's on me."

"Virgin something. Thanks. I'll get the next round."

Jittery inside, Madison slowly raised her gaze. *He* was there, all right, on the balcony in a languid echo of his pose from the night before. No doubt about it, he was looking back.

"So," she said, wondering if Tall, Fair and Distracting could read lips. "Now you show yourself?"

She ran a hand over her body-skimming black dress to rid herself of the sensation that his hands were on her, and braced for a meeting that seemed inevitable.

"Here." The sudden coolness of an icy glass pressed to her elbow made her jump.

"The BBC is at the bar," Teddy shouted over the music, handing her a neon-hued drink. "Want to hobnob?"

She nodded and shouted back. "Be there in a minute."

Raising his glass in salute, Teddy left her. Being alone in this club hadn't really been the plan. Madison looked up again to find that the man she had straddled in that alley was gone from his perch.

Resigned to getting back to her crew, for now, she started for the bar. "I suppose the only way to handle you is with a good dose of truth serum," she said over her shoulder.

Cool fingers closed over hers, stopping her motion,

virtually stapling her in place. A sighed breath, close to her ear, stirred a few wisps of her hair.

There was no need to turn around. Only one man had the ability to affect her this way. His fingers on her wrist sent waves of explosive charges up her arms, made her heart flutter. She didn't appreciate the feeling that told her, in spite of her resolve, and against her better judgment, that she still had the hots for this guy.

"Truth serum wouldn't be my drink of choice," he said in a tone as rich as she'd remembered, and twice as suggestive.

He let go of her hand. Madison lowered her glass to keep from dropping it.

"There isn't actually any drink called O Positive?" she finally said.

"Which is why I usually stick to a good malt whiskey."

Madison faced him, compelled to do so with what amounted to a very bad craving.

"You're here again," he said. "I don't suppose you were looking for me?"

"What would make you think that?"

"Just a wild guess."

She raised her glass. "Actually, you seem to turn up everywhere."

"London is a small place when there's a lot going on," he said.

"Yes. You were out there today. Do you work in the media?"

"I don't, though I have a vested interest in those who do."

"Really? How so?" she asked.

He really was quite something: smooth, elegant

and not actually cocky, but way too confident. Her body was responding to those traits, as well as whatever other kind of magic he possessed. Rationalization seemed to have no say in the matter.

"I prefer quieter times," he confessed.

Even in her three-inch heels, she found that he towered over her. He also wore black, in the form of a soft coat and slacks. His black silk shirt was open at the neck. His brilliant mass of blond hair was long enough to cover his ears and, from memory, as sleek as the shirt.

The guy looked like an archangel gone over to the dark side, and Madison's body was appreciative of the results. She felt a flicker of excitement. Last night in bed, the mere thought of him had gifted her with an easy orgasm.

"Quieter times will help us all if things return to normal as quickly as possible," he said. "It's important for London."

"You do realize that people are missing. Maybe they're lost, or dead," she remarked.

"I hope they are alive, just as you do."

Despite her inner warnings, Madison looked up. "So, if not a member of the media, who are you?"

His eyes were a smoky sky-blue, and flecked with gold.

"I thought you knew," he replied.

"Let's stop with the games, okay? The time for them is over."

He conceded with a nod and the slightest hint of a grin. "My name is Christopher St. John."

"Yes, well, I'd be willing to bet you're no saint," Madison said.

"Most assuredly not a saint," he agreed.

"So, what do you want with me? Insider information? Are you with a London rag, or some other newspaper? For the record, I don't have any new information on those girls, and I regularly engage in sexual escapades with strangers in foreign cities, so doing so with you wasn't special."

His grin widened, suggesting that he knew she was full of crap. She saw a flash of white teeth behind the lips that had greedily trespassed on hers, but no sign of fangs.

He didn't move to press back the hair curtaining the sharpness of his cheekbones. Nor did he show any sign of the smug expression she'd been expecting. He was, in fact, acting more or less like a gentleman.

She took a sip of her drink before setting the glass on the table beside her. Although she was used to men being attracted to her, and adept at shaking them off, she wasn't dislodging the focus of this one. She hadn't meant to dodge his attention, really, because she had questions

But his eyes sought hers now in the same way that his mouth had sought her mouth the night before. He had only touched her hand for a few seconds tonight, and that touch was a heady reminder of how far they could get on lust alone.

More to the point, she wanted a replay of the last night's events right now. He was so damn...*something*.

"I'm afraid I'm busy tonight," she said. "I'm with my crew. Rain check, maybe?"

His grin remained fixed. "Are the gentlemen at the bar here to protect you from me, I wonder, or protect you from yourself?"

Madison blinked slowly to avoid his gaze. If this bastard was going to push every single one of her buttons without letting up, she'd have to take back that stuff about thinking him gallant.

"I'm here looking for someone else," she said. "Maybe you know him? Stewart Chase?"

"Husband?" he said.

"Brother."

"What leads you to believe I might know about your brother?"

"A weapon the police found in his jacket made me think so."

There was a tap on her shoulder. Teddy had returned.

Damn. She had been asking crucial questions, and starting to get somewhere…while also contemplating what Christopher St. John's chest would feel like beneath that black shirt—a wicked thought that was totally out of place and at odds with her agenda.

She wasn't here for a replay. She was here for Stewart. Coveting Christopher St. John, in this circumstance, was an unforgivable sin.

Their game of the night before, that stake in Stewart's possession, St. John's remarks about *them* chasing her, had to be addressed. St. John and everything about this ridiculous club seemed to circle back to vampires.

Of course, she couldn't explore any of this in front of her cameraman.

"Yeah, Teddy?" she yelled.

Teddy made a comical dancing motion with his arms and feet.

Madison looked to St. John, thinking that the man

across from her actually did look too good to be mortal. She hadn't been wrong about that. Or blind.

However, there was no way his voice had been inside her head that day. She had just imagined it.

"Ah. Then I'll leave you to your friends," St. John politely conceded with a nod of his head to Teddy. "We will run into each other again soon enough, I'm sure, Miss Chase."

"I suppose I can count on it," Madison agreed.

But when Teddy took her hand, she felt as though she had just made an error she might soon regret. She had a crazy notion that Christopher St. John did know more about the creatures her brother had been seeking than he let on. Call it intuition. Hell, call it whatever… but their meetings were so strange.

At the very least, he had to know about Stewart's suspicions about vampire presence in London, if he had played along the night before. Besides, Stewart had been to this club often enough to list it in his notes.

A vague disturbance seemed to hang in the air as St. John's eyes met hers one final time. Neither of them took a breath. Her heart raced.

Teddy had to lead her away. Madison turned to look back, struck by a strange feeling that each step away from St. John made the air between them thicker, and that the crowded room had begun to revolve, as if it would take her back to him.

St. John wasn't smiling.

She walked through the crowd with Teddy, without getting far. A brief flare of insight slammed into her like a dire warning alarm.

Whirling toward the direction of whatever had dragged at her attention, Madison watched a shadow cross the stairs to the balcony. As that shadow passed beneath a high-tech wall sconce, a pale, proud face became visible for a fraction of a second.

She was startled. Her body jerked. Tearing herself from Teddy's casual grip, she ran toward the stairs, pushing people out of her way, sprinting after the man she would have known anywhere.

Her brother.

Chapter 10

St. John was watching Madison when her expression grew stricken, as if she'd seen a ghost.

He caught her at the exit with a firm hand on her elbow. Stopping her momentum, he swung Madison around and encircled her with his arms.

"That wasn't who you think it was," he said as she wriggled to get free. "Trust me on this, you do not want to follow that man."

"Let me go!"

Releasing her wasn't a possibility, though they were making a scene by the door and people were eyeing them with concern. Beyond that crowd, St. John scented another immortal heading their way.

"Not for you," he said to Madison. "Do you hear me? What you saw is not for you."

When she refused to settle down and listen, he

picked her up in his arms and headed outside so fast, her glossy scarlet lips parted speechlessly. Even there they weren't alone. The queue for the club was long. The picture he presented by holding her in his arms attracted attention. To get out of this, he'd have to improvise.

He pressed his mouth to hers, absorbing her rising shouts, blowing gentle breaths into her that were the equivalent of an instant dose of Valium.

Her struggles ceased.

"That's it," he encouraged. "Good."

Although her body relaxed slightly, Madison's lips trembled beneath his as if she'd fight this directive if she could get any words of argument out. Those vibrations, so very alluringly feminine, forced St. John to take stock of his balance.

She felt light in his arms. He felt the sleekness of her long, bare legs through his clothes.

Her lipstick tasted like cherries.

The physical desire he had developed for this mortal was beyond his comprehension. Each ragged breath she fought for was sweet, stirring in him memories best forgotten.

But Madison had seen the shadows. Stewart had been moving fast, with a speed few human eyes should have perceived, and yet she had seen him. The truth was that Madison possessed at least some extraspecial senses, just as her brother did. She was showing signs of becoming exactly like her twin.

St. John's arms tensed. His mouth stopped moving over hers.

It was possible, even probable, he thought, that Madison shared her brother's tweaked genetics, and this was the source of the darkness he had detected. But two vampire hunters in one family was unheard of.

He tasted that darkness now, with his lips on hers and her breath in his lungs. If Madison didn't know about the darkness, it meant that her genes had to be latent. However, like her brother, she was seemingly driven toward vampires, instead of away from them.

Bloody hell. It was entirely possible that the Chase twins had shared more than a womb, and had been sprung from a family of Slayers.

As he continued to hold Madison, with his lips resting on hers, St. John's mind raced on.

The attraction between Slayers and vampires was legendary. Vampire hunters had some special cocktail added to their DNA sequencing that didn't dilute or disappear as generations of them lived and died. This was a symbiotic relationship meant to keep the balance between mortals and the monsters that preyed on them. A negative relationship, really, since in the end both Slayer and monster became victims of the very drives that pushed them toward each other.

Was this it? Had he found the key to Madison? The blood in their veins recognized each other?

Or...perhaps he had merely lived too long, and his mind played tricks by offering a respite from the trials of his past in the form of an insatiable attraction to a beautiful woman.

His guess, the one that felt right, was that Madison wasn't completely human, and didn't know that the traits hidden inside her were the same ones that hadn't made things turn out well for her brother.

That morning, he'd made it his task to find out everything about Madison Chase.

The family that had produced the twins had been taken from them prematurely. Madison and her brother were raised by a foster family that they had left as soon as they were able to, due to some kind of trouble there.

Overcoming the trials of their upbringing, the twins were both successful, bright and glamorous. But the loss of her one remaining family member might be the final straw for Madison. Without her brother, her twin, she was alone in the world.

It was entirely possible, he thought now, that Madison had no idea how special she actually might be, if his intuition was right. Slayers were rare enough. Two in one family was a complete anomaly. As his mouth moved over hers, St. John tasted pain. He knew the cost and the toll pain took, but couldn't afford to overthink how Madison's might have affected her.

For everyone's sake, you must leave this city before others take your life from you. He silently sent messages to her. *Maybe then you'll have a chance.*

They were, after all, allies in the war against vampires. His vow as an immortal had been to protect the purity of the original few immortals, and see that their blood didn't get spread around. No one despised the fanged hordes creating chaos on the fringes of mortal society more than he did.

And Madison…

What would make her leave London?

He didn't want to see her hurt. Being a Slayer-in-the-making would do more harm than good, with no skill set to back it up. Fledglings would continue to scent her.

If she refused to leave without her brother, she'd have to be forced to go by removing the one hope she clung to, that of finding Stewart, even if doing so broke her. If she was going to be a Slayer once her inner and outer awareness merged, she'd be needed in the world. Eventually, she would help to keep the balance. They were in accord about this.

As for her recognition of him...

She couldn't know about his true identity or purpose. No one could be allowed to find the Seven. He'd have to distance himself before she found out. He'd have to prove to her that he was no gentleman at all, and send her sprinting away. He'd play the bastard, and watch her run.

The persistent ache in St. John's chest told him he'd do this. He would do it to save her.

Damn though... The back of his neck prickled with a physical warning that the ancient entity in the club who had seen them together had reached the door.

Not only could he *not* distance himself from Madison at the moment, he had to make this moment count, and make it look good.

"No time like the present for a show," he said to Madison, drawing back slowly, meeting her dazed, questioning gaze. "Everyone loves lovers."

He crushed her mouth with his in a sudden, deep, drowning kiss, fighting to make himself believe this didn't actually matter.

He worked to keep his fangs from her as Madison began to spiral upward from numbness, waiting to see what she'd do next, telling himself that she would forgive him if she understood the problems at hand.

What happened was the biggest surprise yet.

She didn't put up a fight, or slap his face. She didn't go on about her brother. She sighed through parted lips.

Likely those lips hadn't opened for him in order to participate in the kiss, and only to protest such treatment, but an explosion of searing passion caught St. John up in a whirling vortex, all the same.

His nerves fired. The blood of the blessed immortals surged in his veins. He kept kissing her, deeply, seriously, as if his life truly depended on this meeting of their mouths, not wanting to confront the disturbing thought that fate might be offering him a final test regarding his vow, after all this time.

He held a being that immortals called a *Recumbent* in his arms: a sleeping Slayer who hadn't yet come into her own. And he could not stop kissing her, or wanting to possess her.

Madison's slick, lush lips opened for him like the folding petals of a night-blooming flower. Their tongues met, darted away, came back in a dance of tension and need that erased the boundaries of enemies in transition.

Enslaved by her mouth, St. John pressed on, unable to help himself, physically enforcing a connection that now catapulted them to an arena where pure sensation ruled. He seemed to be drowning. After centuries, time finally came to a standstill.

His fangs were extended. His cock was erect and aching for her. All the while, his heart thundered in time to hers, as if every inch of their bodies called out to the other for a unification that would have been dangerous in any circumstance, and at the same time sublime.

Levels of awareness peeled back, hurtling him and Madison toward something forbidden, and wondrous. They were nearly there. Not long now, and their souls would find each other through a porthole that defied the rules of life and death. A space reserved for like minds and thirsty souls, no matter what housed those souls.

Dangerous.

Scandalous.

Deadly.

And bloody poor timing.

Meeting Madison in that luminous place where the sun paled by comparison meant that the only thing left would be to take her soul in his hands and twist it out of recognition. Doing so would be the end of her, and a swift exit from his vow.

Noise faded in from the periphery.

Exulted by the open display of mouth-to-mouth sex on the sidewalk, the crowd beside them clapped their hands, laughed and jeered. "Get a room!"

Stop kissing her. Pull away, St. John's mind warned.

Madison was limp in his arms, and not from any loss of spirit. She seemed to be waiting for him to devour her completely. Expecting it. She wanted to lose herself in the strength of his passion. He sensed this in her.

In the end, he had done nothing to help her. He had, in nearly every way that counted, made the situation worse.

Her bare arms clung to his neck, capturing him as surely as if she'd slipped a silver chain around his heart.

Her skin scalded him. Her mouth was an inferno. St. John raked the points of his fangs across her lower lip, leaving a lipstickless line there, a line in the sand of sorts, and a warning of the impossibility of actually crossing a final boundary.

He wondered how bliss like this could end, when he had searched for such a thing for so long without knowing it. When he hadn't been moved in this way for more years than he cared to count, if ever.

But the enormity of his pleasure came with its own shadow, in the form of an interruption.

A fresh, looming darkness stretched across the promise of the light resting in his arms. As the crowd beside them trudged toward the club's door, the etchings between St. John's shoulder blades began to burn as if someone had tripped the tattooed sigils carved into his skin.

Tearing his mouth from the lips clinging to his, he raised his head to meet the gaze of the immortal who stood in the club's open doorway.

A blast of frosty air ripped through the surroundings with a desire-wilting chill. This was a stern warning from the other entity, a pronouncement of that Ancient's disapproval.

St. John didn't want to heed that warning. The bittersweet torment of having Madison in his arms was too great. Her heat spread through him like a violent, raging fire, warming him from the inside out. Until now, he hadn't realized how cold he had been.

The surrounding chill met that heat with a soft hiss. His shoulder blades pinched with a new discomfort as the stripes fused to his skin with the blood of the seven Blood Knights writhed like living things.

This kind of alarm he could not ignore.

How he wanted, against all his principles and the approach of a powerful ancient entity, to throw Madison against a wall and take her in every physical way possible, front to back, teeth to groin. Right there. Right now. He wanted her that badly. He had all but decided.

Yet he could not possibly want her badly enough to ruin what he'd so carefully set in place. Or badly enough to leave so many others vulnerable to the network of evil that had ensnared one of the Hundred, and made one privileged Ancient a traitor to his kind.

By listening to the song of his own longings, St. John might lose sight of the beast he had been after.

With a last brief return to Madison's lips, he pulled back. Madison should have been running by now. He wasn't holding her so very tightly.

A nonphysical touch pierced his mind. Coldness invaded, quickly overwhelming and replacing Madison's marvelous heat. This cold was far more lethal than his ambitious liaison with Madison. This cold would eat the woman in his arms alive if it touched her.

He set Madison down and stepped in front of her to deflect the chill. Although it was imperative that he keep hold of her, and hide her latent abilities from the others, it was equally as important to maintain his disguise. So much depended on that disguise.

Madison moved at last. Sidestepping him, she looked to the immortal in the doorway, then back to St. John.

She was a sight, with her dress creased and her hair in disarray. Her smeared lipstick gave the impression of a chin covered in blood. She looked wild, and so very lovely.

Beneath wide, uncertain eyes, her swollen lips opened. Steadying herself with a bracing breath, she tried to take a step. Satisfied that she could walk, she took another step, then another, her heels making tapping noises on the concrete as she headed for the club's entrance.

There, as she made to brush past the two-hundred-year-old vampire who kept St. John in his sights, she paused, as though some part of her recognized that the entity in the doorway might be dangerous.

Good God...had his kiss made that possible?

Had his good intentions been wasted?

St. John felt the shiver that ran through Madison. He watched her last step wobble. *Do not let him know,* he wanted to shout. *Do not meet that creature's eyes.*

Had she heard? She left the entity in the doorway alone, and said over her shoulder with a vehemence of tone that didn't quite ring true, "Damn you, and the fantasy you rode in on, St. John. If you try anything like that again, I'll sue."

Then she was gone.

Reluctantly, agonizingly, St. John transferred his attention to the immortal gazing questioningly after Madison, not realizing he had just interfered in a life-altering moment, and that nothing from here on out, for any of them, would ever be the same.

Madison made it through the front door of the club before collapsing against a wall. Her hands were shaking. Her entire body shook along with the hands.

Her brother had been here, hadn't he?

Christopher St. John and the old creep in the doorway blocked her from finding out, and now it was probably too late.

What had St. John whispered to her this time?

"What you saw is not for you."

The earlier anxiousness came tumbling back. If

Stewart had been in this club, the fact that she had missed him was hurtful, unthinkable. Whichever way it had gone down, the man with the name of a saint and a mouth like fire had a hand in that. He had kept her from going after her brother.

After regaining her balance, Madison found herself surrounded by Teddy and the other guys, a circle of males that wasn't quite as comforting as it should have been, because as it turned out, she had needed protection from herself. From her attraction to a monster, whether St. John was human or not.

"Ready to go?" Teddy shouted over the music.

Madison nodded. She had to get out of there. Alongside these guys, no one would dare to stop her exit.

She'd made a fool of herself in public two nights in a row and needed some thinking time. She felt confused, frightened. Not one real answer had been found here, unless it was a question of Stewart's possible, momentary whereabouts, and the realization of her own character flaws.

That was something, right?

Teddy handed her a napkin, and pointed to her face. Madison wiped at her mouth, removing the smeared lipstick, feeling stupid. Her walk to the door garnered smiles from people she passed.

"Yeah, I know," she said. "Quite the show."

Although she had a good grip on herself at the moment, she dreaded going outside. Taking a firm hold on Teddy's arm, she sighed with relief when there were no tall, fair strangers on the sidewalk, and no gray-haired creep in the doorway who actually looked like a vampire.

Climbing into a cab at the curb, she couldn't begin to

comprehend the pang of regret running through her—
not only about the possibility of Christopher St. John
keeping her from going after a man that may have been
her brother, but because St. John's kiss had so easily
disrupted her sense of purpose.

And something else about the night nagged at her
consciousness.

Wait a minute.

Madison snapped herself straight on the seat and
blinked slowly to pull up a memory.

She and St. John had been having a conversation
near the dance floor, and neither of them had been
shouting. With the music blaring, she had heard every
word he'd said, when that was impossible.

Goose bumps appeared on every available surface
of her body. She rubbed her arms, pretty damn sure
she actually was going mad. But no, everyone else had
been shouting in order to be heard.

She stopped rubbing.

How could she have heard St. John? Surely not by
any normal means, unless she had suddenly become
adept at reading lips, and he had the same ability.

And if not?

If she took those oddities into Stewart's world, of
which that damn club was supposedly a part...did those
things insinuate that Christopher St. John might be one
of the creatures Stewart had been after?

Could a vampire mesmerize her into wanting and
giving in to that kiss?

Laughable.

What about the sex they'd nearly had on a side
street?

No, she was looking for an out, and setting all blame on Christopher St. John.

All the same, her nerves spiked annoyingly as she looked at her hand, picturing a sharpened stake in it. Her beloved brother's stake. A thing that belonged to Stewart, her twin, who seemed to believe wholeheartedly in his research. Not a hobby. Nothing like that. Who the hell else, other than a true believer, carried a weapon like that around?

Absurd? Well...yes.

Besides, what reason would Christopher St. John, as a man or as some other creature, have for thwarting her plans, when those plans were as simple as finding her brother, and reporting on those missing girls? What would he gain by distracting her?

A more reasonable explanation was that Christopher St. John might just have been the right guy at the right time to tempt her, and it turned out that lust was blind to everything else going on.

Still, once the ridiculous thoughts had taken root, Madison couldn't dislodge them.

In the backseat of the black London cab, sandwiched between the guys in her crew, and trying not to shake hard enough to draw attention to herself, Madison laid her head back, and closed her eyes.

"She saw her brother," St. John said to Simon Monteforte on the street bordering Space. "My distraction worked, but what was he doing here? How did he get inside?"

Simon Monteforte, a formidable creature, looked the part of the ancient vampire. He was as tall as St.

John, and deceptively lean. Under his coat were several layers of steel.

Stone-gray hair, worn straight and long, splayed out over the shoulders of a forest-green velvet tunic as dark as the night itself. Black form-fitting jeans covered all but the tips of expensive polished black boots. Born of French aristocracy, Monteforte retained his original patrician bearing and airs. He had never lost his accent. His love of luxury showed.

He also owned half the block around Space.

Because Monteforte had been around a long time, St. John continued to rein himself in—no easy feat when his heart was in that cab with Madison.

He wanted to look at the street, and didn't dare. Immortals as old as Monteforte could easily smell trouble. They scented lies and deceit like those things were simply new fragrances wafting in the air.

St. John had centuries on Monteforte, and a strength that had once been the stuff of tales. There was no one amid the Hundred, here or anywhere else, for a Blood Knight to truly fear if he exposed his true nature. But he could not blow his cover.

"Besides," he said to Monteforte, "who are we to stop her brother? Stewart Chase killed two young rogues last night."

"So, my friend, did you." Monteforte tilted his head in mock thought. "Or was it five fledglings you took down? I lose count these days when I'm not concentrating."

St. John smiled at the wily immortal's obvious lie. The creature across from him, like himself, probably remembered everything he'd ever done and every idea he'd had. This was both a curse and a blessing for those who had lived so long, depending on the immortal's outlook.

Often, if he didn't watch himself, St. John still heard the voices of the people in his own past, as well as the screams of those he had killed in battle, in the name of honor and the golden quest. After years of this kind of haunting, he had grown used to the whispers inside his head.

At the moment though, those distant voices were silent. His heartbeat continued to echo Madison's. His tattoos burned with cold blue fire.

He willed himself to stay in the moment, knowing Madison was thinking about him, desiring him in a way she didn't understand.

Twitching his shoulders to ease the discomfort centered between them, St. John eyed the creature beside him. As he allowed his gaze to roam over Monteforte's sullen face, the burn on his back became barely tolerable.

Is it you, then, Simon? Is it possible that you're the traitor? My marks think this might be so.

"I suppose you can find her brother quite easily," Monteforte said.

"Why call him out when he does us a service?" St. John asked.

"For the time being, that may be true. There are indeed too many unauthorized, random turnings lately. However, we wouldn't want these kills to go to Stewart's head, so that he desires bigger and better fare."

As Monteforte spoke those words, he stroked the sleeve of his velvet coat with a slender white hand, as if the sleeve were part of a lover's limb.

"It was wise to remove the fledglings from the club

last night," Monteforte continued. "Yet you took the woman with you."

St. John nodded. "As bait to get them out in the open."

The white hand stopped stroking the sleeve. "Did she see them?"

"*Thugs* was the term she used, likely thinking they were after her purse. Since they were trained on her, getting her out of the club and out of the way seemed crucial."

So is this deception. What might you be hiding, Simon? Do I see something in your eyes?

"Thugs." Monteforte pulled a face. "A rather brutish American word, *n'est ce pas?* She doesn't hold to the beliefs of her brother, then?"

"She does not." St. John knew he had to be careful now, when standing close to Simon Monteforte. He had to be sure the pain streaking across his shoulders was in honor of this ancient French immortal.

"Nor does she know what you are?" Monteforte asked.

"It's doubtful that anyone knows."

More caution was necessary here, St. John realized after making that remark.

He had tasted the edge of the secret buried inside Madison Chase. Last night had been a fantastic game to her, when thugs and vampires inherently were no part of her reality. But as a newscaster, she'd latch on to any oddities tossed her way. And as a Slayer, fully awakened to her skills, no vampire would be off her radar.

If Madison believed she had seen her brother tonight, she would hunker down and pursue the issue with talons of steel. Simon Monteforte, the creature across from him, would see her again and perhaps glean her secrets as well.

Another piercing stab between his shoulder blades brought St. John up from thought.

Monteforte said, "You do realize that Miss Chase may become a liability?"

"Any minute now," St. John agreed, hating the need for such deceptions, but noting that the burning chill of his tattoos definitely seemed to be tied to the being across from him.

He took a step closer to Monteforte, just to be sure.

The tattoos screamed with distress.

"You will take care of this?" Monteforte asked pointedly. "Take care of her?"

"Of course," St. John said, watching the old vampire carefully.

"Then I'll bid you *adieu*," Monteforte concluded, and disappeared back into the club like the shadow he was.

"Adieu," St. John echoed, not to the immortal that had just tripped his alarms as a possible traitor to his kind, but to the street where Madison's cab had taken her from him in the nick of time.

One more moment in that heady embrace, out of the trillions of them he had endured since his death and rebirth as what he now was, and he wouldn't have been responsible for his actions.

His fangs thrummed. His skin hurt. The sigils on his back were cold enough to frost the night. He was anxious for more of what the dazzling redhead had to offer, and couldn't be allowed to trip her latent Slayer switches.

Amid all that, he had to look into the fact that Monteforte had become a viable candidate for the term *monster maker.*

Anxiety made him turn.

The taillights of Madison's cab were gone.

He had to deal with Monteforte. That was his job, and he would do it. First, though, he'd make sure that Madison got back to her hotel safely.

"Safe from everyone, other than myself, that is," he said aloud as he took off at a run.

Chapter 11

She was bone-tired, flustered, and a detective was waiting for her in the lobby.

Madison didn't bother to hide her displeasure, and wondered why she couldn't cut a break.

D.I. Crane addressed her crew with a brief nod, and then turned to her. "Can I have a minute, Miss Chase?"

"She's been through a lot today," Teddy said.

"I understand that." Crane took a handkerchief from his pocket and handed it to her.

Madison glanced to Teddy, who shrugged, then nodded for her to use it.

The white handkerchief she used to wipe her face and mouth with came back as red as the napkin at the club had. The detective's white hankie was ruined.

"It's important," Crane said. "Has to do with what we found today."

Sweet Lord, Madison thought. Had it only been that

morning they had discovered Stewart's leather jacket and what he'd hidden inside it? That awful weapon that seemed to haunt her?

She smiled stiffly at Teddy. "I'll be up in five."

"Better make it ten," the detective said, earning a glare from her crew as they headed for the stairs.

"I don't think they like me," he said.

"Does anyone truly like cops?"

"I find that unusual, since we're the good guys."

"You bring bad news. People don't like bad news. I'm assuming that's the case here?"

The detective shrugged. "We've stumbled upon something else I'd like you to take a look at."

"I'm not sure I can take more surprises."

"Oh, I'm fairly certain you're able to stand a lot, Miss Chase. More than most."

Madison wondered what D.I. Crane would do if she asked him if he believed in vampires, and decided to let the question sit, since he was openly staring at the red marks on the handkerchief.

"What is it you want to show me, Detective?"

He removed an article from an evidence bag. It was her other silver shoe.

"We needed to be alone for this unveiling?" Madison asked.

"It's more a case of where we found this shoe, than the shoe itself, that's important."

"Where did you find it?"

"Near an abandoned building by the water."

Madison raised an eyebrow.

"Next to a pile of ashes," the detective said.

"Someone tried to burn my shoe?"

"If that was their intention, they failed. No, Miss Chase, I'm afraid it was a person that burned up."

"What?" Madison's chills returned. The knot in her stomach that she hadn't been able to get to dissolve since landing in London, twisted. "What do you mean?"

"The ash we analyzed appears at first glance to be the remains of a person." He let that sink in for a minute. "The question I now have is why your shoe was found next to him?"

"Him?"

"Figure of speech," D.I. Crane said. "It could just as easily be female."

Madison had a bad feeling about this. She had kicked off her shoes last night in order to ditch some lowlifes. True, the silver stilettos were expensive, but what would a bunch of hoodlums want with only one of them? Why hadn't they picked up both while they were at it, since the detectives had found the other one right where she'd left it?

The immediate reply she heard inside her head was totally insane, but the first answer that came to mind. Maybe that gang had used her discarded shoe to somehow aid their search for her.

But the only instance in which a shoe could have helped in a chase, unless it had a directional chip in it, was if…

Was if those young asses had been vampires, and had used the scent of her shoe to track her.

Which would also mean that Christopher St. John had been right in his inferences about *them*.

"Is something wrong?" D.I. Crane asked.

Madison widened her stance as far as the hem of her

tight skirt would allow in order to remain upright. What she was thinking was nightmarish and unutterable.

"I don't know how my shoe ended up anywhere but where I lost it," she heard herself say. "I left them near the club called Space, as I explained earlier, when you gave me the first one. I don't know anything about ashes, or a body."

She couldn't go on. A paragraph in her brother's notes had mentioned what happened to vampires when they suffered a final death. They were reduced to ash.

Ash.

Suddenly, she wanted to sit down.

She dropped the handkerchief to the floor.

"Miss Chase, were you alone last night?" the detective asked.

"Do I need an alibi?"

She'd have given anything to ask about the length of the teeth they'd found in that pile, but the detective was studying her intently. Being labeled loony by law enforcement wouldn't help anyone here. She could not speak of vampires, and of chasing through the night, away from a pack of them.

"I'd appreciate it if you'd answer the question," the detective said.

"No. I wasn't alone."

"You were with your news crew?"

Madison shook her head.

"A friend?" the detective pressed.

"I met a man at the club."

"His name?"

"St. John. Christopher St. John."

D.I. Crane gave her an odd, unreadable look, then he

nodded and let the subject drop, as if St. John's name was some kind of magic password.

"All right." He glanced at the handkerchief on the floor by Madison's feet. "I'll have to keep this shoe."

"Fine."

The truth was that she didn't want anything to do with that shoe. Maybe a vampire had touched it, and maybe it had just appeared at the scene of a homicide. She supposed there was no way that vampire ash could be checked for DNA, or if the police could track down someone who had died twice.

She looked at the floor. *To hell with you, Stewart, for that grisly thought.*

The detective continued to stare at the red-stained handkerchief. If he was wondering about that wooden stake in Stewart's jacket, he might also be pondering if the Chase twins were homicidal maniacs.

"A few years ago there were cases of homeless people being torched on the streets," she said, needing to come up with an alternate explanation for the one ludicrously taking over her mind. Because if that pile of ash had been a vampire, the world as she and every other human on the planet had always imagined it was a fake.

She put a hand to her forehead.

"Yes," the detective said. "That could be the case here as well. This kind of burn, however, would have required a flamethrower."

Or a wooden stake through the heart.

Madison pressed her hair behind her ears with shaky hands. "Flamethrower," she said. "God, I hope not."

The detective bent over to retrieve his handkerchief. "Well, you're tired," he said. "So, I'll leave you with more advice. It might be a good idea if you keep your crew with you tomorrow."

"You mean in case I might need another alibi?"

Crane tucked the handkerchief into his pocket. She wondered if he was going to check it for DNA.

"Shall I walk you upstairs?" he asked.

"I can manage."

"I'll see you tomorrow, Miss Chase."

"Hopefully not," Madison muttered as he walked away.

Somehow, she made it to the elevator, and heard the ping of its arrival. Before stepping in, she spun back. "Detective?"

He stopped at the door.

"Do you know Christopher St. John?"

"Not personally," he said.

"Is he a credible alibi for last night?"

"Most people around here would think so."

"Do you?"

"What I think doesn't matter. St. John is…highly regarded in important circles."

Trained to pick up on the importance of hesitant nuances, Madison said, "What circles would those be?"

"Just about every one that counts these days," the detective replied.

"I really can't figure out how my shoe got to where you found it," she said.

"I believe you."

With a polite wave of his hand, D.I. Crane exited the lobby, leaving Madison alone with all of the injustices of the world pressing in on her. A world that was shouting for her to consider the possibility that it might be populated by fanged dead men, even though she wanted to think she knew better.

Pressing the button to her floor was a chore.

The elevator, empty, small and ancient, seemed crowded with the thoughts plaguing her.

But Stewart was alive.

And she would find him, if she could keep herself on track.

When she got upstairs she found Teddy sitting on the floor outside her door. He got to his feet. "Everything okay?"

"The good detective found one of my shoes," Madison said.

"He needed to see you in private to talk about a shoe?"

She shrugged. "It's mind-boggling."

"Well, I'll say good night, then. I'm beat." Teddy yawned. "I still have to go over some video footage."

"Do you want some help?"

"No, but thanks for the offer."

"'Night, Teddy," Madison said. "Thanks."

"For what?"

"Being there." Madison pointed to the spot on the floor where he'd been sitting.

Teddy smiled. "You're entirely welcome."

Madison waited with her hand on the doorknob until Teddy had disappeared, almost afraid to go into her room. The tingling sensations at the back of her neck had started up again. Her nerves were humming, leaving her jumpy and on edge. If this was a premonition of something about to happen, it was a doozy.

Shaking off the idea of calling Teddy back, she en-

tered the room with her senses on full alert, and sank
against the closed door without taking another step or
reaching for the light switch. Her eyes didn't have to
adjust to the dark for her to know that the room had
been disturbed.

Her gaze moved to the window that stood wide
open.

Her pulse pounded against her throat, inhibiting
speech.

This was the same reaction she'd had from the beginning. Always the racing heart. Always the almost
visceral need to step closer to a gathering storm.

The man causing this was here. No mistake. But if
the police knew him, and thought him a good enough
alibi, Christopher St. John couldn't be part of any alien,
otherworldly species. As for her earlier concerns, she
had merely read St. John's lips at the club. There was
no second-guessing the laws of such a fierce, animal
attraction.

What she should be doing was returning to the
streets. Anyone with real strength of conviction would
return to the West End to look for further clues as to
Stewart's whereabouts, in case it had been him she'd
seen tonight.

A whiff of the scent of musk hit her.

She blanched, said, "I know you're here."

Christopher St. John's closeness was like a brush
of black velvet on her overworked senses. The surface
of the door felt hard and unforgiving against her tense
back muscles, but there was no way she'd leave it. She
couldn't have moved if she'd tried.

"If you used that window to get in here, I don't know

how you managed it without actually being Spider-Man," she said.

The telling flutter deep inside her was taking over her interior. Waiting for St. John to speak, Madison perceived every other noise, from her own raspy breathing to the sounds on the street outside, but St. John, the trespasser, didn't say a word.

"Vampire got your tongue?" she said.

With an unbelievable speed, St. John was beside her, crushing to the door in a replay of their closeness that first night in the secluded alley. His body was close enough for her to feel every exquisite inch.

"How dare you show up like this," she said, fending off a medley of signals that were the exact opposite of the stern chastisement she'd meant to issue. The sheer, almost mystical power of St. John's masculinity had the ability to make the choicest arguments fade. He was potent, and live with a virile form of raw sexuality. God help her, she was a sucker for those things. She could not turn away.

"Why are you here?" she demanded.

"You may be in danger."

Her voice cracked. "There was a detective here not five minutes ago, and probably still within shouting distance."

"Do you imagine that if I was the danger, that detective could stop me from taking what I want?"

Madison shook her head. "I don't imagine anyone could stop you from doing anything."

Whatever she'd said made him close his eyes. Although she couldn't see that in the dark, she knew he had, because she had shut hers.

She was pinned to the door, and the intensity of

whatever was going on between her and this man was not only insane, it grew stronger by the second. As crazy as it seemed, she wanted to tear his clothes off and feel his hardness firsthand. She wanted to finish what they had started the night before.

None of it was logical, but did it have to be? So many emotions were running rampant.

"Come away from here, with me," St. John said.

"Where?"

"Does it matter?"

"Of course it matters. I've got a job to do."

His cheek, cool and smooth against hers, made Madison's pulse sky-rocket with beats that filled the room.

The bed was a few feet away. She wondered if St. John would take her there and fire up this ongoing, raging desire once and for all, so that she could move beyond it. So that she could think straight, and get this guy out of her system.

When his lips rested lightly on her temple, she sucked in air as if starved for oxygen. He stayed there for a while before angling his mouth toward her chin in an agonizing trail of heat and tempered passion that was all the more seductive because of its soft, ethereal nature.

Nothing bad could be this good, surely? She was a hormonal explosion waiting to go off, and thankful she couldn't fill in his outline. She was glad the darkness hid her face from him. Her lips were quaking with the need for him to find them. The rush of damp heat between her thighs signaled that her body was willing to take this as far as it would go, for better or worse.

In no way could she stop this tumultuous longing now, in spite of the fact that she and St. John were strangers, really, and despite the former, ridiculous suppositions that he might not be human.

She gave the desk a sideways glance. On it sat her computer, containing a hundred files on vampires. The detective had just told her someone had been turned to ash, near her shoe. The shoe she had been wearing when she was with Christopher St. John.

Was it possible that St. John knew anything about this? St. John, who could very well fit the bill of being an immortal, according to her brother. Hadn't she, minutes before, been considering that very thing, because of the intensity of her insatiable lust for him, as well as her ability to think she heard him, and her inability to avoid him?

God...

St. John's lips were on hers now, again. They drifted over her mouth in a flaming reminder of the former make-out session that had tripped every fail-safe switch she possessed.

"What do you want from me?" she asked breathlessly.

"Everything," he said.

Okay. They would do this. Get it over with.

He wore no coat now, making it easier for her fingers to clench the fabric of his black silk shirt. His muscles tensed when she touched him, almost as if the gorgeous, overtly sexual St. John wasn't used to being handled in return.

Tugged free of his waistband, his shirt bunched in her hands. He groaned when she pressed her fingertips into the bare flesh of his lower back. His roving lips paused, poised against her neck, beneath her right ear, above her thundering pulse.

The energy building between them was wild, and whining for release. Emotion? Hell, this was so far beyond emotion as to be laughable. What she needed right that minute was to join St. John on the floor if necessary, to resolve this. All of their scrambled heat needed an outlet.

Possibly it wasn't even this illicit meeting that was causing the emotional arc, but instead, the pain of the last few weeks needing to be replaced by something mind-blowing and special.

"Come with me," he repeated hoarsely. "Away from here."

"So that you can protect me from the bogeyman?"

"Yes." He lowered his voice. "The man you saw outside the club tonight has focused his attention on you, and your search for your brother. He is dangerous. You must take care."

"He knew who I was?"

"Oh, yes."

"Is he a vampire?" Madison stumbled over the term. Though she'd used it partially in jest, there was nothing funny about her need to understand her brother's obsession with fanged creatures, and her own growing belief that things weren't as they seemed. She had felt that old man's strangeness when she passed him in that doorway. For a second, maybe two, she had believed him to actually be one of her brother's creatures of the night.

"Why would that man care what I do?" she asked, feeling his teeth graze her very sensitive neck.

"You bring notoriety to private concerns," St. John said. "Space is close to those interests."

"Some Protector you are, then. Will you issue a

warning, and then offer a kiss to make it all better? Will you keep returning to me as if I were your own personal plaything?"

The sound he made in response to that remark was as silky as his shirt, and wickedly delicious. "Yes," he whispered.

He seemed to be anticipating something. A green light for a momentous sexual escapade? One thing was certain. This guy was all male, all man; no bit of ephemeral mist topped off with fangs. Who could step away from him, or this, when her feelings for him were so insanely intense?

His needs matched hers, washing over Madison in relentless waves. The air heating up between them was new and exhilarating. She'd never felt anything like it, like this, like him, and didn't want this moment to end.

"Are you doing this to me? Making me susceptible to your finer points?" she demanded.

"You're admitting I have some finer points?"

"This close, I'm fully aware of them."

He drew back and smiled. "You knew I'd come."

"I should be questioning how I knew."

St. John's hands reached up into her hair. He held her face so that he could gaze at her in a way she couldn't return in the dark. She felt his attention, though, just as she'd been aware of his smile. Her body knew what was coming.

Her lips parted for him with no further thought. When his mouth claimed hers with an intimacy that was so much more than lips and tongues, it felt to Madison like a continuation of the ravenous mingling of two hungry souls.

When his hands drifted possessively over her hips,

and down the length of her thighs, nothing else mattered except the relief of finally getting to the core of her cravings.

She had to get this unwieldy attraction out of the way, and giving in to that attraction was the only way to do so.

In a slick repeat performance of their time in the alley, his fingers found the hem of her dress. As the material rose over her thighs in an agonizingly slow ascent, time seemed suspended. St. John's fingers were pure sensory bliss. The promise behind the rise of her dress had the impact of a shout.

Cool air on her skin told her that only the thinnest of lace barriers kept him from her now. She'd worn black lace tonight, in his honor. His interest in her partially naked body clearly showed.

Strong hands cupped her bare buttocks, freeing her from the door. With a flex of his arms, St. John lifted her slightly, settling her over him as if they were already fully unclothed, and getting down to it.

Dissatisfied with that, he slipped one hand between her legs, in search of the place that if he were to reach again tonight, skin to skin, would lead him to her sexual soul, if not her actual one.

Her head hit the wall, hard, and Madison didn't care. The flames licking at her were coming fast. She was going down in those flames, and this time, she wouldn't stop them. She had no intention of calling this off. She was completely under his spell.

The movement of his talented hands—over her mound, under the edge of her black thong—hinted at what pleasures were to follow. To ensure that those pleasures did follow, Madison separated her legs and uttered the sultry sigh bubbling up from inside her.

His lips came back to hers with a hunger that rocked her. Her body melted into him. Her hands crawled up the curve of his spine, expecting perfection, relishing in the feel of his bare skin.

She hesitated, surprised when she discovered several raised lines of what had to be scar tissue. The man kissing her had incurred injuries in the past, serious ones to leave such marks. Had someone hurt him badly? Was the cause of these marks an accident, or war wounds?

She knew nothing about him, her mind warned, and yet she desired to kiss those marks away, taste them with her tongue, trace them in the light. She hardly noticed when the pressure between her thighs increased, and how she willingly accepted this.

Then she was on the floor. Not the bed. Urgency demanded that they couldn't get that far.

St. John's weight eased on top of her. He was propped on his elbows, with his face above hers. He still wore his clothes. She wore most of hers. There had been no time to draw this out.

Before her final shudder of expectation, he had pulled her underwear over her ankles. The action, and the knowledge of what it was going to lead up to, was as rich as it was dangerous.

"I—" she sputtered, cut off when he entered her with a slick, partial thrust.

Startled by the sheer pleasure of this, she cried out. St. John made a similar sound, his gasp of surprise threatening to bring her to a peak way too soon.

It seemed to her that his breathy response wasn't indicative of a man's victory over a woman, but of one closer to a verbal manifestation of pain.

She couldn't hold on to any thought for long. St. John was well-endowed and talented. His next thrust, so deep and exactly right, filled her completely, bringing spasms of internal pleasure in what turned out to be only the warm-up. The introduction.

She wanted more. Wanted it all. Was nearly out of her mind with need.

He knew when to back off and make her writhe. He understood how to prolong her obscene craving for him. Holding himself motionless for seconds at a time, he then sent his hips forward, dipping into her slowly, almost maddeningly gracefully, while she clutched at his hips and his back.

She wanted him closer yet, deeper, and opened her mouth to demand satisfaction. But he had foreseen this. His next thrust was harder, slicker. Straight, true, this one stretched her to her limits, demanding full access to what she kept back.

She wrapped herself around him, used her muscles to encourage their connection. She dug at his back and shoulders with her nails, tearing at the silk shirt that remained the only cool sensation in a world on fire, wanting him to share in this crazy, sublime form of torture.

If he felt the pain of her talons, it only drove him on.

A rhythm built between them until their bodies slammed together with a damp, explosive heat. Madison gripped him hard. She beat at him with her fists, in need of something she couldn't yet define.

In the dimness, the eyes above hers, once so blue, appeared a solid midnight-black in his pale face. St. John's fair hair shone like moonlight. Her talented lover brought her to the edge of that peak of satisfaction over and over again, carefully monitoring how long she'd stay there, suspended on the verge of an orgasm. He left her panting, gasping, needing more.

Not one piece of her was left out of this taking. Arms, legs, breasts, thighs, as well as every nerve and cell she possessed, burned for him. The only thing left was to let him have it all, sure that no one could survive much more of this.

Relaxing her insides took effort. When St. John felt that last release, and the internal shudder accompanying it, he took full advantage. Pushing himself into uncharted depths, able to get past the last of her reservations, he stroked the sweet spot she had been saving.

The world dropped away as the intensity of this final action brought down a rain of feeling, emotion, fire and wonder. Madison screamed, not recognizing her voice, and with no idea that she was saying, "Vampire. Goddamn vampire."

St. John's mouth absorbed those curses, and the sob that followed. With his cock still buried inside her, his mouth scorched hers insatiably.

Madison's muscles seized when the orgasm arrived, volcanic, exotic and vicious in intensity. St. John kept her in that shivering, shuddering place where essences mingled and the mind took a holiday. He held her there, sheathed to his hips inside her, and he didn't move or ease up.

Madison rode this cresting wave of outrageous pleasure that made her vision go haywire. Behind closed eyelids, colors revolved, moving rapidly from black to gray to light, like the turning of a mental kaleidoscope, before landing on red. A vibrant, shimmering crimson overlay that overpowered all the rest.

Suddenly, she was no longer soaking up this pleasure, but was out from beneath him.

With lightning-fast reflexes, she rolled Christopher St. John onto his back, and straddled him, on her knees. Her hands, on his shoulders, pinned him down. A strange sound escaped her that was exactly like a growl.

Horrified, and reeling from the brilliance of her climax, Madison launched herself sideways. She opened her eyes, and said in a voice as shaky as the rest of her, "What the hell was that?"

Her lover was quiet for several beats. When he spoke, his tone was husky, his words drawn out. "So," St. John said. "I guess we now know about you."

Madison sat back on her heels, more confused than ever as she pondered what he had said. *Know about her?*

"Bastard," she said. "Do you mean that I've proved to be an easy conquest?"

"I didn't mean anything of the kind," he replied. "It's you who stopped the pleasure."

Had she? The lingering rumble of her orgasm was fading into the distance like an earthquake blowing through. Breathing was tough. The rest of what had happened was a blur.

Yes. She had stopped this.

Was her reflexive disengagement from St. John her body's way of rebelling against such incredible intimacy? Was she trying to protect herself from what would happen next, when Christopher St. John would smile and then leave, having successfully impaled the media sweetheart?

Could she be as vulnerable as that?

The room had gone dark again, but the fright of the red stain behind her eyes wouldn't leave her. Instead of going back to St. John, on the floor, she got up on unsteady legs and backed away. This had been so very good. The best. A first. Jesus, this round of sex had made her hallucinate.

When St. John stood, her eyes remained riveted to him. Having adjusted to the dark, she saw the expression of concern on his face.

He was silhouetted by the light from outside the window. His shirt was open, and torn, revealing the phenomenally bare muscularity of his chest. Crossing his flesh, and easy to see in the dimness, were the scores of scratches she had made while trying to get at him. Each of them had drawn a thin line of blood. Dark blood, of a color approaching maroon.

She couldn't look anywhere but at those scratches, when the awful truth was that she wanted to be in his arms again, and couldn't figure out how to get there.

Sex hadn't resolved anything. What they had between them hadn't even begun to burn itself out. She had to speak. Someone had to.

"I'm sorry." She pointed to his welts with trembling fingers. "For that."

"It's nothing," he said.

"Someone has hurt you before. Those raised lines on your back."

He didn't acknowledge that comment, or explain.

"Did you come here tonight, to do this?" Her gaze dropped to the floor.

"No," he said.

"That's right. You came to warn me to be careful. Did you expect this, though? That this might happen between us?"

"Yes," he replied. "But I came here for another purpose, to warn that you've become an easy target for trouble, whether or not you realize it, and that until you leave England, that won't change."

"I'm used to the spotlight, but the word you used was *danger.* You've insinuated that the man in the doorway of the club is the danger," Madison said. "Why?"

"You are prying into private business."

"I haven't even begun to pry," she said. "And I have no idea what you're talking about. I'm here to report on the missing girls. How could the interviews I've done in regard to that case get me in trouble?"

"It brought you to the club, Madison, twice."

"Lots of people go there."

"None of them looking for Stewart Chase."

The mention of her brother's name was like a slap in the face.

"What has my brother got to do with any of this?"

"I can't tell you that, and suggest that you don't return to Space in your search for answers. I'd ask you not to be alone right now, and that you keep your crew nearby for the rest of your stay."

"Are you in league with that damn detective? I'm not sure what right either of you have to suggest anything like that," Madison said. "If you can't tell me what's behind those cautions, how do you expect me to give them credence?"

"I'm asking you to believe me," he said soberly,

"because I actually have your best interest and safety in mind."

Madison's hand went to her forehead, to the ache between her eyes that had made her world color and shine. "How do you know about my brother?"

"I know that he also has disappeared."

"Why would my going to the club in search of him be dangerous?"

"Because of his beliefs."

Madison blinked slowly, and repeated, "His beliefs?" She added softly, "You know about that?"

"I know about it."

Madison had a hard time taking this in. "I'm not sure how many more surprises or warnings I can take at the moment, to be honest," she said. "You, and what we just did, seem to be the biggest surprise of all."

It was a confession of her scrambled feelings. She knew this, and so did the man across from her. What they had just shared was different, special, mind-blowing, and possibly even scary as hell. But their intimacy, and what he had to say afterward, left her more confused than ever.

Christopher St. John said he knew about her brother's obsession. But she hadn't known about it until recently. So, how did St. John know?

"Tell me," she said. "Tell me how you know about Stewart."

She waited for him to answer, but his nearness was creating more questions than that. Grinding their bodies together on the floor of her hotel room had left her with a desire for him that went far beyond any normal man-woman attraction. She was on fire, even now, with so much up in the air.

"Take a minute," he said without moving closer to her. "Then meet me downstairs."

Things might have been different if he had touched her, or if she had gone to him, and they had comforted each other, held each other. Maybe the questions wouldn't have mattered so much if she had someone to share them with. But they were acting almost as if nothing had happened, when she...God, when she wanted more than anything for it to happen again.

Why couldn't she chalk this up to the one-night stand, and move on, when she so desperately needed to do that?

How could one little spark derail something as important as finding Stewart?

St. John finally moved. He took an item from his pocket, which he set on the sill. "Meet me in the lobby, Madison," he said. "As soon as you can."

"I'm not going anywhere else tonight."

"You asked for my help. I think you'll want to hear what I have to say when we've both had a few seconds of breathing time. Meet me downstairs. It may not be in your best interest to do so, but you will value the importance of what I'm going to show you."

"You will answer my questions? Why not do so first, and I'll decide what to do next."

He looked at her for a long time. "I've had a tip about those missing girls," he said.

Madison leaned on her hands to hide how badly they quaked. She used the wall to keep upright.

"Why didn't you mention this before?"

"We needed to get something else out of the way first."

The sex. Yes, they had needed to indulge in the

thing that was gumming up the works. The problem was that it was obvious, by the tension between them, that it had only made the cravings worse.

Priorities? Hell. Her brother and the Yale girls were at the top of the list, and the urge to straddle St. John had been powerful enough to make her almost forget that.

Smoothing her dress over her hips took self-control. As she shoved the tangle of tousled hair back from her face, Madison's gaze snapped to the window while she called up her courage and her wits.

She stared beyond what was out there, at a city drenched in mystery and intrigue, all those things tainted in one way or another by her brother's horrid files, because Stewart's research haunted her, even now, in these moments with St. John, in a way that defied explanation. Stewart's research just would not go away.

Her feelings of being on the verge of an important discovery, right here, this minute, wasn't only due to St. John's knowledge of Stewart. It was more than that. It *meant* more than that.

She heard St. John's heart beating from a distance of two feet. She perceived his anxiousness as if it were her own. His voice sang in her mind with phrases she shouldn't have been able to hear, and yet she had heard him whispering from the start.

That wasn't all.

The blood rushing through her veins felt unnaturally hot. Her muscles twitched and danced across her bones. The room smelled like wool and musk and forbidden liaisons, and it tasted like sex—sweet and sultry on her tongue.

Beyond those things lay the unmistakable metallic odor of blood. St. John's blood, pooling on the scratches she'd made with her nails, though she could no longer see those marks because of the way he was standing.

Then, there was the red haze that had cloaked the dark.

Frowning, Madison glanced to her left, where the light on her laptop was a niggling form of harassment, telling her to beware of strangers and their intentions, telling her that not everything was always as it seemed, at least in her brother's world.

And Christopher St. John stood there, among all those uncanny perceptions, looking not like a lover, but like some kind of dark, angelic avenger.

"How archaic death by staking seems," she said, voicing a thought instigated by her awareness of the computer. "Unlike using a gun, and firing a bullet, using a wooden stake for a weapon, with the intention of piercing a victim's heart, would necessitate being close enough to look an opponent in the eyes."

St. John eyes met hers. She felt his rapt attention.

"If there were such a thing as vampires, would I be able to kill one, if necessary?" she said. "Would I be able to take you out, if you proved to be a monster in disguise?"

"That's a funny thought," St. John said. "What made you say it?"

"Obsession." Madison struggled for a breath that eluded her. "The tendency must run in my family. My brother was obsessed with London. I appear to be obsessed with you."

More time passed, uncomfortably, after that pronouncement.

"If you won't tell me about Stewart, what kind of tip do you have about the girls? Give me something. Anything," Madison finally said.

"The girls were seen at a hotel near here. I'll take you there."

"Now?"

"It's not public information, Madison. This is for your ears only. The hotel is private."

"Who told you about this?"

"I can't say. You understand about protecting sources."

Madison set her shoulders. "Sex was the payment for that information? With sex out of the way, you'll assist me in the job I've come here to do, in regard to those missing girls?"

"You don't really believe that what we did has anything to do with anything other than what's happening between us on a personal level," he said. "Why even go there."

"I don't know what to believe."

Madison eyed the laptop and the blinking light that haunted her so mercilessly. "You just cautioned me about roaming around. You said going to the club in search of my brother was dangerous, without saying why."

"That warning still stands. More, I cannot say."

She knew that his tip had to be followed up on, no matter what she did or didn't feel about the man who had given it to her, and how cryptic he could be. Other lives were at stake.

"I'll meet you. Give me that minute," she said.

"I'll be waiting."

Those simple words startled her in a way she

couldn't explain. She had heard them in her mind all day. It suddenly seemed that St. John used them here to prove that he truly had been inside her mind telepathically, first conquering that, and then her body.

Christopher St. John appeared to be the bigger danger here, and Madison wondered how she'd move her feet, let alone face him in any kind of light. If he was so perceptive, how could he not know that she was suddenly afraid to leave her room, and that he was partly the cause of this fear?

"I'll bring Teddy," she said.

"I'm not the bad guy here, Madison. Not tonight, anyway. No Teddy. I'll have a car standing by if that will make you feel better."

"You can't carry me?"

She was sorry for the sarcasm, but didn't know what else to say. She longed for his touch as if truly addicted, and sorely needed time away from him in order to recuperate.

When St. John stepped up to her, and again slipped his hands into her hair, she withheld what would have been a telling whimper.

He let several strands of her hair slide through his fingers. He was close enough to kiss her and yet he didn't. He wasn't making this easy at all.

Madison had to move away from the door, away from him, to get a grip on her flailing feelings. She watched him pull his shirt around his bare chest, and reach for the knob beside her.

She stopped him with a question.

"Do you believe in vampires, St. John?"

"Really, Madison. I wonder why you'd mention death by wooden stake, and then ask such a question."

"As much as I wonder why you singled me out in that club and led me to believe…"

"Believe what?" he prompted.

"That you know about vampires."

"Isn't it true that a small percentage of most populations believe in the supernatural?" he said.

"Are you one of them?"

"You're asking if I believe in such things?"

"I'm asking if you're one of them. If you are a vampire."

Madison was sure she saw him wince.

"Not a vampire," he said. "Not in the way you mean."

"Is there another way?"

"Anyone who preys on others, in any way, is a vampire, don't you think?"

"Yes," she agreed. "I suppose you're right. But that doesn't answer my question."

"I'm not one of them," he said. "Not one of those."

"You aren't lying?"

"I don't lie, Madison. I never lie."

"Everyone lies."

"There would be consequences if I did, none of them very pleasant."

"Now you actually believe you're a saint?" she said.

"I have already confessed to having no aspirations in that direction."

"Then why don't you just tell me what you've found out about the hotel and those girls, and save us a trip. That would be saintly enough."

"Because you'll go there alone, without me, and that wouldn't be a good thing," he said. "No story is worth that."

"It would be dangerous to go there without you?"

"You have no idea how much." Christopher St. John left the room, taking his disarming, addictive presence with him, and leaving Madison, half-naked, completely unenlightened, and hungering for him in a way that was too crazy to be tolerated, staring after him.

It was becoming a habit.

A very bad habit.

Chapter 12

Small licks of leftover desire inhibited every step St. John took as he left Madison. Delicious heat. Monstrous heat.

He could have stayed inside her forever. He hadn't wanted the moment to end. But something had happened on that floor. Madison, he believed, had glimpsed her destiny.

Through the closed door, he heard her sigh of relief, and longed to feel that breath on his face. He wanted to see her skin glisten with anticipation, and watch her cheeks flush pink, when going back to her, getting close to her again, wasn't right, or to be condoned.

He hadn't meant to do this. Take her. Indulge. He had known he'd have to stay away from her for this very reason. In the heat of passion, with her body wrapped around an immortal, she had revealed her true colors.

What might have been a fleeting glimpse for her of what lay ahead, was devastatingly real for him.

And yet it truly had only been a glimpse for you, Madison.

She had asked about vampires without realizing her special connection to them. In their lovemaking, she had perceived his Otherness without fully recognizing it.

He had to soak this in, and see his next move. But he didn't like it. How could he? In order to address this with her, he'd have to explain about himself.

It seems that your brother has kept one particular secret to himself.

That secret pertained to what the Chase twins actually were. When Madison had moved from beneath him, it was because her instincts for survival had inadvertently kicked in. Her latent genes had gone into action. Their intimacy had made her see him with half-closed perception.

Madison. Hell. What now?

This was an untimely mess. With repeated proximity to vampires, Madison was beginning to use her senses in a different, predetermined way. Taking that further, if a single dose of Other could awaken her, what might repeated sexual encounters with a centuries-old immortal instigate?

Their blood was calling to each other. There was no doubt about this. Chemistry was sealing the deal. Created to be opposite, he had confused her because he truly wasn't one of the vampires a Slayer could identify clearly.

They were on the same side in the fight against vampires. Again, though, explanations for this would be necessary if she found out about her calling and mistook him for something dangerous.

Why don't you know what you are?

Slayers were usually fully honed by the time they entered puberty. Madison was in her twenties. Her brother had also only recently stumbled on the new image of his future.

Maybe being a twin has stifled some of your ingrained perceptions, overwhelming those perceptions with others.

The dilemma was excruciating.

If he were to remain close to Madison, in any way, there was a chance her nature might take her over completely. She'd be unable to resist following her instincts about going after vampires. It's what they all feared. And what Simon Monteforte had warned him of. Notoriety. Secrets getting out.

In a city teeming with freshly bitten, mindless fledglings and fanged rogues, and ruled by a hundred elegant immortals, how could she keep her identity safe from the Hundred? She'd be driven, compelled to find them, once she woke up. Whatever particles swam in her genetic makeup would demand that she did so. And there were more monsters in London than anywhere else on earth.

Slayer.

St. John shut his eyes to block out the image of Madison with a wooden stake in her hand.

He had done this. In getting as close to her as a man could get with a woman, he had encouraged that dark thing inside her to blossom.

Not only that, he was going to take her to an establishment that reeked of immortality and unedited extravagance, where women willingly came to bleed for the creatures who kept them in the lap of luxury, and who catered to their keepers' monstrous whims.

He'd told her he had a tip, and hated to think what that kind of atmosphere might do to a Slayer who was awakening. But if she got her story, she'd leave the city and be safe from those who preyed on the Slayers who threatened to prey on them.

She had scented his blood. He'd seen this in her. If Madison happened to see a drop on the carpet of that hotel, would that further hurtle her toward her future? Toward the very thing her brother had come here for, before it all went bad?

He had to be careful. He smelled that Otherness in her now, on him, in her lingering scent—the addicting peppery flavor that heralded the reason he'd been drawn to her.

The fact was…he should have known from the beginning. It was a grave oversight. A rueful one. He didn't make mistakes often.

Stewart Chase had come to look for vampires, and had been bitten by the vampires he chased. To ensure that Madison got out of London before becoming a full-fledged Slayer, causing more trouble, hurting herself, he had to leave his attraction to her behind.

Christ, the thought hurt.

Nevertheless, it had to be done.

After all the time he'd spent alone, the woman he'd bonded with wasn't truly mortal at all. Not completely. She was a vampire's natural-born enemy, and would soon have the strength to prove it.

And he couldn't tell her about his own task, or how

important it was for him to maintain his disguise, allowing the Hundred to trust him. To her, he'd be one of the monsters. She'd never know the whole story.

As he got off the elevator, St. John glared at its open door. He'd be willing to bet that if any of his brethren had ever run across a Slayer, none of them had dared to bed one.

He should leave now. If he didn't wait for Madison, she might go back to her room. She might be safe for a while, on her own.

"You might never know what you are."

His voice was hushed, almost angry. "Yet I told you about the hotel around the corner, and that the missing American girls had been there. What media-savvy newscaster would let that tip go unheeded?"

Damn…this…dilemma!

In no way could he actually afford to explain that her brother had been right about London, and that due to Stewart Chase's beliefs, her twin had become monstrous in his own right.

He dared not tell her that by aiding her here, in London, with Simon Monteforte and the rest of the Hundred looking on, more harm would come to her than good, and that because of her brother, her death warrant may already have been signed.

Death warrant.

Simon Monteforte had become a prime suspect in St. John's search for the hidden traitor to the Hundred, and if Monteforte was creating scores of rogue vampires for some sinister purpose, the old immortal could easily send the monsters Madison's way.

Damn and blast. He was stuck. Damned if he helped

Madison, and damned if he didn't. His longing for her was so viciously palpable, even now, he wanted to pry the elevator doors open with his teeth, and get back to her.

"And when you find out that vampires helped to kill the humanity in your brother, what then?" he said.

Yes, what then?

Ignoring the pressures building inside him, St. John paced in the lobby. It was too late to do anything but await his lover, who was not only in serious danger, but ultimately the enemy of every nonmortal creature, anywhere.

It was too damn bad there were so many of them.

When she could breathe normally, Madison went to the window. The item St. John had left on the sill was her cell phone. There was no use in wondering how he had gotten it.

She jumped when the phone buzzed, and pulled up a text message from Teddy. You might want to take a look at the video footage. Something strange about it.

Who in the world, she wanted to shout, had time for more strangeness?

Although St. John wasn't in the room, she felt his nearness. St. John's vibe was subtly sexual, like a kiss of moonlight on sun-warmed flesh. Like swallowing parts of the night, and perilously close to metaphysical intercourse. Her senses were blaring, shouting, warning, that he was waiting for her.

In order to get the information he possessed, she had to see him. If she could help to solve this case, and find her brother, they could all go home.

From the neckline of her dress, Madison retrieved D.I. Crane's business card. She looked at it for some time, hearing those whispers in her head again, this time clearly in St. John's voice. *"Your only chance is to accept what help I can give."*

Palming her phone in one hand and the detective's card in the other, Madison weighed her options.

Then she noticed the blood on her fingers.

She ran her fingers across her mouth, and found another trace of blood. Their lovemaking had been rough. Her mouth hurt.

But there were girls to be found. A brother to be found.

She picked up her shoes and said to St. John, in case he somehow was actually listening with that spooky telepathic connection, "Just so you know, I told Detective Crane I was with you last night. You're the first place he will look if anything happens to me."

Inwardly cursing her ability to place herself in danger in situations where information was at stake, Madison added one more thing.

"It's for them this time. Those girls. Not for you, or because I need to see you again."

She showered off quickly, and stepped past the dress on the floor that still smelled like her lover. She exited the room quietly. Four girls and one man were already missing. Odds were against her possessing the personal magic necessary to keep out of that count if she continually placed herself in the path of danger.

She'd had trouble keeping on track lately, but would have to gear up for the game. Maybe, just maybe,

Christopher St. John really was a good guy, besides being phenomenally good in the sack.

"Yeah, well, I never said I wasn't stupid," she muttered, tucking herself into the corner of the elevator as the contraption began its descent. "If I had, I'd be lying."

Chapter 13

She was not prepared for the breathtaking sight of Christopher St. John in the hotel's ambient light. She had to speak to keep from beating at him with her fists over the chaos he was causing with her resolve.

"I have a funny feeling that your voice speaks to me inside my head," she said.

"The voice of good conscience, I hope," he returned.

"If this leads to those girls, I'll be the first to let you know."

He nodded. "My car is waiting, as promised."

"If the place we're going is around the corner, I'd rather walk." She really needed a blast of chilly London air to cool her off.

Acquiescing, St. John moved aside without touching her, though she was sure he'd thought about it. Worse yet, she had. He had donned a fresh shirt and a black leather jacket, brought to him by the chauffeur of his car, no doubt.

"I hope there aren't any gangs roaming around tonight." Her tone was harsher than she would have liked. Self-defense, she guessed. St. John was staring at her mouth, at the blood she tasted on it.

She wiped her lips with the back of her hand.

"I can assure you those same monsters won't be here," he said.

She felt a stir of air on the side of her face when he waved off his driver. The car he'd alluded to was a black Mercedes. St. John, himself, was a streamlined Ferrari.

He wore expensive clothes and had a chauffeur, and had never actually mentioned what he did for a living. She hadn't thought to ask. Big reminder: she knew nothing about him, and her skills as a journalist were sadly lacking whenever he was around.

Taking a quick visual sweep of the street turned up an uncomfortable lack of people. The incident in her room remained a silent undercurrent between herself and the man beside her as they walked.

"Where are we going?" she asked.

"The hotel is called Germand."

The deepness of St. John's voice was similar to a smooth caress between her thighs. Her mouth wasn't the only body part feeling bruised as she pulled those thighs together.

"Inside, there's a private area where local businessmen and dignitaries often go," he explained.

"Dignitaries? What would four college girls be doing in a place like that?"

"They would have to be invited."

Madison stopped walking. "College girls? That doesn't sound right."

There wasn't any point in explaining about her instincts and how they worked, especially since her initial instincts hadn't been wrong about him. But she knew something. The place St. John was taking her to was *off.* Just hearing the name of that hotel gave her shivers. The Germand wasn't right, somehow.

"Do you go there?" she asked.

"Never."

Somehow, that made her feel better. When St. John walked on, Madison followed.

"I take it someone saw the girls there?" she said.

"They stayed at the hotel for a couple of nights."

Madison stopped again, perplexed. "Are you kidding? Why hasn't that come out?"

St. John turned around to face her. "Maybe they were broke, flattered, and it was an offer too good to refuse. Maybe their parents never told them about the possible perils of accepting attention from strangers."

"The people working there didn't come forward to talk about it, or provide what may be an important detail in the case?"

"The staff at that hotel are notoriously discreet."

"They're also withholding information from an investigation."

"You know sometimes things aren't completely black or white, Madison. However, they did tell me, when pressed."

When he brushed up against her, meaning to urge her forward, unexpected jolts of electricity shot through Madison. Although she kept walking, she gave St. John a sideways glance.

Did he also feel the heat burning between them?

Planning to say something about that, she stopped abruptly, as if someone had yanked on her arm. Scanning the dark street, she was caught off guard by a distant voice. Not St. John's voice this time, but a thin voice, sounding tired, and strained.

Madison forgot to breathe. She felt her face drain of color. She recognized that voice.

"Stewart?" she whispered. "Is that you?"

Seeing Madison spin, St. John dropped all semblance of calm and reached for her. Pulling her with him, he backed toward the building.

"It's my brother," she said. Her face was as white as paper. Her eyes had taken on a haunted cast.

Stewart Chase, damn the beast, had found his sister.

And his own decision not to get close to her again had just blown to pieces.

"It's Stewart," Madison insisted. "He's here."

The new vibration ruffled across St. John's skin with a recognizable chill. It was her brother, all right, but again, not the same one she was expecting, and Stewart had the fangs to prove it.

This new turn of events was a fine mess. Finding her brother would seal the lid on Madison's coffin. She'd know for sure about vampires and Others, and was in a convenient position to expose them, if she didn't attempt to take matters into her own hands first.

Ninety-nine of the immortals comprising the Hundred weren't killers, but they would act to protect their own, if it came to that. Only one of them was a cold-blooded murderer. He wanted to find that one. Especially now, before that killer found the next Slayer.

He tightened his hold on Madison to keep Stewart Chase's presence away from the woman who wanted it most, surprised that her twin had been able to locate her so quickly, when Stewart had only recently been turned.

He hoped that Stewart wasn't so far gone yet that he'd harm his sister, though he'd harm her enough just by showing himself.

Go from here. He sent a silent message to Stewart. *You will hurt her more if you stay.*

"He called to me. He's here." Madison was twisting in his grip. "Where is he? Why doesn't he come out?"

"You may have only thought you heard him."

"Bullshit. I can *feel* him."

"Come on." St. John led her quickly to the sidewalk. "The hotel is just there."

Shaking her head spread crimson curls that were now a blatant contrast to her colorless face. "Help me," she said. "Help me, St. John. Christopher. Please."

Maybe the *please* did it. Possibly it was the stricken look on her lovely face, and the way his heartbeat entwined with hers. He was one of the most powerful creatures on the earth, but in that moment, as Madison's eyes met his, he felt powerless to resist her.

"If it is your brother, he can follow," he said, fisting his hands to keep from taking what he wanted. Madison's mouth. Her body. Her innocence about the existence of monsters.

Due to what he had become such a long time ago, he also selfishly wanted her soul. Because only with her soul surrendered, could he truly have her, truly protect her.

"One thing at a time, Madison. Possibly that one thing will lead to another."

He could almost guarantee that it would.

The Germand's doorman eyed them solemnly, then bowed his head and stepped aside. St. John took one more look over his shoulder, at the street, where Stewart's vibration was like broken glass along his neural pathways. The man had been changed, bitten by the wrong sort of vampire. The Ancients hadn't cared overmuch about the aggressive young American attorney knocking at their door, or what he might have had to say about bartering for their help with the missing girls.

Stewart Chase, in his current incarnation, was a wild card, an anomaly, and still killing vamps. At least for the present.

"I don't like this place," Madison said, balking just past the door.

St. John hardly heard her. It wasn't her brother now who had drawn his attention.

He sniffed the air, and swore beneath his breath. Outside, nearby, more visitors were coming, the likes of which St. John hadn't sensed for quite some time. Monsters he instantly knew the feel and taste of. The atmosphere stank of their imminent journey here. The fabric of the night was shifting to accommodate them.

Surprised, St. John looked from the street to Madison, with real concern. Blood Hunters were on the prowl. Fanged invaders were on their way. *Nosferatu,* an ugly name that made most immortals cringe.

Along with the scent, a full picture appeared in his mind, and the image was damnable. This new plague wasn't coming to London for the sport of killing humans. Not if there wasn't an army of them.

Another spike along his nerves told him these monsters had to be coming for him, personally. There was no other reason for letting a few select Nosferatu loose in a city, other than having a target of consequence. Outside of his search for the traitor among the Hundred, and more and more vampire kills, there was nothing out of the ordinary going on.

The thought stopped him cold. His cover had to have been blown. His commitment here had been compromised.

Having found the whereabouts of a Blood Knight, someone had sent Nosferatu to find him. Creatures notorious for prying secrets from other vampires in the most gruesome of ways would hope to peel back the pieces of his golden vow in order to reveal that vow's source.

Grotesque in the extreme, warrior Nosferatu were strong, mean and driven. They were the minions of a strong master, their Prime, and were vampiric hit men of the worst kind. Soulless hellhounds, bent on destruction. Though a small number of them couldn't take him down, the damage they would inflict on London streets while trying to find him could bring long-hidden secrets into the open. Innocent people might be slaughtered by the dozens. Mortals could finally find out what else walked among them.

Who had done this?

Whoever it was knew about him, and also knew him well enough to figure that he might barter to keep the lives of the people in this city safe. They might assume he'd trade information on his origins, in return for saving the city from a bloodbath.

With an uncharacteristic uneasiness, St. John focused on Madison. Her back was rigid. She fought to maintain an outward appearance of calm when that calm had been stripped from her.

He hoped to God she wasn't picking up on his own tenseness with her up-and-coming Slayer sensitivities. He had pledged to protect her from the darkness, but the presence of these particular monsters, sent for him and spiraling closer, was about to change everything... if he didn't find them first.

In order to save the woman at his side, the only way for him to help her, and so many others now, would be to get clear of all of them and, when the freaks arrived, go after the abominations coming after him.

Someone else would have to watch over Madison in his place.

A nosy detective, maybe.

Madison had pleaded for his help, and he couldn't oblige. He couldn't allow her, or any other innocent, to get in the crossfire of an old feud.

A shock of cold pain between his shoulder blades made him turn. He scanned the room. Apart from the oncoming wave of fanged creatures, this hotel had also been compromised. A noticeable heaviness lay on the air. Shadows hid in the corners. Something sinister had just occurred here.

"I'm sorry," he said to Madison. "We have to go. I shouldn't have brought you here. It's no longer safe."

The stricken expression on the face of the woman with whom his soul had braided told him she awaited an explanation that she would never get. He had to remain here, and face what lay in this hotel's shadows before doing anything else. It took a monster to fight a monster, with any hope of success, if that's what the atmosphere of the Germand indicated.

Anxiously, he grabbed hold of the clerk behind the desk and hauled the poor man onto the shiny oak surface. Peering into that man's worried face, he said, "Get her back to her hotel. Now. Safely."

As the man emphatically gestured for Madison to follow him, another presence filled the room—a green velvet haze that looked for all the world like a patch of lush, verdant grass with the promise of a snake hiding in it.

"No need to scare the pants off the poor devil," Simon Monteforte said in a voice rivaling the night's chill as he fastidiously wiped a drop of crimson liquid from his mouth. "I will see to Miss Chase, personally."

"The hell you will," St. John replied.

Chapter 14

"*Run!*"

The silent command beat at Madison's ears, compelling her to obey. She had never been so frightened.

Looking back and forth from Christopher St. John to the gaunt, sober-featured face of the man she had earlier brushed past in the doorway of Space, she immediately picked up on the strain in the room.

Without waiting for what might happen next, knowing only that she had to get away from that ghastly hotel and the scary apparition in green, Madison turned and sprinted through the open doorway.

No one stopped her.

She ran as if her life depended on it, pretty sure that it did. The quickly covered-up grimace of distaste that St. John hadn't been able to hide from her as he faced the gray-haired man provided the impetus for a fast getaway. Instead of answers to the questions she'd started out with, new craziness had piled up.

That man in the hotel had blood on his chin.

At the end of the short block, where a sharp turn led to her hotel, she realized she was no longer alone. Static pulled her fine hairs to attention. Goose bumps arrived in droves.

Her legs faltered, feeling unnaturally heavy and weak. Without hearing anyone coming, she knew someone was there. The hotel clerk? Another gang of creeps bent on harassing tourists near the long line of popular hotels?

The word *run* replayed over and over like an echo in her overworked mind, in St. John's voice, forcing her to put one foot in front of the other. The entrance to her hotel was only a few yards away, but she ran as if the sidewalk were composed of ankle-deep mud, each step labored and hard-won. Not enough air got into her lungs to make breathing count.

Tired of this crap, disgusted with weakness, she made herself move, and skidded on a damp section of concrete. She broke her fall by bashing the building's wall with her right shoulder, and she cried out. A hand covered her mouth. An arm wrapped around her waist.

Her fear multiplied, though she hadn't lost her wits this time. Using her teeth to try to free herself, Madison bit the palm of the hand covering her mouth, hard, hoping to do damage.

The acrid taste of blood, hot, thick, made her gag, but it also gave her more anxious energy. She kicked out behind her with nearly useless legs, and felt one kick connect.

Take that, prick!

Whoever held on to her didn't seem to notice the kind of injury a well-placed high heel could inflict. Her attacker made no sound and no other move, other than to try to suppress her maniacal energy with one strong arm around her and the hand that kept her from shouting.

Madison refused to give up. Though each struggle required more effort than the one before, she gave it all she had. But it had been a very long day, and she was running out of steam.

An image of four college girls filled her mind, each of them caught in an iron grip on a dark street far from their home. Had their lives ended like this, in fear and useless struggle? She'd be damned if she'd become one of them.

With one last concentrated effort, she again bit the hand covering her mouth. As the blood from that bite ran down her chin, the last remnants of her energy finally failed. She could no longer lift an arm or a foot, open her mouth or fight back.

"Stop fighting, mad one," a whispered voice commanded.

Flailing, Madison felt herself slip, felt the darkness of her surroundings close in...until she became one with the night.

"Ah, my dear St. John," Simon Monteforte said in a voice as dark as the paneled walls. "You'd prefer she takes to the streets alone, without my assistance?"

"Out there, she stands a chance," St. John replied, wanting to follow Madison, and having to carefully hide those feelings.

"You think so?" Monteforte remarked.

St. John didn't bother to nod. He wasn't sure how he could maintain his camouflage with any of the Ancients if he were to test Simon Monteforte's fealty here, among so many of them.

The sound of Madison's heels on the sidewalk had grown faint. He found it strange that nothing else seemed to matter to him at that moment, except getting to her.

"Hurting her would make a mess of things," he said to Monteforte. "There's no reason to do so."

"Yet you brought her here, a place off-limits to most mortals."

"For information about those girls."

"Ah, yes. The missing girls," Monteforte said.

"We can't afford to have another one go missing, Simon. All eyes are on this city already. Haven't you noticed?"

"The other Americans may turn up yet, and then they can all go home and leave us to our own…pleasures," Monteforte said.

"Madison Chase must be with them when they go."

"I suppose you'll see to that, in spite of your earlier pledge?"

"My allegiance lies with maintaining our society and its secrets. Madison might be a nuisance, but is no threat. Getting rid of her won't help any cause."

"Your tune has changed, I see. I find that most interesting, St. John."

"My tune hasn't wavered since I first arrived in London," St. John corrected. "When our goal was to exist alongside the mortals in peace."

"In that, I believe we have fared well."

"Until now, when too many missing people are stirring up public sentiment against those in charge of this city."

St. John took his time with the final question. "Where are those girls now, Simon?"

Monteforte grinned, showing crimson-stained fangs. "You think I know?"

"I believe you might."

"You give me far too much credit, St. John."

"Or else not nearly enough."

In that moment, as the comment left his lips, St. John realized fully that Simon Monteforte was the one he sought. The reek of the immortal's indiscretions sat in this place like another layer of haze. Without the crowd and scent of hundreds of mortals in the club to mask it, Monteforte's foulness was readily apparent.

St. John stared at the Ancient who had to have known his secret identity for some time. Monteforte had unleashed the hellhounds. Did Monteforte imagine those hounds could take a Blood Knight down?

Something else drew his attention.

A prickle of fear twitched the thread tying him and Madison together. It was Madison's fear.

Monteforte was formidable, and needed tending to, but St. John knew he was needed elsewhere. Something had happened to Madison. He had to go to her.

He spun for the door, not bothering to stop when Monteforte called out, "You feel the new darkness on the wind, St. John? Does it whisper your name?"

Free of the weighty Ancient's presence, and out of the building at last, St. John opened his senses. Sniffing the air, he grunted a curse. That new trouble Monteforte had mentioned now tore at his senses as if it had been magnified by the Ancient's recognition of it.

The trouble in the wind hadn't yet arrived, though it was too close for comfort when his strength was needed elsewhere.

The people of London would be lucky if they stayed off the streets in the hours to come.

Facing the direction of the odor of the Nosferatu in the distance, St. John bared his fangs. The unearthly sigils carved and seared into his back were speaking to him in whispers and undulations that confirmed the rightness of the direction of his thinking. Under all of their noses, Simon Monteforte had become a servant of the Dark.

But that wasn't all, certainly not the worst of things. He could no longer sense Madison. She must have lost consciousness. The thread had gone lax, even as his sigils rippled.

Madison opened her eyes, blinked, but saw nothing. She was on her back, on a cold floor.

Sheer fright made her sit up. With darkness enveloping her, and a loss of all direction, a wave of dizziness made her stomach heave.

Flipping onto her hands and knees, she strained for a couple of clear breaths. What she sucked in wasn't pleasant. The air was filled with particles of dust, decay and the awful smell of something rancid.

Crawling on all fours, she tested out her surroundings, afraid of what she'd find. She rotated in a full circle, unhindered. That was good. A start.

The floor wasn't concrete, so it couldn't be a sidewalk. The ground beneath her had the coolness of slick ceramic tile, with grooves in regular intervals. She counted four large tiles by crawling forward and backward and feeling with her fingers, and more tiles to her right and left. She was indoors, then, on a floor. Her attacker had left her, without bothering to tie her up.

"Stupid bastard."

Her searching fingers found something soft that gave her a start. She backed up, sliding over the hard floor on bare, throbbing knees. Nothing happened. No one pulled her back.

Inching forward again, she reached out, closed her fingers over the soft object. No bad consequences presented themselves.

Sitting back on her heels, Madison pulled the object through both of her hands. A sweater? *Yes.* Long-sleeved, loosely woven and smelling faintly of perfume.

Her heart gave a gigantic thump. Waiting in silence, she half expected her attacker to laugh, and sighed with relief when no laughter rang out.

Crawling farther, the silence creating pressure in her ears, Madison found another item that felt like a canvas bag. Fumbling, she wrenched the bag open and moved her hands over more fabric. Another sweater, and a pair of jeans, easy to identify because of the unique smell of the denim. With further scrutiny, she concluded that whoever owned these clothes was small-boned, thin.

Excitement made her heart lurch. Clothes meant that either she'd been tossed onto the floor of someone's residence, or someone had been here recently. *A young woman.*

Her mind spliced that information together, driving Madison to her feet. Again, she waited for danger to strike and said in astonishment and relief when it didn't, "Okay."

Since she was free to move about, she might also have the freedom to leave this place.

With the sweater grasped tightly in one hand, and the other hand held out in front of her, Madison shuffled forward. She found a wall, and next to it the arm of a chair.

The smell of decay grew stronger. Gagging, Madison felt around, paused, recoiled when breathing became difficult. The object in the chair was large, stiff, cold and unmoving.

It was a body.

Swallowing a scream, she backpedaled with her pulse exploding, then she dived forward again, refusing to lose the wall. Maybe there was a door or a window in that wall.

Hand over hand, with the sweater dangling from her fingers and the blood pounding in her ears, Madison felt her way across the room until she found a crack. Tracing the crack, she discovered a doorknob that turned in her hand.

Breathless, frightened, she took a cautious step forward and felt the chill of fresher air on her face.

St. John strode through the night, alert, determined.

Stopping on the side street bordering Madison's hotel, he glanced once at his surroundings, then looked upward. Gripping the building's brick exterior with both hands, he began to climb.

Madison's window was open. Knowing immediately that she wasn't in that room, he hauled himself in, landing agilely on both feet. As the skin prickle of warning washed over him, he closed his eyes to process any new scent that might overlap hers, and snapped his fangs in frustration over not finding any.

The room was just as he'd last seen it. Some of Madison's things were spread out on the bureau, personal things he wanted to touch.

The doorknob to the hallway rattled. St. John turned his head, and gathered to spring.

The door opened slowly, but no monster stood there. On the threshold was one of the men from Madison's network, wearing a startled expression and a wrinkled shirt.

"Who the hell are you?" that man demanded.

"I might ask you the same thing," St. John replied, unfisting his hands.

Chapter 15

Madison didn't bother to wonder why no one kept her from leaving the dark room. She was absorbed in getting away as fast as possible.

She ran down a dim corridor punctuated by other open doors until she found stairs heading down. There was only one wall next to the staircase. The other side showed a gaping hole of nothing, open to the night. The meager illumination of distant streetlights helped in her race for freedom.

After descending four floors, she hit flat ground. Only then did she stop to take stock of her surroundings, because she had to. She'd need to find this awful place again.

She made quick mental notes. *Shabby building. Deserted. Derelict. Big dark holes where windows should have been.* Due to the unsoundness of the structure, the whole thing may have been slated for destruction. What was left of it sagged on its foundation; just the kind of place for keeping a kidnap victim, or hiding a body, though her kidnapper had been inexperienced enough to have forgotten to lock the door.

What about the body?

Glad she hadn't had to see it, she knew help would be needed for those details. Police.

Madison took precious seconds more to look herself over and get her trembling under control. Everything seemed fine, which under the circumstances was a blessing. She still wore her dress, and both shoes. Her knees were bruised, her fingernails were chipped, but if she had been able to get away so easily, what had the guy gained by accosting her on the street in the first place? She hadn't carried a purse or wallet. She didn't own any jewelry.

"Not a robbery, then."

Her fingers were cramping from holding tightly to the sweater she'd found. Her mind raced. One thing was crystal clear. Detective Crane had been right in that pieces of clothing were turning up all over the place. At least, thankfully, this sweater didn't belong to anyone in the Chase family.

What if that body turned out to be one of the Yale girls?

She had to get help, when the biggest problem facing her now was having no idea where she might be.

"Damn it to hell and back!"

The curses she uttered followed her through the dark as ran down the street in search of a car to flag down.

* * *

St. John was too worried about Madison to consider the mortal in the doorway anything more than a hindrance.

"I'm looking for Madison," he said, already moving toward the window.

"How did you get in?" the man demanded.

"How did you get in?" St. John countered.

The man held up a key. "It was under my door. Madison must have put it there."

St. John had no time for explanations or hiding his next move. He sat for a moment on the sill before swinging his long legs outside, said, "Tell her I came by," and jumped.

He landed on the sidewalk in a crouch, with one hand touching the ground and his chin lifted. The malignant odor of the rogues was stronger, though they weren't advancing as fast as he had anticipated, and were still outside of the city.

What good was hurrying, he supposed, when they and their counterparts had been after him, unsuccessfully, for centuries. When animals like these had plagued the Seven for an eternity.

As he straightened, he wondered how Simon Monteforte been able to fool the rest of the Hundred about his position within the community. Monteforte had hidden his darkness from the other creatures, when fooling the Hundred wasn't easy. Nearly impossible, in fact. Yet the old monster would now call attention to the beings who actually ruled most of London, and quite probably cause a rain of bloody terror to fall upon the innocent bystanders who got in their way.

No doubt Monteforte pined for the Grail, like so

many others before him. He would shake the foundation of the Hundred to gain the knowledge St. John possessed. Thinking to bargain with the lives of the people in London, he would demand to know the resting place of the most holy of religious relics, sought for centuries and protected by the Seven Blood Knights bound to it.

Monteforte desired the magic that went with the chalice of Christ. No doubt he believed that with the Grail in his possession, Monteforte would have power beyond belief, and command the Seven.

Mason LanVal, the last of the knights to be added to the Seven, had been entrusted with the task of hiding the Grail, and was its keeper still, as far as St. John knew. Had Nosferatu been sent after LanVal, as well? Perhaps monsters were emerging all over Europe, hoping to track down his reclusive brethren.

Monteforte. Traitor.

Very bad news, indeed.

He had found what he'd been seeking, but was torn. Tonight, he had made a promise to keep a special mortal safe. His vow, meant for protecting the masses, or as many of them as he could manage, had truly enlarged in scope.

"Where are you?" he called to Madison, sending his senses outward. "I know you're near."

He looked down at his feet. She had been here, on this spot. He saw her in his mind's eye as a shimmering outline of pale gray mist.

"I can smell you, little Slayer."

Her fragrance lingered, hanging on the damp night air like a cloud partially tainted with the iron odor of fright, and blood.

Icy knife pricks of discomfort returned.

He had told Madison to run, and she had done so, blindly. Instead of sprinting to what she would think of as safety, however, she had met someone else along the way. Some*thing* else, smelling not quite so sweet.

He instantly recognized the image forming next to hers in his mind. Stewart Chase. The twins had indeed found each other here, not long ago. And all because St. John had left her alone for what was, in his world, an insignificant amount of time, but was in hers direly significant, the difference between life and death and another type of existence after real breath was gone.

St. John tried to appease the gnawing marks on his back that continued to pain him. Even without Nosferatu on the way, his dealings with the Hundred, and among them a traitor of the worst kind, this particular meeting between Madison and what was left of her brother could have bad consequences for everyone.

Monteforte would know this, too, and that in splitting his allegiances, St. John would become weaker in regard to any one of them.

The screech of sirens roused St. John from thought. The sirens were close, slicing shrilly through the heaviness of the otherwise deceptively quiet London night. Intermittent with those sirens, he heard the approach of a car.

He spun, slamming his stinging back against the side of the building, and waited for the arrival of the woman he felt with every sense in his body. The flame-haired object of his soul's desire was coming back to him. Stewart, bless that damn hybrid, hadn't harmed his sister.

When the car pulled up, he saw Madison through the window. He couldn't rush out there and tear the door from its hinges. What he could do, though, was offer up a prayer of thanks for her return, even though his prayers were seldom, if ever, answered.

As the detective's car came to a stop in front of her hotel, Madison shivered. Her inner radar told her that St. John hovered just out of sight.

She wasn't sure she could withstand another encounter with him just now. Yet she couldn't wait for it.

He had warned her to run because he believed the creature in the Germand hotel lobby had been extremely dangerous. She knew he'd been right. Just the sight of that hotel had caused a flare of unease in her. And there had been still more danger on the surrounding streets.

"You'll need to come back to the department with me to make a statement," Crane said, cutting the engine. "You have time for a quick shower and a change, that's all."

Probably sensing the distressing way he had put that, he hurried on, more gently. "You look like you need that shower, as well as a good, stiff drink."

Madison searched the dark. "They'll find out who's in that place, and who the sweater belongs to?"

"We'll do our best."

The detective got out of the car, crossed to her side and helped her out. She hated the fact that she needed his arm in order to stand.

"I'll take you up," he said in a tone that let her know he'd accept no argument.

"I can shower by myself, Detective."

"Of course you can, so I'll wait in the hall."

He wasn't smiling when Madison looked. His forehead showed deep furrows as he said, "You saw St. John again? Could the blood on your hands be his?"

"No. Not his."

She didn't dare address the reason why the detective had been spying on her, and instead thought about the Germand hotel, and how wrong it had felt leaving St. John there. Had it only been hours ago that he'd held her in his arms?

"Is something wrong?" the detective asked.

"Funny question, isn't it, given the circumstances," she said.

She realized as they passed through the lobby that she'd begun to hate this place, and every hotel like it.

"There's a hospital a few blocks away. It might be a good idea to stop there," D.I. Crane said in a tone of honest concern.

"Thanks, but I really do need that shower."

Her stomach was queasy, but Madison couldn't recall the last time it hadn't been. As for the weak-kneed condition currently crimping her style, well, that had to go. She was smarter than this, stronger than this. She was alive. She hadn't been hurt by whoever had abducted her. In fact, she had gotten away without much fuss at all, as bizarre as that was.

Her journalistic side wanted to know why she had been allowed to leave the scene of a possible homicide, and why her abductor had let her walk when he had to figure she'd go straight to the police. The detective beside her had probably asked himself those same questions.

Would he also consider that whoever had taken her to that apartment might have done so for a very specific reason? So she would find the body in it?

The clock over the lobby desk told her she'd been gone an hour. One freaking hour, when it felt like twenty.

She eyed the detective as they approached the elevator, finding it interesting that he'd give her a pass to return to the hotel for a quick cleanup, when that kind of leniency surely had to go against police policy in any country. She had been part of a crime scene. Even after they'd taken samples from under her nails, she remained the bearer of important details, and a credible witness.

Contrary to Teddy's analysis, British D.I.s weren't stupid or notorious for fits of lovesickness. Nevertheless, too damn many things were popping up that any skilled journalist would have gone after with lights and cameras blazing…which was exactly what she intended to do.

As she and the detective stepped into the elevator, the smell of the blood on her hand made her stare at her fingers. She'd bitten some guy, acting like one of Stewart's vampires. She had tasted the awful stuff twice tonight, and wondered how vampires could like it.

However, the dried blood on her hands seemed to signify something of real consequence. And damn if that didn't always bring her back to Stewart, and the way his insane explanation for the events of the past two days would go down.

Vampires. In London.

As the elevator started up, Madison delved into her memory of her brother's files, unable to help herself. Because there had been, she was sure, blood on the old man's lips at the Germand.

Blood that may not have been his.

Stewart had written that there were two Londons, one for the living and one for the dead, and that the two worlds had collided in the worst possible of ways. He had suggested that innocent people were suffering the consequences of the secrets known only to a few savvy souls.

What if there were actually such things as vampires, and everything she'd been through was tied in to that?

What if what she had seen on the old man's face at the Germand had been blood, as in he'd been drinking some?

What if vampire existence somehow explained the disappearance of the four Yale girls who had been seen at that hideous hotel, and Stewart knew it and that's why he'd come here?

Vampires, in London.

For real.

Screw the shaky stuff. She had a job to do and by God, she would do it. Finding that body tonight only served to up the ante.

"I remembered something," she said to D. I. Crane. "I'm sorry I can't recall where the information came from, but it was to check out a hotel around the corner called the Germand. Do you know it?"

The detective nodded. "Fancy place for fancy people."

Again, she thought of the image of the old man in green.

"Can you send someone there to investigate whether the girls might have been there recently?" she asked. "Right away?"

"I can, and will," he said, eyeing her quizzically. "It was a good tip? Trustworthy?"

"As good as it gets."

She was shivering again, and positive that Christopher St. John waited for her. He felt close enough to touch.

Who was St. John, really?

He had rubbed his hands over her on a dance floor, and had taken her, body and soul, in a hotel room. He had stepped in front of her on the street, and in that awful hotel, in an attempt to protect her.

Protector. Beings who were liaisons between immortals and humans. This was the term she had bandied about the night she'd met him. And just after he'd offered his assistance with this case.

St. John. With his easy access to all sorts of clubs and private hotels, was there any doubt that he might also be socially well placed enough to be able to pull the strings necessary to get her a shower and her current chaperone?

Had the Protector, in lieu of not being able to do his job, recruited someone else to do it for him?

She gave the detective a covert glance before her gaze strayed to the bloodstains on her hands.

The dried blood was the same color as the blood that had pooled on St. John's scratches. Not the faded hue of dried blood, but much darker, older.

Her stomach tightened. A flash of white heat seared across her neck. This meant something, surely?

It certainly didn't have to be proof that Christopher St. John had lied about not being mortal. Or that the old man in green in the Germand's lobby had been unearthly.

So, how could she prove these things once and for all?

"Proof," she whispered, earning her a second raised eyebrow from the detective beside her. "I have one stop to make," she said when the elevator stopped at her floor.

"No time for that," Crane said.

"I just have to let my crew know I'm okay. It'll take a second."

Crane didn't actually nod, though he didn't look happy about this.

Passing her door, continuing down the corridor, Madison stopped, lifted a hand and knocked. In spite of the ungodly hour, the door opened and Teddy stood there, looking not worried, but excited.

"There was something on the tape you wanted to show me," she said. "You sent a text about finding something strange in the footage you shot yesterday?"

If Teddy replied, she didn't hear it. Her heart rate was escalating. St. John had entered the building. Her body knew it and was already heating up.

She had to see that footage. She had to see it so that she could put Stewart's obsessions behind her, and get on with her own.

She knew exactly what she'd be looking for on that tape: a man in the doorway of a pub. A man who would show up on that tape because he was mortal, not some idiotic version of her brother's wicked imagination. That was the vampire deal, right? No captured image for the undead?

D.I. Crane grunted his displeasure over allowing her to stretch the leeway he'd allowed her. As his hand closed on her elbow with a subtle pressure, Teddy switched on the monitor.

The picture came on the screen. Madison zeroed in, ready to laugh, feeling relieved.

She watched other newscasters scrambling to get to the scuffle going on in the distance, and paid attention as the camera turned in Teddy's capable hands.

"What the—?"

She stared in disbelief at the doorway as the camera swept past it. She wanted to shout for Teddy to rewind.

Empty.

Christopher St. John was not in that doorway.

But St. John had been there. She had seen him. Possibly Teddy had taken too long to focus the lens.

"Did you see that?" Teddy asked excitedly.

Her cameraman rewound the tape, and pointed at the screen.

Dazed, trying to rally, Madison saw the face in the crowd that Teddy was alluding to. So did the detective beside her.

"That's Janis Blake," Teddy said, rewinding again. He looked to Madison for confirmation. "Isn't that one of the missing girls?"

"Damn well looks like her," Crane replied, loosening his grip on Madison.

The two men in the room would assume she was as stunned as they were to see a familiar face in the crowd—the face of the youngest of the missing Yale Four. They might even have been right if this had happened two days ago.

Unfortunately, she was stuck in the loop of video footage preceding that flash of the missing girl's face, seeing the pub's doorway over and over in her mind, and picturing Christopher St. John standing in it.

The room went unnaturally quiet. Madison observed the scene around her as if it, too, was being played back on a machine in slow motion.

The detective studied the screen, with one hand on his phone. Teddy beamed, realizing he had made an important discovery. The room, for her, had gone hazy. Her ears filled with static. In that scratchy noise swam a memory, a message meant only for her, and for times like this.

"You will crave this touch as much as I will."

And there was something else, another voice over-lapping St. John's.

"Mad one," the voice tonight, on the street, had whispered. She remembered that only now.

"Stop fighting, mad one," that voice had directed.

Fending off a rising panic, Madison swallowed a cry. Only one person in the world used that nickname for her. *Mad one.*

She flashed back to the hand on her mouth and the fact that the abductor hadn't really harmed her. Black-ing out had nothing to do with him hurting her; she just hadn't been able to hang on.

She'd been so scared.

But she hadn't been tied up in that awful place where she'd been left. Escape had been easy. The ab-ductor hadn't meant to hurt her. He meant for her to find that body.

Her abductor hadn't been just anyone, reason now told her. It had, in fact, been her brother. Her twin. Stewart. No one else on the planet knew his nickname for her.

The wall felt hard and unyielding against her injured shoulder. She was shaking, had been shaking nonstop for what seemed like hours, from distress and fatigue and so damn many loose ends. Now, there was light.

No!

Hell...

She had provided the police with a blood sample from her attacker, and it might have been Stewart's DNA they would discover. She might have bitten her brother's hand.

Locking her jaw to keep the shouts trapped inside, Madison reached for the doorknob. She had to see St. John. She had to confront him. No matter what he was, if he had connections, she'd ask him to use them to get her brother back.

The detective's voice stopped her from leaving. Slowly, and with her heart revved by a new kind of panic, she turned to face him.

Chapter 16

A foul wind, impossible to ignore, reached St. John as he stood beneath Madison's window. The Nosferatu hadn't yet breached the city proper.

They had been sent to find the royal blood in his veins and in the veins of the other Knights offered immortality, exactly as his Makers had long ago predicted.

Evil, it seemed, never gave up or gave in. The thirst for greed never waned.

Peeling himself from the wall, St. John rolled his aching shoulder blades. What was happening in London, and about to get worse, went so far beyond the concept of right and wrong, as well as the most basic, normal perceptions most people had of the world, as to be unrecognizable fragments of those ideas.

Ruthless monsters were coming, due to the fact that

a traitor had infiltrated the Hundred, desiring to upgrade his personal stockpile of power.

With his etched skin searing, St. John searched the street, setting mental boundaries for the battle to come.

In his mind, the haunting refrain of a question issued through moist, parted lips plagued him.

"Are you a vampire?"

After all this time, St. John wondered if he might be losing his mind.

"Can you skip that shower?" D.I. Crane asked Madison as she went to leave Teddy's room. He turned to her cameraman and said, "I'll need that tape."

Madison's hand was frozen on the door. He hadn't mentioned anything about St. John. When he looked at her again, she said, "I need my purse and my credentials. I'll skip the shower but I need a quick cleanup. I've got blood on my hands and knees."

Crane nodded as he opened the door. "We've got to get back to the station with this information."

"Back?" Teddy sounded confused.

"I'll have to go with the detective," Madison said. She didn't sound like herself, and wondered if anyone noticed.

"At this time of night?" Teddy said.

Madison shrugged, hoping she looked nonchalant, feeling like hell. Now wasn't the time to go into what had occurred. Explanations would take time she didn't have.

The news world would be rocked by what was on this tape. This network exclusive would advance the careers of everyone on their crew, but at this moment, she couldn't have cared less about her job. St. John was near. Her brother was near. Answers as to what the heck was going on were required from both.

"There's something I was supposed to tell you," Teddy said, as if just remembering. "A man stopped by."

Madison looked to the detective to make sure he didn't sense her sudden stiffness, and found him making another call.

"What man?" she asked.

"Don't know," Teddy said. "I wasn't paying attention. I only remember that I'm supposed to tell you that he came by. I must have been groggy, or too excited about the tape. Sorry. I think he knocked at my door."

Madison controlled her reply. "It must not have been important."

"Want me to go along, wherever it is you're going?"

"I'll have her back before breakfast," Crane said.

Teddy made a point of looking at his watch. "That's about an hour from now."

"Is it?" The detective seemed surprised. Probably his night had also been long.

"We have another briefing in the morning," Teddy reminded her. "You look like hell." He turned to the detective. "We're going to air the tape. It'll be a gut-busting exclusive for us, and Madison has to be there to present it."

"I'll be there," Madison promised.

Teddy handed her the key to her room. "You must have dropped this by my door."

The preoccupied detective was checking and re-checking his messages, adept at texting while walking as they headed for her room.

"Five minutes?" Madison said to him, when they reached it.

"Four," the detective countered, leaning a shoulder against the wall, and continuing to fiddle with his phone.

Madison closed the door behind her, drew in a long breath and said to Christopher St. John, "I know you're here, and I know what you are."

Chapter 17

"Do you know?" St. John countered from the shadows of her hotel room.

Madison feared that her heart might jump right out of her chest, it was beating so fast.

"Show me, or prove me wrong," she said.

"It would hurt me to see the disappointment on your face, either way."

"More than everything else has hurt me?"

"What do you think you know?" he asked.

"A question for a question is a clever parry, St. John, but won't work. What I want is a confession."

Madison stared at the figure in front of her, and blocked out the soft rap at the door.

"Miss Chase," Crane called from the hallway. "Only four minutes."

"You found Stewart," St. John said.

"He was out there. I was right."

The silence following her remark eventually filled with his whisper. "He didn't harm you, then?"

"Why would you think he'd harm me?"

St. John didn't answer the question. He said, with relief in his tone, "For that one thing alone I owe him."

He stepped forward. "Are you afraid of me, Madison?"

"Scared out of my mind. And I now think you know more about my brother than you're letting on. I believe you might have purposefully kept me from going after him at the club, and also on the street tonight."

St. John's voice was like sifted gravel. "It would have been in your best interest."

"Did you know that Stewart was there?"

"Yes."

Feeling faint, Madison stood her ground. "Why would you keep me from him for any reason? Something is wrong with Stewart. I get that. But he is my brother."

"Your brother came here after creatures he was sure hid in the shadows."

"You think I don't know that? I've thought of nothing else since I arrived in this city. So, are you admitting that he was right to do so?"

"He was right," St. John conceded. "You would have found this out soon enough on your own, but the knowledge places you in more danger."

Madison shook her head. "Stop it. You're freaking me out, and I'm freaked enough already."

"You said you know about Stewart." St. John's voice was tender, which made things infinitely worse. "Do you also understand what he has become?"

"I know that he's possibly gone off the deep end, and that he is hiding."

"Is that all?"

"Isn't that enough?"

The protest she'd been about to use stuck in her throat. A chill rippled across the back of her neck. Gathering her courage, Madison raised her hand, and placed her fingertips against St. John's mouth, sure she had heard what he'd said, and that he hadn't moved his lips.

"Isn't that enough?" she repeated.

"Not by far."

Beneath her fingers, she felt the shape of something she envisioned in her nightmares, but had never expected. She swayed as if she'd been struck, and reached for the light switch.

The room flooded with light that was blinding in intensity after the darkness she had endured. What that light showed her was alarming.

The chiseled face across from her wore a pained expression. The eyes looking into hers were part blue, and also midnight-dark. Too dark to be human.

God help her, Christopher St. John was a vampire.

"Show me." Her tone was sharp with despair. "I need to see."

He smiled sadly, and there they were. Between the lips that had kissed her gently, and savagely, and torturously, were two long, white, lethal-looking points. Fangs.

"You lied," she charged weakly.

"No," he said. "You asked the wrong question."

This time when he leaned forward, she twitched

with anger and fear and frustration. She had nowhere to go to get away from him, and from the pain of this.

"Tell me they're fake," she said, knowing this was a last-ditch effort to make sense of what she was confronting.

"I wish I could," he said. "You have no idea how much."

The door handle beside them jiggled with an interruption of metal and wood. D.I. Crane's voice rose in pitch. "Miss Chase? Madison?"

Her fingers untangled from the jacket she had inadvertently clung to as that jacket was dragged from her grasp. Cold invaded the room as St. John backed away from her.

Christopher St. John had teased, tempted, shown his true nature and left her. In the blink of an eye, he had gone, leaving her room the same way he'd gotten in. That damn window. She hadn't seen a thing after the fangs. Her eyes had been closed.

"Stewart…" she sobbed. "I've found one of them. Damn you, brother, I've…found one."

She had gotten close to the embodiment of danger, had been physically intimate with a creature of the night. A real one. No trick of the light. No fantasy. Not her imagination.

Stewart had been right, all along.

Madison stared after St. John. He had fangs. Possibly he wasn't alive at all…and yet the throb deep inside her, the one connecting her to him, was more insistent than ever.

Impossibly, she wanted those fangs on her. She wanted him inside her. How did a person reason with insanity?

They weren't *people.* This wasn't just any frenetic love affair between strangers. In some rule book, somewhere, a liaison like this one had to be forbidden.

St. John was a vampire.

And he was magnificent.

If there were vampires all over London who could mesmerize with a look and a kiss…heaven help everyone.

"Heaven help me."

She remembered again the wooden stake hidden in her brother's jacket, and how it had shocked her. She remembered believing that she saw, in her mind, Stewart limp to the London Eye, possibly wounded, to hide that stake.

Her brother had come here to chase vampires, and there seemed to be plenty of them around.

St. John was a vampire. And her brother was alive.

"Miss Chase? Time to go."

She'd nearly forgotten Crane in the hallway, and wasn't sure about opening the door, or what the detective would see when he looked at her. She wasn't sure if she could stand up straight, or if her face held telltale signs of her inner struggle.

Was it possible to look relatively normal when the earth had tilted off its axis?

There were vampires in London, and she had seen them firsthand. She had, in fact, gone a lot further than that.

She swallowed back the urge to shout St. John's name. She had to internalize the fear, and she could do so. She would handle this. She'd have to. It wasn't over.

It was far from over.

There were vampires in London, and one of them had her name on his lips.

Had her brother been showing her a body, she now wanted to know, or trying to get her away from Christopher St. John?

She had stopped shaking. That, too, seemed odd.

The truth didn't actually set one free, as the saying went. Truth could be terrible, unbelievable, earth-shattering.

"Forgive me, brother," she whispered, with a last glance to the window.

A final thought came to her as she watched the curtain blow, perhaps out of a need for just one minute of normality in a world that had gone insane and was pulling her down with it.

Teddy had been wrong about there being an hour until breakfast. A gray English morning was set to dawn.

"So, now you know."

St. John looked up at Madison's window. "You know about me."

Daylight was minutes away. He had to start walking, and couldn't make his legs work.

No one knew why vampires and other monsters needed the night to animate them. He had never heard one plausible explanation for the phenomenon, other than that death had always been equated with darkness. Though he was old enough and strong enough to tolerate some light, it was inconvenient as hell.

He turned with a concerted effort that strained his ligaments, and raised his face. In the small wedge of time when darkness slipped into submission and the horizon grew colorful, he usually felt the most alive, and almost normal. Almost mortal.

While humans began to stir in their beds and the monsters went to ground until the return of night, he walked and breathed and thought things over as if he were still an integral part of the human landscape.

Today was different. Because Madison knew, and he'd left her with that.

At least she would be safe for a few more hours.

Often, he had yearned for simpler times. Lately he'd been thinking about going back to where it all started—to Castle Brocéliande, in Brittany—in search of a respite from the world. The castle where he had traded his old life for immortality might still be there. He had never gone back to see. He had been unwilling to face the place of his death, and the site of his rebirth into what he had become.

"I have sipped from the Holy Grail," he wanted to tell Madison. "The blood that chalice contained was a mixture of my Maker's and another's blood that once stained the famous cup."

He didn't tell her this in a way she would hear. She couldn't know that the golden chalice had been passed through time by careful hands until it eventually wound up in the possession of the three special creatures at Castle Brocéliande. And that the beings there had chosen St. John and his brethren for a special task that saw them killed and resurrected—bringing them back from death with their souls turned inside out and their bodies strengthened for a new purpose.

He wanted to tell Madison that he had experienced life as a mortal, with its pain and hopes and death, and that he remembered parts of his former life, his last breath and what had come after.

He needed to explain to her that he would never forget his first sight of the five men who had preceded him as Blood Knights, and how much they meant to him.

"Seven new beings of molded muscle, sinew, cold flesh and purpose became the servants of both the Grail and the holy blood in our veins," he whispered to the dawn mist, and to Madison over their unique connection. "We rode forth from Castle Brocéliande's gates on black steeds that matched our emblazoned shields. Seven men, who were no longer men, but something more, bound to each other and hungering in ways no one else could imagine. Immortals."

Lance Van Baaren. Mason LanVal. Alexander Kent. He was often left hurting for the companionship of the creatures most like himself who also had traded their mortal souls for immortality.

"Who else but they knew what I need, and what I feel? The regrets, the desires."

His building lay ahead with the promise of refuge. In a perfect world, he would have brought Madison here and loved her within an inch of her life, saving that last inch for the decision she'd have to make in order to join him. He had actually considered going that far. Not offering just his heart, but immortality, and a love that would last forever.

"And danger rains down from all directions."

With Nosferatu coming, and Simon Monteforte uncovered as the traitor, all he wanted to think about was *her*. Madison. The radiant woman with the shrewd blue eyes that fate had tossed in his path as if offering a bone to a ravenous beast.

He had to settle things with her before the Nosferatu arrived. A dark hand had disturbed the fabric of London, and threatened to distort it further, but she had to understand that Stewart's ravings about vampires had been correct, though his warning had fallen on the wrong ears.

St. John would not barter with Monteforte, a heinous example of a modern-day terrorist. Monteforte might assume to know how his mind worked, but that assumption would be a mistake. Nosferatu could not kill a Blood Knight. There was only one way to end his existence forever, one unique key to a final death for each of the Seven, and neither sword nor fangs came close to being his.

He dared not involve the rest of the Hundred in this situation. He couldn't afford to show his true self to them, or anyone else. Although his goal here in London had been achieved, and the traitor among them exposed, the situation remained fragile.

In the meantime, the detective outside Madison's door should be able to protect her. For a while, anyway.

Luckily, the sun was about to rise. Simon Monteforte would be going to ground, locked away somewhere until that sun went down.

Madison, can you hear me?

Her face appeared all around him as he walked.

"My strength is not endless," he said. "Still, I will honor my promise to help you."

Come to me tonight, he sent to her, using their bond. *By nightfall you must find me, Madison. Hurry. Do not delay.*

He knew the second she received this final message, and that its arrival stunned her. As he lifted his face to the pink brilliance of the rising sun, thinking of Madison's warm, lush body and worrying that she might never come, now that she knew about the fangs…the sun, like so many other things in his age-old existence, finally began to betray him.

Chapter 18

For the tenth time in as many minutes, Madison pressed a hand to her neck, searching for possible puncture marks that might explain her ability to hear Christopher St. John as clearly as if he sat next to her.

Looking out the window of D.I. Crane's car that hadn't yet left the curb, she said, "Have you gone to the Germand?"

"Officers are there now," the detective said.

"Have you found out anything about that apartment where my abductor took me?"

"You mean in the four minutes you were in your room?"

Madison filed away the detective's cynicism. She had no idea how long she'd actually been in that room with St. John, or where he had gone after he'd jumped out her window. She strained to see the faces passing on the street at this early hour, searching for St. John and Stewart among them.

"I'm afraid so," Crane said, cutting his eyes to her.

Madison faced him directly. "What did they find, Detective? I can take it. Trust me."

He took a minute to think that over, appearing not too sure. As the sun began to rise between the buildings, he said, "It was a girl, as yet unidentified."

"Not one of those—"

"No. Presumably not one of the missing American girls. Another young one, though. We can't get an ID until more tests are done. I'm telling you this because you were there last night, and I'm asking for this information to go no further. This is off the record. Is that clear?"

Madison nodded. "What happened to her?"

"It seems," Crane said, "that there was a wooden stake sticking out of her chest."

Madison sat very still, trying not to scream. Then she said, "Not through her heart, then. The stake would have to pierce her heart if she were one of them. She wasn't. That's why she could be found, and why she wasn't reduced to a pile of ash."

Horrified that she'd said those things aloud, she stiffened. "I'm sorry," she said. "I didn't realize…" D.I. Crane nodded warily.

"So," the detective finally said. "You did know what that weapon in your brother's pocket was, and what it potentially could be used for."

"My brother didn't do that," she said. "In case that's what you're thinking, Stewart would never hurt anyone."

Would he harm a vampire, though? she wondered.

The detective seemed to be waiting for her to come up with a better excuse for why such an odd weapon had been in Stewart's possession, now that a similar weapon had been found at a crime scene.

"I can't explain that to you," she said before he could even ask his question. What she didn't add was the idea that Stewart, after all his research, would know better than to miss the heart if the victim had been a vampire, and if killing a vampire had been his objective.

A wooden stake through the heart was supposed to explode a vampire, turning them to ash, to dust. There would be little left to identify, like the ashes the cops said they had found near her lost shoe.

That's how the story went. Stake through the heart, and gone, baby, gone. Yet the girl in that apartment hadn't gone. And Stewart had taken his sister there why? To find that girl, and make Madison wonder what the heck was going on.

News flash. I know they exist.

God, yes, she knew they did.

And she knew that her brother was no homicidal maniac, so he couldn't have been the stake wielder. Someone else had killed that girl.

"I can't go to your department," she said. "My head is splitting. I need to lie down. Please, Detective, give me just a little more time." She glanced at the detective's wristwatch. "I have a job to do in thirty minutes."

She needed to figure out how she could clear her brother's name. A clear head was necessary for that.

She wanted to believe that vampires were killing people, and making it look as if Stewart had a part in that. To frame him? To stop him from going after them?

She had to help. She would hunt the vampires down

in the only way she knew how. The media. She would shine the light of camera exposure on London's vampires by regaling them with unwanted attention.

D.I. Crane spoke. "The time of death was estimated as the night before last. The same night you lost your shoe. That's a strange coincidence, I believe."

"Come to me tonight..."

The unspoken invitation came with the jolt of a charge that streaked through Madison's body like a lightning bolt. She uttered a gasp of alarm.

"It's been too much," Crane said. "Take a deep breath."

Deep breaths weren't going to do it. Madison recognized the thrum in her body and knew its source.

"By nightfall you must find me, Madison. Hurry. Do not delay."

There was no doubt whatsoever about whose voice this was, and how freaked she was, hearing it.

Crane continued to study her, as if waiting to see if she'd faint. But he didn't know her, or what caused her shakes. He didn't know what she was capable of when cornered. Hell, maybe she didn't even know.

She had to stop herself from running to her vampire lover, and the effort that took was rough.

A girl with a stake in her chest, she sent back to St. John. *What would you know about that?*

"All right," Crane said. "I'll see what I can do to let you off. I'll be at the announcement this morning. One missing girl is alive and walking around London, and that's a good thing. Janis Blake is out there. Let's focus on that."

Madison said, "I have a feeling the Hotel Germand may turn up something."

The detective seemed about to reply, then didn't. Maybe he had some intuition of his own as to when to let things go.

And to hell with you, St. John, she added inwardly. *I'm nobody's mind slave or future blood supply.*

As she went back inside the hotel, the concentric rings of madness seemed to close in. The dead had risen up in this city, and how many people knew?

She wished to God that she didn't.

It was a new night.

The undercurrent of darkness running beneath the streets of London angered St. John. The grooves in his skin burned as he waited for the pack of Nosferatu to hit the city.

They had already infiltrated the outskirts. Other things were following in their wake, stuck to the darkness like barnacles on a whale's back. Shades and vermin usually relegated to their own spaces were feeling the terrible presence of the Hunters and experiencing their own kind of perverse glee for the desecration ahead.

True night was about to befall London if he didn't find those monsters first, and take care of them.

In the distance, he heard Madison's voice. The television set behind him replayed that morning's newscast. The world had been stunned by the footage of Janis Blake in the crowd the day before. Madison's network had celebrated a coup, yet he knew that Madison wasn't joining in that celebration.

He knew also that she wasn't coming to him. He didn't blame her. He had allowed her to see the truth, and by doing so he had hurt her.

"I understand," he said, tugging lightly on the invisible thread stretched tightly between them.

The walls of his lair were several feet thick and heavily reinforced with silver-coated steel. Silver was a decent vampire deterrent that he had been reborn with the ability to tolerate. If he could get Madison here, she would be safe.

He had little time now to do what was necessary, when time had always been the enemy. He had to kill Nosferatu and round up Simon Monteforte, the pompous, velvet-clad, ancient French deformity that had set those Hunters upon him.

And Madison?

"Don't you see that I can't rest until what's between us is settled?"

He was, in fact, already heading for the door.

Madison had grown sicker as the day wore on. Though London and the rest of the world buzzed with the news about the Janis Blake sighting, and things were moving in the right direction for one of the Yale Four, she couldn't concentrate on that. Secrets were eating away at her.

Ignoring St. John's call had become nearly impossible. She wanted to scream, shout, if that would make him stop.

He couldn't get to her. A detective stood in the hotel hall, at her door, and another cop lounged downstairs. Like a shadow, Crane had been in the crowd all day, following her around when she did her interviews. He hadn't said a word about the Germand.

Resting a hand on the window frame and her forehead on the glass, Madison gazed out. Night had fallen.

A full moon hung in the sky, visible between a long block of buildings and a bank of navy-blue clouds. Seeing that moon brought on another violent attack of anxiety. Light from the big silver disc seemed to amplify St. John's voice. *"I understand."*

"Nonsense," she whispered back. "Leave me alone."

She wasn't sure of the exact moment the hair on her arms began to rise. After noticing it, she found herself standing near the head of the bed with her right hand gripping the crudely carved bedpost. She couldn't recall how she had gotten there.

She didn't want to go to bed.

Truly, her mind was slipping.

Back at the window, she threw a wary glance to the street below. She saw a shadow, and shook off the feeling it could be anything other than a shadow.

Then she saw another.

A filmy gray when seen against the pools of moonlight, the shadow moved from the street to the corner of her building, where it disappeared.

"Stewart? Is that you?"

He couldn't get in to see her with cops all over the place, knowing they were probably looking for him. She had to see him, talk to him.

Without weighing the consequences of her actions, Madison sat on the window sill, waiting for the rush of blood beating at her veins to subside. Then she swiveled her body around and climbed out onto the ledge six stories high.

Chapter 19

There were police on the street next to Madison's hotel, and more inside. The detectives were on guard.

From the shadows lent by the moon in its full phase, St. John watched the officers on the street round the building. Looking up, expecting to climb, he sobered when he saw the figure on the railing outside Madison's window.

"My brave, foolish love," he said. "Pity the poor bastards who'd try to keep you in line."

Swinging up the brick, hand over hand, and from floor to floor by way of the ornamental railings and the ledges beneath them, he reached Madison before she had turned around far enough to search for a firm place to put her foot.

Perched on the railing, he said, "If it's a quick fall to your death you're after, you're well on your way."

She turned her head. "Go to hell."

"Actually, I've been there, and wouldn't want to go back."

"Then just go away."

He pictured Madison shimmying up and down the trees of those Florida orchards she smelled like. "You're six stories up," he said.

"It's none of your business," she snapped.

"I beg to differ. A lot rides on your ability to stay alive, my own feelings among them."

"What feelings would those be?"

"Oh, I have them," he said. "Never doubt that."

"What I doubt is anything you say. You lied to me. I wonder how many times."

"I never lie, Madison. I told you that."

"So you said, but have you looked in a mirror lately?"

St. John grinned. She had scored with a vampire slam dunk, or so she thought. If the situation with the Nosferatu wasn't so dire…if he was free to expand his relationship with her, at least for a while…he would help her to comprehend what each of them soon had to face.

"That's a myth, you know," he explained quietly, so as not to scare her further or make her loosen her hold on the railing. "That we can't see ourselves in shiny surfaces."

"Damn it, why can't you leave me alone?"

"We're connected. Haven't you figured that out? I hear your thoughts almost as easily as I hear my own."

"Yeah? Well, tell that story to the video equipment that didn't pick up your image in the doorway of the pub."

"You didn't get me on film because I saw your cameraman coming."

He saw her think that over, then shake her head, dismissing his excuse.

"Stewart and I are connected," she corrected. "You and I are…"

"Lovers," he said. "Possibly even closer than that."

She winced. "I wasn't coming to you tonight."

"Then why are you hanging from the side of a building in the middle of the night? What are you planning to do when the officers below stop you?"

"Shit," she said. "Are they down there, too?"

"Several of them, any one of which might look up at any moment."

"I thought Stewart…"

She didn't complete that sentence, and didn't have to. He also felt Stewart Chase's nearness, as well as the closeness of two filthy Shades.

Madison could not go down there, whether her brother was close, or not.

He looked at her. She wore the same clothes she'd worn for the camera that day. All black, not in honor of the girl who had been seen alive in the crowd, but for the few still missing. Flared skirt. Soft sweater. None of it prime climbing attire.

Her bare left leg, stretching downward in search of a ledge, was hindered by the fabric of the skirt presently trapped by the railing. The Shades in the alley would sniff that bareness out, and hope the vampire killer in their midst would bring them some dinner to make up for missing a live mortal.

As she reached the stone ledge with the tip of her shoe, Madison let her hands slide down the wrought iron until her foot had a firm placement. She suspended there between two hotel floors without completely letting go of the upper railing, naked from the tops of her shoes to the tops of her thighs.

St. John took stock of his reaction to this before speaking.

"You're hurting, seeking," he said. "By coming with me tonight, you'll hear some of what you want to know, and I'll be sure you're safe."

"I think I'll pass."

"Don't be foolish, Madison. You're wondering why all this has happened and I can help to clear some of the puzzle up."

"You're not human. You look human, and act like one, but you're not. My brother came here after you, and those like you, and I...I didn't believe him."

Her voice faded. Her eyes glittered. St. John thought he saw dampness beneath her lashes.

"I can yell, and the cops you say are down there will come running," she said.

"They won't find me. I can't let them, or I'll be late for an engagement."

"Don't let me keep you. And besides, I'm almost certain the fly-like-a-bat thing is a joke. Possibly the only joke regarding vampires," she said, looking at him. "Isn't it?"

"What will you do if you get by those on guard?"

"Find my brother."

"I see. You know where he is, then?"

After a hesitation, she said, "Somewhere close."

"London is a big city, and you are not free of its dangers. If you assume vampires are the only hindrances in the dark, you'd be gravely mistaken."

"I'll take my chances."

"And if that detective finds you out here, he'll lock you up in a padded cell."

"He'd see you, too, barring the bat thing."

By the time she'd said those words, he spoke to her from the floor above her. "No flying. Just fast."

"Go to hell." She had whispered this, and was looking paler.

"I need some time, and your trust," he said. "I need to make sure you're safe while I take care of something. Please humor me. It might be all right if I have your trust."

She said nothing.

"Forces are about to be unleashed that will have innocent people caught in the crossfire of an age-old struggle for power if I don't get to them first."

Madison didn't move, or respond.

"If those forces get through, London may become the first of many cities to fall before the darkness," he explained.

"I know," she said.

"How do you know?" He studied her face, sculpted by moon shadows.

"There's an undercurrent," she said. "I feel it."

"What's this undercurrent like?"

"Like a dark river running beneath the city, under my feet, that's flowing in the wrong direction."

"How is it affecting you?"

"It scares me, almost more than you do."

Her explanation startled him. He saw that it also alarmed her to have confessed such a thing. Madison's eyes were wide and fearful, though she looked every inch the Slayer, with her muscles tense and straining for a hold on the railing, and her face as white as the moon's.

Her explanation about what she felt was stunningly similar to how he perceived the oncoming movement of the Nosferatu. There was only one way for Madison to perceive monsters in the distance. She was catching up to her destiny, on a fast track.

"Bloody brilliant," he said.

Madison's face, when she looked up at him, told him that she maintained hope of there being a viable explanation for what she had been sensing, and that she expected the truth from him, no matter how much he might have lied to her before.

She had bitten her lip hard enough to draw a few drops of blood. Seeing that, St. John's hunger raged. Not for the blood, but for the hides of every outside force that would try to take him from her.

"Tell me," she said. "Why am I feeling this? Feeling wrong. Feeling things? Hearing you inside my head?"

"Because you were born to do so," he replied. "You and your brother."

"How?" She closed her eyes as if what he'd said pained her. "Why?"

"You are vampire hunters," he said. "Just as someone in your family had to be, before you. Our word for what you are is *Slayer*."

She seemed to listen. Nevertheless, as he moved to catch hold of her arm when her grip on the railing loosened, Madison made good on her threat to scream.

Chapter 20

Madison found herself in someone else's room when she was finally able to draw a breath. A strange suitcase sat open on the bed. The bureau drawers were open.

St. John was beside her, looking every bit the supernatural creature he was. His fair, wind-blown hair served to highlight his serious expression. His eyes glowed with a blue-black fire.

They stood there, staring at each other, hungering for each other. She was sure he'd hear her heart racing, and that St. John would see the fear in her eyes.

When the muffled noise of big men on running feet on the street caught her attention, St. John took hold of her wrist, and pulled her to the door.

"I wish you could trust me," he said.

Before she could think of anything to say, his lips

were on hers, softly, gently, in what felt to her like goodbye.

And God help her, her own lips softened beneath his, independent of her will to get away.

She felt him stiffen. Then his body gave in, as hers had. His mouth ravished her, kissing her savagely and almost cruelly. For a few brief seconds, Madison felt as if she were drowning in the sensual, seductive shadows surrounding St. John that she had feared to find.

He didn't give her time to finish a single thought. Parting from her, yet remaining just inches away, he said hoarsely, "Wake up, Madison. It's the only way I can leave you. Wake up. Find your strength. It's there, waiting for you, hiding near the surface. Call it up. Call it now, and watch the dark."

Reaching around her, he yanked open the door. She let him push her into the hallway corridor, and then raised her face to him.

"If I'm what you say I am, you'd be on my list."

"Someday," he said sadly, "maybe I can explain. I'm sorry that it can't be tonight."

"How can I trust you?" she asked in frustration.

He smiled, and ran a finger over her cheek. Then he called out, "Here! Up here."

When the door to the stairway slammed open and Crane stepped out, St. John said to the detective in a low, barely audible voice, and with the force of a command that rang in Madison's ears, "I'm counting on you. Don't let me down."

And St. John—vampire, saint, Other, Protector, lover—disappeared.

"What the hell were you thinking!" the angry detective demanded, catching hold of her.

He smelled faintly of cologne, hair gel and wool, scents that stood out as recognizable, now that she'd noticed. The hallway smelled like carpet and dust and paint and peeling paper somewhere close. Over everything lay St. John's unique scent. A vampire's scent.

The detective hadn't once looked St. John's way.

Madison didn't answer his question. Didn't even try. What she was thinking would get her booked into an asylum if it were to be vocalized. St. John had known this. He had used his mesmerizing voice to direct the detective beside her, and it was possible that Crane didn't even know.

As for herself…

Slayer?

Vampire hunter?

Instead of freaking out, her thoughts were for Stewart. Did he chase vampires because he had to? Because he was born to chase them?

She stood here now in one piece, having been up close and personal with a vampire. And yet Christopher St. John had done nothing to harm her, unless having sex with him amounted to some kind of abuse. On the contrary, he acted like a bodyguard. He seemed to always have her back.

Peculiar behavior for a bloodsucker?

Could St. John truly be the Protector in Stewart's notes?

"Madison," the detective began. "How did you get up here to another floor when I had a man outside your door? What was that scream?"

The explanation was so unbelievable, she couldn't use it.

I'm here because of an undercurrent that feels filthy

*and like the end of the world is coming. And, by the
way, Christopher St. John says I'm a vampire hunter.*

By allowing those words to take shape in the real
world, they began to make some kind of sense. But
could she afford to lose her sense of normalcy? Forever?

*"You're feeling this because you were born to do
so,"* St. John had said. *"Wake up."*

Well, she was wide-awake. Her head hurt. She felt
sick. That red haze had appeared behind her eyes again,
as if she were bleeding bad thoughts internally.

"Let's get you back to your room," Crane said.

She was so damn scared, she couldn't speak.

"Are you okay?" he persisted.

Madison shook her head. Her throat felt tight. The
floor, and the carpet covering it, were absorbing some
of that terribly dark undercurrent. Whatever was coming had gotten closer. The dampness of that metaphorical river soaked through the soles of her shoes.

Her senses were on overload. The darkness. Vampires being real. The lingering imprint of St. John's
lips on hers. Her scream had been a manifestation of
all those things.

"Maybe you were sleepwalking?" Crane suggested
rather wryly, his patience starting to wear thin.

"Yes," Madison said, paying little attention. The red
haze was coloring everything now, from the walls to
the detective's tanned face. An odd flutter began in the
pit of her stomach, and spread to her limbs. She began
to sense a new awareness of each muscle in her body,
and to feel how tense those muscles were.

"Please," she said. "Get me out of here. I need to
find my brother."

"We have people out looking for him," Crane said. "Is that what you were doing outside your window? Attempting to get out, and get to him?"

"Yes."

"I would have taken you anywhere you wanted to go, in my car."

"You would have frightened him off, or taken him in."

The detective cleared his throat. "You could have fallen from pretty high up," he said. "It was a stupid thing to do."

It was the only way to escape you all, Madison wanted to shout, wondering why she was keeping St. John's secret. Wondering how St. John could have cloaked himself from the detective, like he was the invisible man.

The detective's expression was one of puzzlement. He would be thinking he'd just witnessed a sample of the madness plaguing her, and he'd be right. He'd be supposing it was possible that he and others had made a mistake by trusting her to help them. About that, too, he'd be correct.

Vampires had gotten in the way.

Vampires had been in the way from the start.

"I'll take you to the hospital," he said. "You may be in shock."

Madison nodded, resigned that she'd have to ride this out while she decided what to do next.

Crane punched the elevator button, and looked her over once more. "Whoever told you about that Germand hotel had good information," he said. "The girls were there, at that hotel. Whoever gave you that tip de-

serves a reward. If I had my way, we'd close the godforsaken place down."

The girls…had been found.

The American girls.

"All of them?" she asked.

"Every one."

She had lost all sense of color now, as if she looked
out through scarlet-tinted lenses. Her legs felt weak.
But she could do this. She was determined to get outside, and then to someplace where someone could help
her. Even if that meant finding Christopher St. John.

Intuition now told her that if she didn't find him,
the nightmare might never end.

"I can almost guarantee you're not asleep," Crane
said, his appraisal as steady as his grip. "Though you
do look dazed."

She couldn't look at the detective. The dark undercurrent beneath her had grown stronger and was
shaking the ceiling, and the walls. Somehow, she understood that monsters were coming, and that's where
St. John would soon go. He was going to face them.

The detective didn't notice the quaking surroundings. When she stumbled, he said, "We'll get you
looked at. Maybe a sedative will help."

He had noticed how badly she was twitching,
though. He wrapped one arm around her waist.

Trying to calm herself down and stop the convul-
sions was useless. The harder Madison worked at it,
the more the shakes took her over. She'd been trapped
by her own outrageous behavior, and was going to pay
the price. What could she do now? Push the detective
out of the way and run? Run where?

"Truth serum would also be nice," Crane said. "I'd

give an eyetooth for some of that stuff in my job. Right about now, my gut says you might not have been telling me the truth, or all you knew about this missing girls case, from day one. And though you helped work miracles with that Germand tip, the rest is downright frustrating."

All Madison could do to maintain her slipping sanity was to grit her teeth and act meek, when her energy was beginning to buzz and soar, and the red haze covering her vision was the color of Christopher St. John's blood.

The darkness outside the building was a relief. The chill was necessary to her ability to breathe. In the dark of the night, the redness tinting her vision faded.

The hospital Crane took her to looked like a big beige box, sterile, benign. The heavy odors of alcohol and antiseptic blocked out any trace of her connection to St. John's lingering scent.

No vampires here, Madison told herself, wondering how she knew that, and how she was going to ditch the detective after making it plain that she was ailing, and not a lunatic.

She'd be safe here at the hospital, she supposed. But if she couldn't perceive St. John, maybe he wouldn't be able to find her, either. And what good would hiding do, in the end, when nothing could be gained that way? Could a doctor, or the detective, explain to her what the dark under her feet meant?

D.I. Crane, her self-appointed bodyguard, leaned against a bookshelf, looking as fatigued as she felt. The lines on his face had deepened. He hadn't smiled one time.

The honeymoon was over.

"Don't you have business to attend to?" she finally asked as they awaited the doctor on call.

"You're it," Crane replied.

"I can take it from here."

"I'll just make sure that's true."

He observed her a bit too carefully, she decided.

"I'm here of my own free will, Detective."

"So am I," Crane said.

Not the truth, she wanted to tell him. A vampire had issued a demand for her safety with the mental voodoo in his repertoire, and Crane had unknowingly become St. John's puppet.

If St. John could command the cops, would nothing prevent him from doing whatever the hell he wanted to?

A few minutes more, she decided, and then she'd be out of here. Someone would tell her where St. John lived. He'd tell her what the darkness was, and what she was supposed to do.

When the doctor arrived, he first glanced to her, then to the detective. She saw something unsaid pass between them.

"Possible shock. Possible sleepwalker," Crane explained.

"Another one?" the doctor asked.

Crane shrugged.

"There appears to be an epidemic of sleepwalking every time we have a full moon," the doctor, whose shirt was embroidered with the name D. Dillon, remarked.

"Why would that be the case?" Madison asked.

"It's as good an alibi as anything else for unusual behavior," Crane said.

Madison listened for sarcasm in this odd pronouncement, and came up short. The detective had been serious.

"Of course," he continued, with another glance to
the doctor pressing a stethoscope to her chest, "if you'd
care to elaborate on what you were doing crawling out
of a sixth-story window, we can probably forego the
meds."

"I told you. I was tired and trying to get away from
the scrutiny of cops at my door."

"Actually, you told me you were going out to look for
your brother. So which is it, sleep deprivation messing
with your actions, or slipping out to find your twin?"

To the doctor, Crane added, "Can you just give her
something so she can sleep, and a secure room she
can do that in?"

"I think I can manage that," the doctor agreed.

"Screw the meds," Madison snapped. "I'm all right
now."

"That's a matter of opinion." Crane showed her a
text message on his cell from someone at his department that read, Keep her there.

"Besides," Crane went on as she tried to get to her
feet. "What do you have in mind in terms of a destination, if you were to leave?"

"I need to find Christopher St. John's house," she
said.

"Sorry," Crane said. "That's just not an option."

When Madison glanced down, a needle was heading for her arm.

She felt a sharp prick, tasted something funny in
her mouth, and the walls went slack.

* * *

St. John spun to face the west.

The first Hunter had arrived in London proper, and was nosing around. Its feel was slimy, and oiled up the air.

He cursed in the old English language, out of a habit too ingrained to break. Leaving Madison in the detective's hands was the only way to track this new burden. He had put all of his considerable weight behind the request to keep her safe and out of the way. But he felt Madison stirring. He felt her growing rebelliousness.

Theirs was a preordained attraction—the mesmerizing relationship of one kind of hunter to the species she was designed to hunt. A female to male pairing was how the vampire versus Slayer thing usually manifested, creating a unique bond between opposites that was so deep-seated as to be sexual in nature.

Definitely sexual in nature.

Each time he closed his eyes, he felt her sultry heat.

Madison couldn't have sidelined this attraction any more than he could have. The draw of a Slayer to her target, and vice versa, went back in history nearly as far as vampires had been in existence.

The origins of the enticement for a vampire and a Slayer to find each other were ingrained needs set in place for that purpose. Cells calling to cells. One kind of life calling to another kind. A signal from one genetic mutant to another that had evolved over time.

Slayers were the second universal check against one of this world's many anomalies. Protectors like himself had been the first line of defense in maintaining balance in the world between species.

Although the tale of how the first Slayer had been

born and activated wasn't information he possessed, the goals and objectives driving Madison, once she realized who she was, would be similar. Rid the world of the plague of vampirism. She had to be made to realize this.

Her brother had been the true anomaly here. Stewart had been a male Slayer with no roots to any of his opposites, carrying the Slayer building blocks only because he had shared a womb with his twin. Stewart therefore hadn't been as strong as Madison would ultimately be. He had the urge to find vampires, without the internal backup necessary to perform the task.

Still, Christopher St. John wasn't a vampire, and explanations for what he really was couldn't be forthcoming to a Slayer or anyone else, whether he wanted her or not. He was different. Not a vampire, but a chosen immortal. His life was to be kept secret.

The thought of losing Madison sickened him. His tie to a vow that separated him from all others sickened him. And yet he would go endlessly on. Alone, if he had to. If Madison refused to use their connection to further their bond.

He sniffed the air and looked up at the sky.

It was possible that the detective could handle a Slayer coming into her own for a while, though the arrival of a full moon wasn't going to help. A full moon brought out all sorts of Others. Vampires, Madison truly would be sorry to find, weren't the only species trolling the streets.

Traitors like Simon Monteforte also walked among the shadows. Stewart Chase's bane. The ancient entity that Stewart had found in London had changed everything.

Recognizing Stewart as a Slayer and a potential problem to his own plans, Monteforte must have sent his dogs after Madison's brother. Something as simple as one word to the wrong monster had removed one Slayer, and now threatened another.

The haze was starting to lift. Pieces on the game board were already shifting. Yet St. John couldn't be in two places at once, no matter how fast he was.

He would take care of the Nosferatu, and teach Monteforte a lesson. He prayed that Simon would be waiting when he returned from sparring with the monsters, and that he could get his hands on the Frenchman's pasty neck.

The tattoos carved into his back undulated in anticipation of the events to come, reminding him that through those sigils there was one other possibility of help open to him for aid, should he need or decide to take it.

Using the power of those sigils, a call could be made to those of his own brethren still able to heed the signal they themselves had created for such a purpose.

Who among the other Blood Knights, he wondered, resided within calling range? He had no idea what direction their existence had taken them.

And he wanted Simon Monteforte for himself.

Contracting his muscles to savor the thought of seeing even one of the Seven again, St. John again sniffed the air.

"Stewart?" he said. "Come out."

The infected Slayer, so close St. John could reach out and touch him, didn't oblige.

"I would never hurt her, Stewart. Not ever. This I

swear," he said. "Just as I never would have harmed you. We fight for the same things."

No reply.

"Monteforte," St. John said. "He's the one who found you?"

"Monteforte," came the echo from the shadows. And then Madison's brother's scent faded rapidly between the buildings, as if it had just wafted away.

Confirmation. Damnation.

St. John smelled the air again, turned his head and let out a low growl of displeasure.

It wasn't Nosferatu that captured his attention at the moment, though, or vampire hunters. It was *her*. Madison was going to slip D.I. Crane's net and get into trouble. Her intentions surfed his skin like a bad sunburn.

Can't have that, my love.

Not even if it meant postponing his meeting with the monsters for a while longer. Letting those creatures get closer.

Spinning, he said to the fetid odor in the distance that was the Nosferatu's unique calling card, "Not long now, I promise."

Then he raced for the hospital where Madison Chase, and his heart, lay.

Chapter 21

Madison's limbs felt heavy. Her throat was dry. But she was awake.

She kept her eyes closed.

"She's been out for ten minutes," a voice said.

"Can we lock the door?" asked another.

"Sorry. It is a hospital, when all is said and done. Don't worry. She'll be out for two hours, at least. Have you gotten any rest, Crane?"

"You saw the news?"

"You've found one of those four girls."

"We've found them all."

"What?"

"They're in pretty bad shape. We had a tip that led to finding them. This woman on the bed gave us that tip. I can't go into it any more than that. All four girls are on their way here right now."

"Well, thank heavens for that. I have a large stash of sedatives here if you need a little something for the stress."

"You know I can't do that, and that I appreciate the offer."

"Actually, I wouldn't have offered if I'd assumed you'd accept."

"You didn't have to tell me that, Doc. I thought maybe you were being nice for once."

Sensing someone's approach by the sound of rubber-soled shoes on a linoleum floor, Madison kept still and squeezed her eyes tighter.

Under the sheet covering her, she fisted her fingers, grasping for an object out of reach: a sliver of the bedpost in her hotel room; a wooden weapon like the one tucked inside her brother's leather jacket. It was true that she knew what those things could be used for. She wondered if something as simple as a stake could be used against whatever was heading their way, and if St. John would be able to stop its progress.

"She's moving," a voice noted.

"She isn't comatose, Crane, just sedated."

"Can I leave her in your care for an hour, at most, while I check on those girls, and make sure their parents are with them?"

"Of course. Miss Chase will be fine here."

"She won't get out?"

"Crane, if she gets out after what I've given her, she's not human."

Guessing I'm not completely human, then, Madison concluded, waiting for the opportunity to get to her feet.

* * *

The first Blood Hunter had reached Wimbledon, heading in a straight line for the city. Its presence was vague because it had used the Underground tunnels en route to its destination.

This monster's master had trained it well.

He would soon find out how well.

But first, a detour.

London's Central Hospital rose before him. As was usual on a weekend night, the place bustled. St. John went in. He headed for the E.R., tracing Madison's scent on the ceiling, the walls and the floor.

The detective had been wise to bring her here, where her sweet scent could be partially masked for most of the creatures looking for it. No doubt Monteforte would be salivating for the taste of another budding Slayer, now that he'd seen her.

Foregoing the elevator, he opted for the stairs. His skin continued its pattern of twitches and undulations under his black sweater as he strode to a room where Madison's scent was the strongest.

She wasn't there. The bed was still warm.

"Madison, you little fool," he whispered.

He went through the adjoining door, and into the next room, which was also empty. Then he started back down the hallway, driven by a vicious need to find her.

He came face-to-face with the one man he didn't particularly want to see at the moment. "You've lost her," he said cuttingly to the detective who had stopped to return his stare.

Crane anxiously looked past St. John. "Hell. She's gone? That's not supposed to be possible."

"You were to watch her," St. John said.

"Do you give the orders in this hospital now, too?"

"Isn't it common sense, Detective, to keep her out of trouble while searching for her brother? At least, I'd have thought so."

"Not that it's any of your business," Crane said.

Arguing wouldn't get him anywhere. St. John passed the detective in a hurry, nearly brushing shoulders with him in the narrow hospital hallway. Two steps beyond the cop, he paused with the hair at the nape of his neck bristling. Turning his head, he gave the detective a last glance, and grimaced.

"What?" Detective Crane snapped, anger creasing his features.

St. John kept walking.

Back on the street, he dialed up more of his senses. Picking up the faint trace of the fragrance of orange blossoms nearby, he started in that direction.

Madison continued at a sluggish pace up the street, slowed by drugged limbs and feeling as if she were dreaming.

The night seemed darker than usual and saturated with smells. The old bricks of the building facades she passed gave off odors of weak, trapped sunlight eating away at rampant, aged mildew. The sidewalk stank of the thousands of feet that had used it that day.

Without her cell phone and wallet, hailing a cab was useless. Though her hotel wasn't far, she had no intention of returning there. The guys would be celebrating their video coup. Their work would pick up again in the morning. Joining them probably would be expected, but was also the first place D.I. Crane would look for her after discovering she'd escaped.

She needed a breath of fresh, untainted air, and wasn't finding it. Unsure of where to go, what to do, or how to deal with the truth about the existence of vampires, she found London doubly ominous now.

Before seeing St. John's fangs, she had vowed to pressure the monsters in the media. That idea had fallen away, with no viable way to resurrect it. By shining light on monsters, she'd be placing her entire crew in danger, and maybe a good section of London's human population.

"Where are you, St. John?"

Did vampires prefer the lower floors of buildings? Basement apartments? Coffins? London was huge. The odds of finding him without outside help were slim, and she'd left the detective and his resources behind.

What she could do was test her own version of speaking to him via their strange internal connection. It was only fair for communication to work both ways.

Nothing to lose.

Waiting for a break in the line of people on the street, she looked up and spoke loudly. "Okay, St. John. You're all I have. Bring it on. I'm here, and I'm listening."

"Good," he said clearly, in a voice that definitely hadn't come from inside her head.

Madison had appeared before him like a desert mirage, spreading flickers of familiar fire throughout his body that he now knew were meant to be warnings, but what the hell.

She leaned against a building with her eyes raised skyward. Her face and lips were bloodless. Dampness gathered on her forehead. The cloying odor of drugs hung in the air.

His heart lurched when she met his gaze.

"It worked," she said, just as she had on the dance floor the first night he'd seen her in person. "Imagine that," she added.

The desire to hold her beat at him as fiercely as if they were normal people finding something special in each other in a normal world, when nothing could have been further from the truth.

St. John held himself back.

"They gave me a sedative." Her words slurred. "I'm probably helpless if your intention is to harm me."

"Harming you never entered the picture," he said. "I'd have thought you had figured that out by now."

"Your nature is to…" She left that remark unfinished, took a rattling breath and started over. "Can you get me off this street? My legs aren't working properly. People are staring, and will recognize me. I haven't the money for a cab."

"Will you trust me now?" he asked her.

"Do I have a choice?"

Her eyes held to his as if she'd seek the truth there and know it when she saw it. If she had any intuitive knowledge of how this meeting affected him, she gave no indication.

"I give you my word that your safety is foremost in my mind," he said. "You know that I'm not the only one looking for you."

"The detective is a good enough guy." She lowered her gaze. "It's just that he can't fill in the blanks. Only you can do that, and you'll have to if you help me now."

"Can you walk?"

"Made it this far, didn't I?"

"You're less than a block from the hospital," he said. "I can see it from here."

Her eyes rose to his again, briefly and unfocused. "Am I to believe what you say because you never lie?"

"Quibbling over semantics seems silly when there's so much at stake," he countered. "In any case, you asked for my help, when being near to me at the moment is an added danger."

"Is that some kind of disclaimer?"

St. John smiled. "I suppose it is."

"That old man in that hotel lobby has it out for you," she said, surprising him again with her insight and her candor. "Am I right?"

"I believe so."

"He is a vampire?"

He nodded. "A very old one."

Madison blinked slowly. "I knew it without knowing how I knew it. So, where will you take me?"

"To my home."

"No. Not there. It's too intimate. Too private and personal. I was going to find it. But now that I see you, I…"

"You'll be safe there," he said. "Only there."

"Safe from who?"

He knew what she meant, and that she was thinking of a kiss and a hardwood floor and the potential hazard of his fangs.

"Protector," she muttered weakly, though St. John perceived her strength and wits recovering with an astounding swiftness that only someone with her kind of secrets had the power to pull off.

The bit of darkness he had discovered when he had

first observed her now lay like a fine film over her skin, changing her skin's tone. Some of that darkness curled upward, foglike, over her spinal column.

In addition, his scrutiny turned up something else.

In the center of Madison, a new skill set was building, even as she drunkenly staggered. Her body was uploading a program that was her birthright to possess.

That tiny illumination inside her would soon get brighter. Already she'd find strengths to tap into if she figured out how to access them. She'd made it here through the meds.

When he roused from thought, he found her attentive.

"I have to know," she said, "what that look was about. What our strange relationship means, if it isn't supposed to be."

"There's so little time left, Madison." He offered her his hand, assuming she'd back away, as she had done the first time he had wanted to touch her.

Then again, he had to acknowledge how far they had come since that original meeting, where she'd been nothing more than Stewart Chase's sister, a potential media pain in the backside, and he hadn't shown her his teeth.

Clearly, and in spite of everything since that first meeting, Madison's hunger remained, relayed to him by the soft gleam in her eyes.

Yet also inside those big blues of hers lay another clue about her oncoming evolution. Sparks of liquid silver swam there, as if a ghost were sharing her vision. The ghost of what she was to become, not long from now, if he kept her with him much longer.

She knew about the dark river coming their way.

She was maturing before his eyes, with no way for him to turn back time, or start over. By remaining close to her, he would have no way to stop her transformation, and transformation might be her only way to cope with what lay ahead.

He just didn't care about any of that. He no longer wanted to take one single breath, real or otherwise, that didn't contain the scent of orange blossoms.

Madison was special. She was, in essence, a fighting machine with a nose for the supernatural, and the enemy of all those who had begun their new lives by drinking the blood of another. She was halfway to her heritage already, and sparring with the learning curve.

"So very little time," he repeated as she voluntarily placed her fingers on his upturned palm. "I will explain as much as I can before then."

She had touched him because she wanted to, had chosen to, and the pleasure this gave him was extreme. Hers was the first touch he had allowed, in any manner, in a few hundred years.

His heart beat faster, keeping time with hers. Without thinking of an action that possibly harked back to the days when chivalry ruled the land as the foremost rule of behavior, he brought her knuckles to his lips.

"Too easy," she said breathlessly. "Need answers."

"You won't like what you hear," he warned. "You might not remember what came before those answers. I'll regret that, Madison. I'll regret it deeply, I swear."

No longer hindered by having to keep some of his identity hidden from the woman beside him, St. John swept Madison into his arms. Not because she needed to be carried, or even would allow it, but because it might truly be the last closeness offered them, and he wanted to take full advantage of the minutes left.

Turning on his heels, gripping her tightly, he and the Slayer he had bonded with, for good or ill, became one more shadow in an already troublesome night.

Chapter 22

Wind whipped through Madison's hair. Buildings moved past as if they were made of rubber. Streetlights left thin streams of luminous thread suspended in the air.

The surroundings passed by at a fantastical pace as she and St. John rushed through it, seemingly shredding all known theories of time and space.

St. John hadn't lied about being exceptionally fast. He was also stronger than anything she had imagined. She hoped that her trust in him was warranted, but a debilitating fear of vampires hadn't entered the picture. Her stomach hadn't turned over.

Cohesive thought patterns were returning. She no longer felt heavy with fatigue. The reason she allowed St. John to carry her was that he was so much faster than she. And because he still had a fight ahead.

Her plan had always been to be self-sufficient, and most people perceived her to be. Madison Chase, they thought, was strong, independent and forthright. Her very private fear was that by giving in to St. John, or anyone who got close enough to mine the gaps in her plan, she'd lose some crucial part of herself. That was a feeble thought, she admitted now, when a vampire had hold of her and she had delved her fingers into his thick blond hair for no other reason than she liked the feel of him.

This special being carrying her had helped her that first night to escape the rogue vampire gang who'd had her in their sights. He had checked to make sure she was all right, she now felt sure, using her hotel window when she was at her most vulnerable, unconscious, asleep, without disturbing her.

St. John had provided the information about the Yale girls being at the other hotel and had taken her there, intending to help her find them. Because of that, the girls had been found, Crane had said. The girls were safe.

Jesus, they were safe.

St. John and his tip about the Germand hotel had proved that he had a tender side. He had proved this over and over, as a matter of fact.

He had come to her after her ordeal in the abandoned apartment, keyed up and worried about what she had been through. His features had registered pain and guilt and sorrow over having left her open to that awful event.

They had kissed, screwed their brains out and shown evidence of their feelings for each other in one way or another each time they met. A quickly formed kinship had taken the place of fear and wonder. In spite of what St. John was, and what he'd told her she was, they always found each other.

Finally, most importantly, St. John had allowed her to see him, sharing a confidence that could turn out to be harmful to him in the long run. He didn't have to let her know his secret, or view his fangs. He had trusted her.

In all their time together, and through all those things, he had not harmed her in any way, or shown an inkling of an intent to harm her.

The truth was...she had feelings for him. Deep feelings. For a vampire.

Vampires, he had told her, had been people once upon a time. Some of them could and did adhere to the path of virtue. Not all of them were evil bloodsuckers.

Bigger, stronger, twice the presence of anyone else. That had been her first impression of the man on the club balcony. This remained as obvious to her now as it had then. It was indeed a special kind of being that held her.

"God help me," she whispered. "I think I'm falling in love with you."

When she again looked up, they were exiting an antiquated elevator, the kind historical warehouses used, made of an open-weave iron mesh with visible cables.

Time regained its foothold after having brakes applied to its wheels, dumping them into a lofty open space filled, not with dungeonlike darkness, but brilliant wood floors and long spans of floor-to-ceiling glass.

Bewildered, Madison stared at St. John's refuge as her head cleared away the last remnants of the sedative.

"No one has seen this place," he said, setting her on her feet. "Except you."

Madison faced him. He still had a stabilizing hand on her elbow. "What are you, really?" she asked.

"First. Can you repeat what you just said?"

"I said I think I'm falling in love with you."

She watched him close his eyes.

"So, now that I have admitted that, what are you really?" she pressed.

"Immortal," he said.

"Another term for vampire."

He shook his head, corrected her gently, his voice little more than a sigh. "Not a vampire, Madison. The source from which vampires spring."

"You…make them? Make vampires?"

Another shake of his head tossed his golden hair away from his cheekbones. She would have touched his face, had they been real lovers having a reunion. As real lovers, human lovers, she would have remained in his arms.

"I do not make them. I fight against those who do, as you soon will," he said.

"You've got that wrong. It's my brother who carries a stake."

Without pausing, she spoke again. "You are older than the vampires on the street, and in the club, right?"

His affirmation was a nod.

"You are different," she pressed.

"Yes."

"There is a distinction, then, between the term you used, *immortal,* and vampires? A real difference?"

"A vast one."

"I have to know if there are others like you. Not vampires. Immortals."

"Only a few."

"In London?"

"There are immortals in London. Old vampires we call Ancients."

"Not like you, though. Not exactly like you."

"No. Not like me."

"Stewart wrote that the club, Space, along with half of London, is owned by vampires." She gestured to the stunning room around her. "This is yours?"

"Not material gain by way of tyranny or theft," he said. "Only a long succession of careful acquisitions."

She nodded, feeling the pressure of time's passage, and St. John's need to confront what lay beyond those windows.

"The creature in Germand's lobby is a vampire, you said. An old one."

"Vampires are what most Ancients originally were before they learned to control their appetites."

Madison waited out a beat of silence before continuing. "If they don't feed on mortals, how do they sustain themselves?"

"As a vampire ages, it loses the necessity for sustenance."

"Does that mean they live on air? Regular food?"

"They must take in blood now and then, when necessary, but only if it's offered freely. That's the way it's supposed to go, anyway."

"Except when they feel like biting somebody for fun, like in the good old days?"

St. John remained patient, his voice quiet. "The Ancients in this city are supposed to forego their beginnings and their pasts. They've evolved."

"All of them?"

He frowned. "They have taken vows to, if not fit in with the mortals surrounding them, come close to doing so. They stay away from people and are lucky to have made it this far without being hunted and killed. They are well provided for with stocks of blood, kept stored for needs that arise, and willing donors who are well paid for their services."

Though Madison winced at the *donor* part, she took all this in ravenously.

"They have formed their own community here," St. John continued. "They do more good than harm, for the most part."

"How many? How many of the old ones are there?" she asked.

"I can't tell you that for reasons which will soon be made clear."

"Can an Ancient die? Again? Can you?" She didn't wait for his reply. "Just how ancient are you?"

"Older than you. Older than the rest."

"Are there females among these Ancients?"

This was a selfish question. The thought of females like him, tall and elegant and hurtfully beautiful, brought on a wave of jealousy she could barely contain.

St. John read this, and smiled. "None. No females."

"Why not? If you mention the words *weaker sex,* I'll stake you myself."

Something she had said caused him to smile again. Madison sensed a fresh round of heat beating at the air between them.

"Actually, I'm not sure why," he finally replied.

"You've never asked?"

"It never mattered."

His answer took some time to absorb. She'd been correct, then, when she had touched his bare back and thought his reaction odd. He hadn't been handled by a female for years.

How many years?

She wanted to be the only one to ever touch him, and ever get near to him. She felt an icy blast of jealousy for this creature beside her that was so very much the male she wanted.

"If you're not like the others, why are you here?" she asked.

"I have a task to do, and have been building up to it."

"Where does the term *Protector* come in?"

"I serve the Hundred in a guiding capacity, when I choose to. I help them to deal with mortals and keep their secrets, a job that suits us all, for now."

"Mortals like me," Madison said.

She held up a hand, as if asking him to hold off on answering her. "Why would they believe you'd serve them in any capacity, if I can see the flaw in that in about two seconds, and that you're so much more than they probably are?"

Did he smile again? She thought he did, though the darkness outside the glass wall now hid all but the outline of the contours of his face.

She was aware of the line of his shoulders. Aware of the fall of his hair and the lean hardness of his hands. She tried desperately to erect a barrier against the notice of those things, hoping to section off her feelings. It was more than the masculine attributes of this figure beside her she craved, though the exact meaning of what she needed from him still remained out of reach.

"They don't know everything about me," he said. "And serving them serves my purpose."

"Now I sense a change in you, St. John," Madison said.

"That purpose has almost been satisfied, after a very long time."

Madison watched him, soaking up every detail.

"I believe that my brother came to London to find all of you, for a reason I can't comprehend," she said. "Not to kill you. Not as a vampire hunter. Stewart used the case he was working on as an excuse to get here, where he had something else in mind."

"Yes," he said. "It is possible that your brother had other motives."

Excited, Madison pressed on, desperate to know everything.

"Possible, or probable?"

She placed her hands against St. John's chest, ready to shove the answers out of him if necessary. Finally, they were getting somewhere. Half the questions had answers. Surely he sensed her frustration over him withholding the rest.

Against her palms, she felt the hardness of muscle and bone beneath his sweater. She felt a beat, and wanted to damn this creature whose heart worked much in the way a mortal man's would, each stroke strong and sure and as fast as her own. Each stroke seeming to bring her closer to him.

Beside her stood a being whose pulse was a mockery of life. The forces invigorating him should have disappeared, fading to nothing on the day he had died.

God, yes. St. John had died.

Did the remembrance of that death pain him, as it pained her to think of it? Was that the source of his dark demeanor?

She knew in that moment that she did truly love him, in spite of all that. In spite of knowing about him.

The acknowledgment of her emotions wasn't a shock. It was depressing. St. John was a special being, even within the tiers of special beings. He had a job to do that might soon take him from her. And though he'd said she was special, she was still mortal, and would eventually, after finding her brother, go home.

Twisting the fine weave of his sweater between her fingers, Madison felt the steady throb of his heartbeat reverberate in her forearms, shoulders, chest and the pit of her stomach. She had always tuned in to Christopher St. John as if they were fatefully connected. This made them closer than normal, and incessantly intimate.

"If Stewart wanted to chase vampires, he could have done so anywhere. But he came here, Christopher," she said.

It was the first time she had used his given name. Madison observed how his expression softened.

"Your brother came here to find himself," he said, his velvet voice husky. "He tried to distance himself from you, having to leave you behind in order to find answers."

Her grasp on his sweater tightened. She didn't have time to think about ruining the expensive cashmere, or the fact that St. John was already facing the door.

"His wasn't a completely selfish action," he said. "Your brother also came here to find those girls, hoping to pick up their trail, meaning to ask for direction from those who could find out what had happened to them."

"The Ancients," she said.

"Yes."

"You knew who he was?"

"I saw him once. By that time, it was too late to help."

"Too late? What do you mean?"

The immortal male she clung to remained silent for a short time. Then, as if he had considered what he was about to say from all angles, he said, "Stewart killed a vampire when eyes were watching. No one could have saved him from what came after."

Hearing this, Madison wanted to change her plea. She wasn't ready for this. How could anyone be ready, no matter how desperate they were for facts?

"What did Stewart want to find out about himself?" she demanded.

St. John's hands covered her own, inflicting a level of pleasure and support that by all rights should have been torture. Madison allowed the sparks flickering between them to fuel her depleted energy.

Her voice emerged strongly. "I love my brother. I deserve to know what happened to him. You must see that."

Yes, she was feeling stronger now. She felt ready.

"The police believe I'm withholding evidence and hiding Stewart's whereabouts," she said. "They assume I'm purposefully hampering their investigation, and will charge me eventually unless I give them something. I don't have anything to offer them. I don't know where Stewart is, or what he is doing."

"Maybe that's a blessing in disguise," St. John suggested.

"Not a blessing. I think you know that. I think you understand. They think he might have killed a girl."

"Yes," he said so softly that Madison wasn't sure she heard him at all. "You deserve to know more, though not from me."

"From you," she argued. "I want to hear it from you. Who will tell me if you don't?"

She planted her legs apart in case the information he might eventually provide turned out to be as outrageous as everything else so far. She decided not to let him go until she had something more, and planned to block his exit if he tried to get away.

"Stewart can tell you. He should tell you," he said.

"If he could be found."

St. John nodded, and hesitated again, as if considering what she'd said. "Your brother was bitten," he finally said.

"Bitten?" Madison repeated.

"Stewart was what you are. A Slayer. He thought his strength might help when facing the Ancients. The problem was that he wasn't strong enough to actually find them. The old one he did discover was the wrong one. I know this now. Stewart didn't have a chance to get the information on the girls that he sought. Fledglings found him, sent by a bigger monster. Too many of them. I'm sorry, Madison."

Madison tried to make sense of this explanation, without success. "Bitten," she said, reeling from the idea. "Are you saying that my brother is one of them now? He is a vampire?"

"Not one of them, exactly."

"Then Stewart is alive? He's okay?"

When St. John didn't immediately reply, Madison knew that more bad news was coming. She snapped her body straight. As if to steady her, St. John pressed his chest tightly to hers.

Her ears filled with the sizzling buzz of a lightning streak, and the sound hadn't come from outside the wall of windows, where the moon shone brightly. The charge had originated right there, from St. John's touch. He continued to affect her this way.

But instincts about what he might say next were warning her to beware, pay attention, run away, suggesting that she actually was unprepared for the explanations to come.

She hung on, filled with dread.

"Madison," he began, using her name like a lover's caress. "Your brother is killing vampires. He is staking vampires because he has to. Stewart is killing them because that is his destiny, even though he has become something like those he chases."

Madison saw in the smooth planes of St. John's hard, proud face that he had told the truth. He had given her what she had asked for. It was up to her to connect the dots.

Stewart was a Slayer *and* a vampire.

Was that even possible?

What kind of special monster did that sort of mixture make?

St. John broke away from her. He moved toward the windows and looked out. His face, his expression, his demeanor had changed again when he glanced back at her.

With trepidation, he said, "You'll have to let the

rest ride for now, my love. Time is up. The first of the Nosferatu has arrived."

Madison had no idea what Nosferatu meant, though the word was more terrible than anything she had heard so far, and struck fear into her bones.

St. John was going to face some dreadful beast. Maybe more than one. He seemed calm enough about the upcoming engagement, when a dark river was carrying monsters closer.

Christopher St. John's expression was gentle when he looked at her, showing his worry and his concern for her. Monsters had arrived, and his thought wasn't for himself.

Looking to the window, and the red-tinted night outside it, Madison felt like screaming.

Chapter 23

"If you stay here, you'll be safe."

St. John said this from the doorway, and in a way that made Madison want to weep.

"I've taken great care to keep this place hidden," he said. "Possibly for just such a night as this one."

Madison moved toward him, willfully making her feet move.

"I have to go," he said quietly, his voice the draw for her that it always had been. "So much depends on what happens now."

"Who is going to help you? Does the detective know?" she asked.

St. John shook his head. "Stay here, Madison. I'd have you safe, you know. Always."

"My brother is still out there."

"I couldn't stop them from biting him. I didn't know

until it was too late. You must believe that I would have tried to stop it."

She nodded. "He helped me. Stewart didn't hurt me. He isn't a monster."

"I don't know what he is now," St. John confessed. "No one really knows."

St. John pulled her hands from his sweater, and held them clasped in his for a few seconds longer. "Wait for me here, my love," he said. "Please."

"Not knowing what will happen to you out there?"

"For now," he said. "Just for now."

"What if I do love you?" Her voice was faint. "What happens then?"

"It would make everything I have ever done worth-while," St. John said.

His voice echoed in the wide expanse of space he had called his refuge. It echoed inside Madison.

She had told him the thing she had barely admitted to herself. Love, she had said. What if she loved him.

It was a fascinating word to describe the complex emotions that had somehow entangled them both. There was no explanation for how it had arrived be-tween two beings that had spent so little time together. But what was time, after all?

Did caring for another person, really caring about them and what happened to them, constitute being in love? Did the fact that she ached for St. John prove the truth of her feelings?

When she opened her eyes, she was alone.

Her immortal lover had gone.

"It would make everything I have ever done worth-while," St. John had said, if she loved him. She didn't know how she would cope if he didn't return.

Her brother had come here to help those missing girls, and that had gone wrong. She had come here to find Stewart, and how would she categorize what had happened to her since?

Although she had felt strong the moment before, the room began to revolve around her as St. John's presence faded. She seemed to feel those enemies closing in.

However, this wasn't about enemies. The spinning sensation had been caused by the recognition of a title that she was afraid now defined her. A title that could keep her from St. John forever, if it were true.

That word lit up her mind, lit up St. John's apartment, reflecting off the windows, hitting her eyes with an uncomfortable glare.

Slayer.

She was what her brother was, St. John had told her, and it had been Stewart's downfall.

It wasn't a choice or an option, St. John had led her to believe. Genetics determined who would be a vampire hunter. *Born to it,* was the way this went.

Her parents had produced a set of Slayers without letting their children know. Their silence, before their deaths, had resulted in Stewart being nearly killed because he wasn't strong enough to hold his own when he came here.

Nearly killed.

She clung to that. St. John had said her brother had been bitten. Not killed. He hadn't used that awful death word.

There was hope. In a world threatened by darkness, there was some light, and she was starved for light.

"I believe you," she whispered to St. John. "I trust you."

She had to confess everything.

"If what you say is true, I see the horror of the future. I will be the one running through the shadows with a wooden weapon in my hand. I will be seeking fanged creatures that will know how to fight back. I will do so in your honor."

When the flash of rightness came, streaking past her vision in prisms of multicolored light, Madison realized it was a sign of her soul opening up to what had been hidden there.

Slayer.

She held tight on legs that no longer wanted to support her. It all seemed too much.

After taking a step, she crumpled to the floor, refusing to give in to the waiting void that offered a temporary respite from the world, its secrets and what part she would play in it after this, if she chose.

How could she make it work, when she loved an immortal soul that she had been born to fight?

Love...

Opposites...

St. John had gone to confront a wave of unspeakable terror taking shape. *Them. Nosferatu.* But he had seen to her safety first. He cared for her that much.

Using the window for support, Madison picked herself up. Pushing back her fear, she sent her senses inward, in search of the thing St. John said had long lain dormant inside her.

What she found instead was Stewart's voice, calling. "Maddie. Mad one...."

It was a voice she had to find.

St. John emerged from the Tube station through a blocked-off exit used by underground workers. He soon found what he was seeking. The creature was grotesque in the simplicity of its design, a tall, slender beast with the bone-pale face of the dead.

Nosferatu. Eternally damned, savage vampires with the bite of a bear trap and no remembrance of a soul. Creatures with no thoughts of their own, and no heart-beat.

At first sight, its features were human enough, save for the mouth and eyes. With its dead-white skin, its lips glowed red, as if it had been snacking on some poor soul on its way here.

Its eye sockets were black, bottomless holes, sur-rounded by circles of more blackness. Sparse, stringy hair, as white as its face, covered only the bottom por-tion of its head, curtaining large pointed ears.

The rank odor of death trailed behind this Hunter like a kite. Moldy earth, fetid flesh, death trapped in a body. Once free of the exit, the monster moved with a gliding motion, as if on skates, never seeming to ac-tually touch the ground.

Its long, threadbare coat kicked up dust and debris as its arms swung menacingly at the air. This ungodly entity, not of the earth or what lay below, had been created to mock both places as a mindless beast on the rampage.

St. John observed it from the rooftop above, stand-ing half hidden behind a sign made of the same kind of steel beams that reinforced his apartment, though these beams weren't silver-coated. Vampires couldn't detect anything through exposed metal. Metal, like sunlight, could hurt them, become the true end of them if coated. If silver pierced unholy flesh in the right place, they were dust.

In this day and age, a silver bullet through the head or through the empty cavity that had once held a heart was the quickest way to take down a monster like this one. A quick, final death that could be issued from a distance.

But that was too easy.

Since his own new existence had begun with drinking from a golden cup, he was exempt from the problems of metal. He had exposed himself to all kinds after that, and had for long years carried both shield and sword.

This hideous Nosferatu had caught a scent. Lifting its chin to sniff the air, it then swung around, searching for the source of the smell, failing to look up, perhaps sensing and disliking the heavy tonnage of beams.

The game of the moment had become hide-and-seek.

Unable to trace what it had scented, the beast's narrow head cocked once before its body went completely motionless, like a statue carved from a block of flawed marble. It didn't blink because it didn't have to, didn't breathe because it had no need for air, and never had to fake breath in order to fit in with any other kind of society.

Not even its long coat moved.

St. John heard its thoughts, and they weren't pretty. The mantra was a cycle of hatred, disgust and bloodlust looped together. He felt its venom and the chaos holding the white carcass together.

This sucker was a forerunner, the first trickle of a nightmarish stream of monsters on their way. It was also alone at the moment.

St. John's tattoos became a barely tolerable ball of

fire, calling up the strength of his background, urging him to action. For the sake of the people of London, who might get in the way at any moment, and for the sake of everything he'd given up in his own past in order to prevent such a circumstance as this one from happening, he had to deal with this crazy sucker and the flood of others behind it, quickly.

Walking to the edge of the rooftop, he braced himself. With the wind on his face and his power rising swiftly to the surface of his skin, he began, measure by measure, to shed his disguise.

Chapter 24

Madison's heart hammered. Restlessness returned.

"Stewart?" she said.

She pressed her forehead to the glass.

The street below St. John's apartment was dark. A big moon rode the sky behind a bank of black clouds.

St. John was out there somewhere, chasing demons. Her brother was out there, too, waiting for her.

The glass felt cool against her fingertips. The night beyond the glass resonated with indistinguishable shapes, and movement. Even St. John's refuge wasn't immune from the pressure of those things.

She didn't know how to help St. John. If she tried, she might distract him. She could go after her brother, though. One of those shadows on the street below might be Stewart. In finding Stewart, she'd find herself.

As she turned for the door, rage began to build inside her for whoever had hurt her brother. She didn't feel particularly brave or courageous. The thought of having to go outside, for any reason, made her stomach roil.

Damn it, though, she had to go out there, ignoring St. John's *"Please."*

Unable to stand the suspense, and with her missing courage overruled by sheer determination, Madison headed for the door.

"I'm sorry," she said to the ghost of Christopher St. John. "You, of all…people, should understand."

"You're looking for me?" St. John called out to the monster on the sidewalk, landing quietly beside it.

The thing had no tongue, making a reply impossible. Nor did it possess a functioning brain able to process surprise or fear. Nosferatu were terrors designed only for one purpose—to hunt their prey. They were ghosts of the worst parts of the human psyche. Animals, really, with one-track desires.

They wouldn't notice St. John's glowing white skin that had burned through his clothes, or the ripples of extraordinary muscle fueled by a mythical resurrection. They wouldn't be afraid of the halo of golden hair radiating outward as if he were a dark angel, or the reddened gleam of his Maker's blood tinting his eyes.

The beast's black sockets trained on St. John. He felt a shudder of satisfaction run through it.

St. John smiled. This one wasn't so very old, and therefore inexperienced.

"They sent only one of you?" he remarked as the creature moved first one arm, then the other, as though thawing from a deep freeze. "You do know what I am?"

The creature lunged so fast, it became a colorless smear. St. John, with equal speed, sidestepped the thrust of a specially made knife, pulled from the monster's pocket. He had only seconds to study that weapon, forged of both gold and silver, one of those ingredients the same as the chalice that had changed him.

Someone had their facts straight about the Grail, too. But most facts having to do with the Seven who drank from that holy cup were erroneous.

The Nosferatu spun in place and lunged again, catching the edge of St. John's sweater where only traces of it remained, clinging to his waistband. In a burst of extraordinary speed, St. John raised his arms, spreading the blooded sigils carved into him—the sigils that responded to the Nosferatu with an almost audible whine.

Cool London mist clung to his bareness as he widened his stance. The scars crisscrossing his body became livid reminders of past battles, each one of them scalding the cooler skin around them.

His tattoos burned hotter than the depths of the hell the monster beside him had sprung from. Not a cold burn this time. Powerfully hot.

His power focused.

He felt himself growing further into the terrible entity he had been created to be. The one he had to be in order to best the worst of the villains.

More muscle was there for the asking. His shoulders stretched, pulling at his bones. He heard his spine crackle with a live energy conceived of centuries of righteousness, after having being born in the dark. The two worlds met in his body, throwing sparks and shadow that were divinely beautiful and fiendishly terrible.

The Hunter came on, fast, strong, determined. Before it had moved too far, he had the thing by its throat and its weapon in his hand. As the Hunter's eyes locked with his, St. John sunk the knife deeply into the creature's gaunt chest.

"Are you an example of what I can expect?" he said to the monster. "Because that would be nice."

There was an explosion of body parts, and a rain of mottled gray ash. St. John watched the ash fall, thinking that killing this beast had been alarmingly simple for a Blood Knight in pursuit of peace. There had been no fight to speak of. Not this time. This had been a warning. Merely a hint of what was to follow.

More monsters were coming. Two of them had entered London from another direction. Another slithered in their wake in the old tunnels beneath the city.

Their approach filled St. John with rage.

With the weapon grasped tightly in his hand, he paused. Raising his eyes to the sky, he was struck by a new pain. Madison had left the safety of his refuge. Her voice reached him along the thread tying them together.

"I'm sorry. You, of all...people, should understand."

Muttering a sharp *"No!"* across the link connecting him to her, St. John sucked in a lungful of the crackling power that was his immortal birthright, and turned back toward the city.

Madison crept from the safety of St. John's building with her nerves on fire.

Stepping to the street, she waited, listening for footsteps, finding some and thinking that vampires probably moved soundlessly, and that footsteps meant the two figures she'd seen from the window had to be people. Humans. Mortals.

If she possessed the special genetics of a vampire Slayer, shouldn't she have been able to tell the difference between men and monsters?

Other than the footsteps retreating into the distance, the night was eerily silent. Long shadows, cast by the moon, made the street look seriously *noir*. She sensed nothing. Not one special trait kicked in to help her.

Setting her shoulders, gritting her teeth, she stepped off the curb. She walked to the center of the narrow street. There were no passing cabs or cars. The moon shone from straight up in the sky.

Ears straining, she felt the slow seep of a rising panic, not knowing which way to go, or what to do.

She ventured a call. "Stewart?"

Movement behind her spun her around. She hadn't heard this coming....

That was her last thought before a black-eyed monster, its appearance unimaginable even in nightmares, threw her to the pavement with a simple flick of its wrist.

The arrival of the Nosferatu sat like a bad taste in St. John's mouth. The fear of them meeting Madison, if that were to happen, fueled his outrage.

He twitched the thread connecting her to him as he sprinted street by street toward his apartment, and found that thread unreasonably taut. Across it, he heard Madison's scream.

Utilizing every bit of the power he had so carefully hidden, he raced on, fearful for the first time he could recall, and calculating how long it would take him to get to her.

Turning one last corner, his speed too fast to raise dust or debris, he slammed to a halt in front of two of the monsters he had sensed.

One of them leaned over Madison, who was stretched out on the ground.

"At last," Simon Monteforte said. "We see the Protector in action."

St. John flicked his eyes to Madison. Her breathing came in gasps, but her heart beat strongly. The Nosferatu hadn't harmed her because she wasn't on his radar.

"What is it you want, Simon?" he asked, his tone deadly serious.

"Look at you," Monteforte said. "You're some kind of freakish angel, not one of us. You've never been one of us, and the others are too self-absorbed to see it. You glow from within, special, pale and pretty. You have the blood of angels in you, as well as your Maker's. Due to this, you have hidden yourself well from the Ancients. But you haven't fooled me. I want to be like you. I want you to tell me how to make that possible."

"What is it you want, Simon?"

"The thing you've kept hidden from us. From me."

"Name that thing you'd do all of this for," St. John said.

"Power."

"I'd have thought you had enough power. You are one of the Hundred."

Monteforte waved that suggestion away with a subtle twist of his fingers. "That's ninety-nine vampires too many."

St. John stood his ground, his bare chest reflecting the moonlight, his arms tense at his sides.

"What you want isn't possible," he said. "You know it."

"I will have the Grail, St. John."

"The Grail is a legend."

"As are you, supposedly, and yet your light blinds me. Which one of the Seven Blood Knights are you? The first? The last? I've paid a lot of people, some of them immortal, some not, to find out about you. And here you were, in our midst, the whole time."

St. John observed the ancient traitor closely. Monteforte stank of this selfish greed. With Nosferatu by his side, under his spell, and Madison at his feet, Monteforte posed a real threat. He'd hurt Madison if given the opportunity, in order to hurt St. John.

However, St. John's expanded senses perceived another visitor in the shadows of the overhang of the building to his right. Someone not on the Nosferatu's radar, either, since the monster hadn't turned to look. Oddly enough, neither had Simon Monteforte, whose attention remained locked to St. John as if the old vampire's greed had indeed blinded him to anything other than getting his way.

St. John's sigils pulsed, the danger in them building until his back was crawling with movement indicating the promise of what he could do to the old vampire in seconds if Madison hadn't been involved.

It was a strange time to discover just how much he loved her, and to realize the extent of the agony he'd suffer if he were to lose her, or leave her behind.

"What would you do with the power you seek?" he asked Monteforte to gain time.

"Rule the world, as you and the others of your kind could, if you chose. Surely you've considered doing so?"

Monteforte gave a signal that amounted to little more than a slight raising of his hand, and the black-eyed monster took a gliding step forward.

Something else moved, as well. The shadow lurking near the building came on fast, and St. John heard Madison's intake of breath when she, too, identified who it was.

By then it was too late for Monteforte to ignore his surroundings. Casually, as if facing a conspirator, the old vampire glanced sideways. He said to Madison's brother, "I thought we took care of you, Stewart. Pity you didn't stay down."

When confronted with so many monsters, hell had no option but to break loose.

Chapter 25

The horrid, twisted creature holding her had let go. Scrambling sideways, Madison knew better than to run to any of the beings here for assistance. There wasn't a mortal among them.

"Stewart," she said.

Her brother didn't respond, or look her way. Stewart's face, free of the shadows that had hidden it, told her all she needed to know.

Stewart was parchment-pale, and gaunt to the point of starvation. His face was sharp, cold and soberly intent. He wore a dark shirt, partially tattered, and an old pair of jeans, torn at the knees. His hair was disheveled, with long streaks of gray running through the red-auburn color.

He didn't look strong, or completely alive. Yet Stewart had again arrived when needed, as though he had been keeping watch over her all this time.

With a snap of her head, she swept her gaze to St. John, who had also become someone else. Some*thing* else. Bigger. Painfully beautiful. Altered both in shape and content, he radiated power that was visible as it crossed his skin, as if power were waves of moving muscle.

He was the personification of the knights of old, and radiated with the glory of angels. A human made more than human. A being apart from the rules governing reality.

Madison could hardly look at him, and yet couldn't make herself look away. She had heard the conversation between him and Monteforte, and the old vampire's accusations: something about St. John being able to rule the world if he wanted to.

His half-naked body gleamed with the luster of a south-sea pearl as he met the wiry, black-eyed monster rushing at him. The dichotomy of the twisted flesh of the monster meeting with St. John's fierce, deadly light, was breathtaking.

The impact of their bodies hitting was loud in the quiet of the night. The monster moved with incredible speed, but it was clear from the start that the beast had no chance against its superior counterpart.

St. John reeked of power. The air had become electrified with it.

And he had purposefully left the gray-haired vampire he had called Monteforte for Stewart to deal with—which suggested to Madison that Stewart had met the velvet-clad monster before.

This was the Ancient that St. John had said was the wrong one for Stewart to have found, and was the

creep in the Germand's lobby. Simon Monteforte was
the beast that had betrayed her twin's confidence.

Madison didn't know where to look, or what to do.
The fighting had started in two places, and her attention remained glued to her lover.

On his back, covering an expansive space from
shoulder blade to shoulder blade, a fiery design burned
in the night as if it were a live flame. The tattoos looked
like a blaze of wings about to unfurl. Unearthly. Beautiful. Angry. Unlike anything else in existence.

He had told her there was no other like him.

Shaking off her stupor, Madison finally tore her
gaze from him to see that her brother had circled the
old gray-haired vampire. In Stewart's gloved hand a
knife glinted wickedly in the moonlight. Silver. Metal
for killing vampires, if the aim was true.

The vampire St. John had addressed as Monteforte
wore a feral expression of sly cunning. Her brother's
face remained dangerously expressionless, as if emotion had been stripped from him, along with parts of
his former life.

Monteforte was wild, and frightening. He seemed
to her a deadly foe in the sheer length of his existence
alone. Still, her twin moved as though that didn't matter. Sustained by vampire blood passed to him through
the savage bites of Monteforte's vampires, and therefore maybe even Monteforte himself, her twin, because
of his heritage and his destiny, had beat the odds of
death's two-fisted knock.

It was too damn incredible an event to go unnoticed
on a public street. Alerted to movement in the shadows, Madison jumped sideways to meet it. Through

their bond, she shared St. John's awareness of another monster, not too distant, on its way.

She didn't have time to confront that oncoming shadow. Another shadow beside it pushed her out of the way and stood in her place.

Madison held her breath.

If this was another Nosferatu, the good guys here, no matter how strong they were, would be outnumbered.

Uncertain now as to where to look, fearing for her brother, wanting to watch St. John, she felt her chest begin to ache from the riotous beating of her heart.

She had to do something.

Madison flung herself at Simon Monteforte, ramming into him with every ounce of strength she possessed. Monteforte tilted sideways. Recovering quickly, he rounded back to Stewart.

Her brother had been prepared. He swung himself off-balance as Monteforte struck with both hands, and righted himself with a graceful lunge. Stewart's arm came down in an arc, slashing at shadows, his silver knife coming up red with the old vampire's blood. But the knife hadn't hit its mark. It had been impossible to see, let alone find Monteforte's chest, in his flurry of seemingly effortless moves.

Nevertheless, Monteforte had been struck. And that one thing created a lucky gap in the fight.

Scenting the blood, St. John's ravenous Nosferatu made a sharp turn. An error in judgment that allowed St. John's strong fingers to find its throat.

With the force of a whirlwind, St. John yanked the beast backward. The monster fell back, writhing against its capture, too energetic and focused on the scent of blood in the air to be held for long.

But St. John hung on to it, his muscles corded, and a look of defiance on his face. It was a terrible dance of power. And it gave Madison the courage she needed.

She lunged again at the monster keeping pace with her brother, and who was flinging blood from his wounds in all directions.

Tossing herself at the old vampire a second time, she knocked him into her brother. Stewart moved with a practiced precision, whirling in place, raising the knife, bringing it down.

More blood tinted the blade of his knife, but the old vampire continued to move.

God, how she hated vampires!

Stewart didn't register the slightest bit of fear. Madison was terrified. Across her overworked, inflamed nerve fibers, she sensed the imminent approach of the newcomer. Not only one newcomer, she sensed, but two.

Fueled by fear and a surge of adrenaline that shot through her, she hurled herself at Monteforte, who appeared suddenly to her right. Instead of connecting with anything solid, two strong hands caught her and flung her aside.

Rebounding from the wall, ready to go at it again, Madison hesitated when she recognized one of the newcomers on the scene. He stood on the outskirts of the area of fighting wearing an expression of disgust on his lined, familiar face.

That newcomer was D.I. Crane.

St. John threw the Nosferatu to the ground, aware of the bloodlust that had overcome its instructions to take a Blood Knight down.

The scent of its own master's blood was driving the creature mad. If he let the Nosferatu loose, it would go after the source of that blood, potentially helping to solve everyone's immediate problems. But his thought was for Madison, who didn't need to witness what a frenzied vampire could do. Or what he, himself, would have to do to stop the monster.

With the beast trapped between his foot and the pavement, he threw a calm look over his shoulder at the tall figure that had come late to the party. *That damned detective.*

Too late now for excuses or disguises. The cat was very obviously out of the bag. And though he didn't need help, Stewart Chase might. He had given Stewart a chance to take his own revenge out on Monteforte, but a second pair of hands when dealing with an aged entity like Monteforte was probably always welcome.

Especially when Detective Inspector Ellis Crane was so much more than a second pair of hands.

St. John glanced up at the moon, then down at Crane, who stood beneath the overhang of the buildings.

"Wrong party for you," he said to the detective.

"Every party in this city is my party," the detective snarled in reply.

St. John shrugged, and nodded to the detective. "Want to get your hands dirty?"

"I'd like nothing better," Crane said, tossing a revolver to Madison with the harsh directive, "Silver bullets," and "Watch your aim." Then Detective Inspector Crane began to let his own beast out.

The wet, flesh-morphing, bone-cracking sounds of a man shifting into another shape made Madison cringe.

What was happening to the detective went flagrantly against nature.

The detective's shoulders widened. He grew taller, as if the moon overhead was stretching him closer to it. Muscle built upon muscle, as if someone had just poured more onto his frame.

His face lengthened. More bones cracked and heaved. He tipped forward from the waist, as if the whole process hurt him greatly. And when he stood up again, seconds later, a creature that was half man, half beast looked out of big black eyes from a feral-featured face above a body covered by a brown fur pelt.

It was official, Madison thought. She had entered another dimension.

The detective's gun felt cool in her hand, and heavier than she'd have expected. She knew what silver bullets were for. Killing monsters of all kinds.

The good detective was a goddamn werewolf, and had come prepared because of the full moon and the antics he'd said ran amok beneath it.

With trembling hands, Madison raised the gun, thinking she should fire on them all—all of London's monsters. Narrowing her focus, squeezing the trigger, she went for Monteforte, who was clinging to Stewart with fingers like talons.

Kicked back slightly by the force of the shot, she heard nothing from the old vampire. Seconds later, a great howl split the night. God, had she missed, and hit the werewolf instead?

No, not the detective. He growled deep in his throat with a sound that was scary as hell.

Madison spun in place in time to see him leap toward the shadows on the curb, where another impossibly frightening, twisted creature had appeared. Setting her stance, she again used both hands to hoist the gun. Aiming at the quick-moving Monteforte, she fired.

Her brother suddenly stopped wrestling. The shadows dancing with him coagulated, showing an angry Monteforte holding his chest.

St. John let loose of the monster he'd been holding down, and in a blurred instant was at Madison's side, taking the gun from her, pressing her out of the way, his wide shoulders hiding the view of creatures killing creatures in a last-second turnaround.

But anyone for miles could have heard the terrible noises these beasts were making, Madison thought. The night rang with gut-wrenching nightmarish sounds of flesh tearing and gluttonous beasts ravaging each other.

St. John, beside her, tried to disguise those terrible sounds. "Good shot, my lovely, beautiful Madison," he whispered to her. "It's almost over, my love."

An explosion rocked the area. Then another, followed by a third. Three explosions, after which a rain of thick gray ash began to fall, appearing like snow, smelling foul. The ash of the final death of three vampire abominations obliterated everything in the area, other than the moonlight.

A hand appeared on St. John's shoulder, pushing him aside. Stewart's face peered into hers, tense, white, skeletal.

"I'm sorry," she said to her twin. "I didn't know."

She started over, feeling sobs choke her throat.

"I'm sorry for ruining your revenge with that gun. And for what happened to you. And for what you are."

Throwing her arms around him, she hugged her

brother tight. He didn't immediately respond. It took him a minute to hug her back. When he finally closed his arms around her, it felt as though she had found that missing piece of herself again. It felt like heaven. She had her brother back.

But Stewart pulled back and stepped away. Mutely, he turned to go.

"Wait! Stewart, wait!" she cried. "It's okay. I swear it's okay."

Could she blame him for being wary, though, when Stewart knew he had become another kind of demon?

"We're going to go home," she told him. "We're going to be together, no matter what. We'll both see to that, and whatever it takes."

She turned to the werewolf, who thankfully had changed back into a bare-chested detective glowing with sweat. She had to find her voice. "My brother didn't harm that girl. He will swear to that."

"Then I'm sure he will tell me everything he knows about it," Crane said, his voice gruff. "But I believe we have found the killers, thanks to your tip. St. John may have to do a bit of complying on his own, as to how to take care of that in a world where none of us are welcome. We'll have to spin the tale of that one girl's death into something believable—not to make light of it, you understand, but to protect the public."

"You went to the Germand?" St. John asked Crane.

Madison looked to her lover to find him St. John again. Merely that, on the surface, anyway, though his skin still seemed lit from within.

"The Germand. Disgusting place," Crane said. "No offense."

"You found the other girls?" St. John asked.

"All of them. Seems everyone wants to meet a vampire, and the girls were enticed by the prospect until they were actually faced with reality."

The detective paused for a grimace. "I don't get that. Blood is ugly. It tastes like hell. But we're lucky we found them. Janis Blake had escaped once, and they'd caught up with her. The girls were hysterical when we found them."

All eyes shifted to Stewart, who nodded. His voice emerged roughly, as though he hadn't used it lately.

"I found that dead girl," he said.

"Yes, well, your DNA, taken from your sister's hands, will be of no use, of course. The lab will cop to making a mistake, since the sample will be all messed up. The good news is that there is nothing to tie you to that murder. Nothing at all."

Crane turned to St. John. "The girls have fang marks on them. Some bastard bloodsucker had been snacking on them. Will this mean they also will be hungry eventually?"

"Did they drink, in return?" St. John asked.

"Not as far as I know. They were glad to be found, and have been taken to the hospital. Their parents have been notified, but if they're..."

"Give them a transfusion right away. Invent an excuse for that. If they didn't drink, or receive blood in return, they will likely be all right."

Loose screws...

Loose ends...

Madison's head hurt like a son of a gun.

She observed the scene in front of her, made up of St. John, in all his chiseled splendor, and Crane, looking mostly normal after his big, freaky surprise, and her brother, still there, whatever the hell Stewart had actually become…to find them all looking at her. Expecting her to what? Scream? Swoon?

"Yeah, right. Like that's going to happen," she said to them. "And it isn't as if I'm going to be able to tell anyone. Who the hell would believe it?"

"What about the Hundred?" Crane said.

"You mean the Ninety-Nine? You know about them, too?" St. John asked.

"No Lycan worth his salt can't tell a vampire from a hole in the ground," Crane said.

St. John grinned, looking very much like the St. John Madison was so uproariously in love with.

"I don't suppose they'll miss Monteforte," he said. "I'm not sure they ever knew about you," he added to Stewart. "Not for sure, anyway. I'm damned certain most of them didn't have any idea about what went on at the Germand. They can't afford to allow that kind of blasphemy against their rules."

His smile widened, showing two gleaming white fangs. "You will need to stop staking everything that moves, of course."

"Does the Hundred know about the detective here?" Madison threw Crane a look, still shaken up by that big, furry surprise.

Crane smiled back with a very wolfish expression that was in no way apologetic. "It's likely they do," he said.

"It's tough to hide the smell of a werewolf," St. John explained.

The detective grinned again. "That's what your look meant in the hospital hallway? You tagged me? Well, I wouldn't be so quick to call the kettle black, vampire. Most of you smell like burnt toast."

"And you," Madison whispered to Stewart. "What about you? Are you all right? Enough to come home?"

She directed a question to St. John. "Is that possible?"

He nodded. "Ocean liner. Darkened room. He can make it work if he wants to. He'll have to explain what the hell he is, and how that works, first."

Stewart's slump, Madison knew, was caused by the extremes of a relief he had no doubt lost sight and hope of. Though infused with vampire blood, enough of her twin remained in the mix, thanks, she supposed, to his Slayer base.

She wanted to cry with happiness over that one small thing. Her brother hadn't been taken from her forever. Hope shone in his eyes.

Although there was stuff to be cleared up, the Yale Four girls were alive. St. John was here. Stewart was here.

She doubted this kind of mess would happen again anytime soon in London. As St. John had said, a fringe community like those old vampires couldn't afford the attention.

So, what about her?

Where did she fit in?

Her network would be waiting for an update as soon as the story of finding the girls broke. She was going to break it. In spite of standing there in the moonlight with a vampire-hunter hybrid, an immortal she loved more than anything else on the earth, and a werewolf cop—all of those things part of London's dirty little secrets—she still had a job to do.

In spite of everything.

And because of everything.

She still had the energy to do it. Help clean this up. Put a shiny new spin on the news.

There were vampires in London, the biggest story of all, the story of a lifetime, and she couldn't tell that story. Her life, and the lives of many others, depended on her silence.

The world depended on it.

"Shall I take you back to your hotel?" the werewolf detective asked her.

She couldn't have taken a first step, if she had accepted that offer. The almost heart-rending expression of sadness on St. John's face kept her rooted in place.

That sadness told her she had one more thing left to do. She had to make peace with her own immortal obsession.

When he held out a hand, as if he had heard her thoughts, her brother stepped forward.

"It's okay," she said to Stewart. "He is the Protector, you know. My Protector. Can you go to my hotel, Stewart? Will you go, and wait for me there, please? I can't lose you again. We'll do everything possible to make you comfortable, I promise. The detective can let you in. Cops have ways to do that. This—" she gestured to St. John "—is important."

Crane and Stewart eyed each other warily. They were different species who had come together tonight for a common goal, but they didn't have to like it.

This was important.

She placed her hand in St. John's, feeling the familiar charge that hadn't lessened one bit. She wondered if this would be their last night together, and if he would move on now that his task had been accomplished.

He was one of Seven Blood Knights who could rule the world if they wanted to.

"One more night is not enough," St. John sent to her.

When she met his eyes, she said, "Not a Slayer. Nothing resembling a Slayer. There was some mistake. I was scared to death out here."

Before her next breath, and in a surge of motion that left her last remark trailing, they were running, together, toward shelter.

Chapter 26

St. John's bare body, perfectly proportioned and as powerful as poured steel, was a thing of beauty in whatever incarnation, and carved by a master artist's hand. A partly unsteady hand. Evidence of that artist's slip of the chisel showed in the long lines of ridged scar tissue that glowed whiter, grittier than the rest of his undisturbed flesh, and curved around the sides of his rib cage.

In what now seemed like ages ago, Madison had felt those ridges with her fingers and wondered who had dared to hurt him. She now knew that many of his enemies, mortals and vampires alike, would try to do the same if they understood what his presence among them meant. Christopher St. John was no friend to vampires or monstrosities of any kind, though he had been born one.

Supposedly, she was his enemy, though they didn't view things that way. Big lessons had been learned during these days and nights in London. Not everything that appeared as black and white had to be perceived as polar opposites, when a vast area of gray ran between. Although most people considered this gray area negatively, an awareness of how vast that area was had changed her.

Meeting Christopher St. John had changed her.

He'd been mortal once. His life had been taken from him, exchanged for another kind of existence. He lived in that gray zone as an elegant, honorable, noble immortal whose past remained a mystery and whose immediate future rose above her as she gazed up at him from the bed.

She also lived in that gray zone, because she loved St. John with every fiber of her being. Someone, somewhere, might damn her for this, she supposed, but Madison didn't care. She thanked the heavens that he so obviously felt the same way about her.

Many loose ends had been tied up at last in London, but this one dangling thread remained above some unanswered others.

Their future.

They were in his refuge. She didn't remember anything between being on the street and on her back, in his bed.

He was completely naked, pale, perfect and more beautiful than anything she had ever seen. It was the first time she had seen all of him.

Eyeing the fullness of his erection, her body reacted with a quiver of anticipation. The word *glorious* came to mind.

Would the sky fall in if two beings created to eradicate each other came together in this way, repeatedly?

She'd seen no evidence in herself of the traits her twin possessed, except for the dangerous attraction to vampires. Particularly her attraction to this one.

Just now, with her breath coming in great gasps, she wanted a physical culmination of their feelings.

Just this one last time. At least.

The scent of his bare skin filled her with heat as he came closer, as he leaned over to place his hands on the pillow behind her head. As she looked at him, taking in the exquisite length of his magnificent body, a beating, soulful longing made her heart soar.

This was the same longing she'd felt from the first sighting of him on that balcony, in the monsters' club, magnified a thousand times and manifesting here, inside her chest, and between her legs. If this was to be the last time, with him, she didn't know how she would cope.

"So much to do," she said to him. "And you see only me."

"You imagine I could see anything else?"

His expression was tender, sober, provocative. His eyes captured hers with a glint of blue-black fire.

"Do immortals remember what to do in times like this, after a fight?" she asked.

"Why don't you be the judge."

The tickle of silky hair on her cheek made her reach for the wide shoulders she wanted crushed to hers. She sighed with pleasure when his long arms wrapped around her, lifting her from the mattress.

He sat down beside her, holding her inches away from him for an agonizing minute more.

"I don't think you do remember," she said. "It's not supposed to take this long."

"You're afraid you will change your mind?"

"Hell, no."

His laughter mingled with the sound of fabric tearing. Madison felt a chill of cooler air, realizing without looking that she'd been rendered as naked as he was, and that she had been the one to forget the details, such as clothes getting in the way.

Even then, St. John didn't immediately release her. His lips stroked across hers, sending jolt after jolt of red-hot current through her, each strike turning up the heat and causing moisture to rush to the place she wanted him the most.

The hungry, completely savage meeting of their mouths came like rapture. The slick dance of their tongues sent her heartbeat into overdrive and her breasts straining upward, hard and aching for the attention of his heat, hoping for just one touch.

He laid her back without breaking the contact of that kiss. Her arms encircled his neck, muscles contracting to pull him to her until she felt the smooth seduction of his chest against hers at last.

Skin to skin…

She had imagined this would be a vigorous taking—his hardness, her need. But his kiss became deeper, slower, producing a similar effect to having his hands slide down her body, covering every inch.

She arched her back, ran her hands over his shoulders, mindful of the fiery tattoos that had glowed like a bonfire, feverishly tracing the grooves she found between his blades.

More sound came from her throat when she found those muscled shoulders rippling, and feverish.

Touching him there seemed to strip from him his ability to restrain himself. He murmured something incomprehensible as his body slid onto hers, stretching them both out on the sheets.

As he breathed her name into her mouth, his erection found the home that would welcome him. He wasn't one of the Seven here. He was Christopher St. John, lover, giver.

He eased only the swollen tip of his cock against her, holding back, seeming to need this kind of restraint.

Madison's body opened to him without effort or resistance. Her legs separated to grant him full access. She was damp, anxious and waiting, wanting to see where this meeting would take them, when she had to go home to Florida soon after.

When her moan of invitation reached him, St. John drew his hips back. Slowly, he sank his cock inside her, one glorious inch at a time.

It wasn't enough. Not by far.

Clutching at him, wanting to shout with the pleasure of the sensation of having him inside her, Madison spoke into his mouth. "Prove how much you want this. Prove it now."

Her remark caused another motion of his hips. He pressed into her with a faster, livelier thrust that he followed with more, until he wrenched a series of cries from her lips, locked to his.

Each sound she made quickened his pace, and drove him deeper between her legs. Madison tried to hold off the pleasure by squeezing herself around him. She didn't want this to be quick, or over too soon. She didn't want it ever to be over.

Mindless of the old injuries he had sustained, she clawed at his back. Her need was endless. He seemed to be sharing every sensation, which was perhaps why he was in no hurry to reach the place inside her that wanted him so desperately.

When he backed off, she growled. When his fingers traced her collarbone, and dipped between her breasts, she uttered a breathy protest.

Nothing else mattered in that instant, not her straining breasts, or any other body part. She wanted this. She wanted him. Why wasn't he listening to her? How could he wait?

His fingertip was cool against the flush of her overheated skin as it circled the raised pink flesh of her breast. He gave her a devastating smile before lowering his mouth there.

With a slow lap, his tongue danced over her. In reaction, she clutched at his hair. The draw, as he suckled her, struck all the way to her bones, ending up in a deep place between her thighs, near where his cock waited to satisfy her.

Writhing on the mattress, she arched her back, liking what he was doing, lost in the sensation of his mouth on her.

He wasn't inside her now, but so damn close.

His hand glided over her stomach, and between her hip bones. At the same time, his talented tongue aided his next draw on the tip of her breast. Her insides began to ache. She felt each throb of her pulse, and couldn't tell which sensation mattered most: mouth, fingers, lips? She refused to give up or give in to the whole, not wanting to miss any part of this.

It was so very good.

It might be the last.

God, not the last!

His lips gave a last soft pull on her breast before his face came close to hers. His eyes sought hers with an intensity that drove her mad with desire for the promise she saw there.

"Don't even presume to read my mind," she murmured.

His eyes were all black now. She heard the drop of his fangs.

It was as if their souls knew what came next.

His plunge struck hard, rocking the bed on its foundation, reaching her core. Her breath whooshed out. Emotion released, spiraling upward within her to meet with the largeness of her need, crashing into it, spilling the emptiness out, filling it with something altogether new.

The air on her face became a colorful burst of brilliant light. Electric blue. Pink. White. She became one with that light as it ripped through her, scattering her senses to pieces.

Her body rose upward in a violent jerk of intensity. The edge of her physical pleasure was joined by her mind, and soon after that, her soul. She and this special being were wrapped together, not just along some nebulous thread, but everywhere possible. In all ways possible.

One more slight move of his hips, and he had her completely. Swept along by the explosion that rocked her was the ultimate gratification of a need being beautifully fulfilled.

Her lover began to shine. His back began to burn white-hot, scorching her fingertips. Madison felt as if they were lifted from the bed, from the world, wrapped intimately together.

There was a sensation of wind, or maybe the air caused by the movement of wings, on her face. The place St. John took her to was brilliant, colorless, and yet filled with light.

Images filled her mind.

Knights riding on black horses. Black shields emblazoned with crests of fire. Stern, pale faces of men fighting, then gliding through gardens of grass, red roses, and gurgling, water-filled fountains. And in the center of that fountain sat a sparkling golden cup, its rim covered in blood.

Her cry of ecstasy went on and on, echoing in the room, mingling with the visions, as her orgasm merged with St. John's long, deep groan of satisfaction.

It felt like hours before the climax backed off, and faded. It felt like hours before she even began to come down to earth.

The room had gone quiet after their cries and shouts. In the new silence, neither of them moved...until that quiet was severed by the unmistakable crunch of splintering wood.

Madison opened her eyes to find herself not beneath St. John, but on top of her lover, straddling his naked body as she had done once before, but this time holding a narrow length of wood, its sharpest edge centered on St. John's chest, where his unearthly heart continued to thunder.

His hand surrounded hers, on that stake, the weapon she'd sworn never to possess, as if he'd stop her from using it. As if she might have used it.

Bewildered, dazed, Madison blinked and met his eyes.

"Instincts," he said.

A slow grin lifted his face, a damnable expression she immediately adored, and a sign of his new ease with her.

The tips of his fangs gleamed from between the fullness of his lips. And though she wasn't so sure how she felt about the fangs, she loved those lips, loved the way shadows caressed his angular face.

In a Slayer, this would have been a problem. She didn't want anyone to remove St. John from the equation, from her future, by using such a weapon—especially herself, due to hidden instincts she refused to accept.

But she hadn't shown any tendency toward being a vampire hunter. So how had she ended up with a stake in her hand?

"We'll probably have to invest in a furniture store until you learn to control those instincts," he said. "You just destroyed the bedpost."

"I'm no Slayer," Madison protested. But she had pointed a weapon at him before realizing she had moved, seconds after they had climaxed together.

"No Slayer," she repeated.

His grin remained fixed. His eyes were softening, showing a hint of blue in the center. His tender expression registered empathy, because he also had become something other than mortal, once upon a time.

"You said that you can make monsters," she said breathlessly. "Will you make me one?"

"Like me, you mean?" He removed the stake from her fingers.

"Can you do it? Make someone like you?"

"Yes."

"Have you ever?"

"It is forbidden."

"Will you do it to me, anyway?"

"No, Madison."

"Because I'm something else already?"

"Even if you hadn't held that stake in your hand, I'd refuse."

"How else can we be together?"

St. John's smile wavered. Madison saw on his face dueling emotions of satisfaction and suffering that made her chest tighten.

"Are you saying you might learn to love me, Slayer, as the monster you may think me, or that you merely want a rematch?" he asked. "For old times' sake."

In response, Madison again found the crude stake clutched in her fingers. Swore to God, she didn't remember moving. Finding the weapon a second time had been as automatic and mindless as the first time.

St. John, able to move much faster, didn't stop her when the point of the stake touched his skin. His expression didn't change from that gentle, sad, knowing smile.

"Do you want to bite me?" she asked him. "Not *will* you do it, but do you *want* to?"

"I want to," he admitted.

"Will you always want to?"

"Just as you will want to point that thing at me," he replied.

"I didn't want to point this at you."

"You are waking to your destiny. It takes work, effort and vigilance to tamp those instincts down and then learn to control them. We will learn to adapt."

He'd said *we*. A flutter resulted, close to the place he had just found and conquered.

"I want to go home. Take Stewart home," Madison said.

"There are vampires in the States," he pointed out.

"I don't care if there are. I don't want to care."

He nodded, and said in a manner that told her he had considered the question before, "I wonder if Florida really smells like oranges."

Gauging the meaning of this caused Madison to feel anxious for a very specific reason. Back to that term...*we*.

There should have been concern over this. Yet the marvelous being beneath her had proved trustworthy several times over in the brief time she had known him. He had helped to lead the authorities to the missing girls. He had reunited her with her brother.

Christopher St. John had rid the world of one set of very bad vampires, and in the process, had saved her ass a couple of times. And he was better than brilliant in bed.

Better than anything in bed.

Her immortal lover had well earned her trust. As strange as it seemed, he also filled the pockets of emptiness that she had long harbored.

He was smiling, damn him.

He'd read that in her mind, too.

"Some of Florida smells that way," she said, answering his question long after he'd asked it. "Do you have a sudden craving for fruit?"

"Ever since I met you," he said.

Madison smiled, widely, fully, expectantly. That simple reply was his way of telling her that he would go with her to America. He didn't seek permission because he knew what her answer would be. Communication along the thread binding them worked both ways.

They were going to be together. Their unique relationship, merely beginning, had a long way to go, but looked promising.

Understatement.

Madison's face flushed. Intelligence warned that she should be running in the other direction. St. John's task in London had finished. She assumed he'd have another. He was, after all, the Protector.

Maybe that new task would be aimed at taming her and her terrible new instincts. Maybe he was *her* Protector, after all, and had been meant for that particular task, all along.

"In time, you'll tell me about my genetics?" she said.

Maybe he'd tell her what his title actually meant, and about his life before and after being granted immortality. Maybe he would tell her about that image of the garden, and the fountain she'd envisioned in it.

She'd given up trying to picture St. John the mortal, the man, but there were enough of the good parts to make her realize with perfect certainty how badly she wanted him with her, whether she accepted her own bizarre destiny, or not.

"Yes," he replied. "I can do that. I can tell you some of what you want to know."

"Some?"

His smile met her.

And well, damn. She had no idea how to make this work. More questions would arise. More answers would come. In the meantime...

There were vampires in Florida.

And plenty of beds.

Florida. A state large enough that freaks like Stewart and St. John and herself might go unnoticed if they behaved. With two Slayers and an immortal the likes of Christopher St. John about to descend, Miami's rogue vampires didn't stand a chance.

Mere centimeters above her lover's pale skin, Madison moved the tip of the stake, drawing her name in the air.

Slayer.

She said, "If that's what I'm going to be, whether I want it or not, I'd better face facts."

When St. John smiled up at her in earnest, the light in his face eager and hopeful, the blue in his eyes again receding into a flat, liquid black, Madison knew what this meant. She knew it before acknowledging the feel of his erection.

Handing him the stake, and with his hints about *forever* in her mind, Madison tossed the hair out of her eyes, squeezed her legs tighter around his hips... and smiled back.

* * * * *

MILLS & BOON®

Want to get more from Mills & Boon?

Here's what's available to you if you join the
exclusive **Mills & Boon eBook Club** today:

✦ *Convenience – choose your books each month*
✦ *Exclusive – receive your books a month before
   anywhere else*
✦ *Flexibility – change your subscription at any time*
✦ *Variety – gain access to eBook-only series*
✦ *Value – subscriptions from just £1.99 a month*

So visit **www.millsandboon.co.uk/esubs** today
to be a part of this exclusive eBook Club!

EBOOK_SUBS_2014

MILLS & BOON®

Maybe This Christmas

Author of *Sleigh Bells in the Snow*

Sarah Morgan

Maybe this **Christmas**

COMING SOON
OCTOBER 2014

* cover in development

Let Sarah Morgan sweep you away to a perfect
winter wonderland with this wonderful Christmas
tale filled with unforgettable characters, wit,
charm and heart-melting romance!
Pick up your copy today!

www.millsandboon.co.uk/xmas

MILLS & BOON®

The Little Shop of Hopes & Dreams

* cover in development

Much loved author Fiona Harper brings you the story of Nicole, a born organiser and true romantic, whose life is spent making the dream proposals of others come true. All is well until she is enlisted to plan the proposal of gorgeous photographer Alex Black—the same Alex Black with whom Nicole shared a New Year's kiss that she is unable to forget...

**Get your copy today at
www.millsandboon.co.uk/dreams**

MILLS & BOON®

Why shop at millsandboon.co.uk?

Each year, thousands of romance readers find their perfect read at millsandboon.co.uk. That's because we're passionate about bringing you the very best romantic fiction. Here are some of the advantages of shopping at www.millsandboon.co.uk:

* **Get new books first**—you'll be able to buy your favourite books one month before they hit the shops

* **Get exclusive discounts**—you'll also be able to buy our specially created monthly collections, with up to 50% off the RRP

* **Find your favourite authors**—latest news, interviews and new releases for all your favourite authors and series on our website, plus ideas for what to try next

* **Join in**—once you've bought your favourite books, don't forget to register with us to rate, review and join in the discussions

Visit **www.millsandboon.co.uk**
for all this and more today!

LS_WEB